You Buy Bones

**Sherlock Holmes and his London
Through the Eyes of Scotland Yard**

Marcia Wilson

Paperback ISBN 978-1-78092-809-8
ePub ISBN 978-1-78092-810-4
PDF ISBN 978-1-78092-811-1

Published in the UK by MX Publishing
335 Princess Park Manor, Royal Drive, London, N11 3GX
www.mxpublishing.com

Cover layout and construction by
www.staunch.com

Prelude: Somewhere on the Cornish Coast

The two men huddling around the lonely camp-fire against the gloom were similar in height and build if years apart in age. In a particular-ness of dress and demeanor they might have been father and son within the demands of their duties—if the father had lived much harder than the son. Tonight they were united in the garb of common labourers in threadbare greatcoats over slops,[1] grey-blue shirts over corduroy trousers tied at the ankles with packing twine, and coarse cowhide boots better fit for trapping the cold against the foot than keeping it warm. Fitting to their temporary identities, they were no credit to the nose.

"Is it supposed to have those green bits?"

The elder never looked up from stirring the coals about the cooking-trivet that had begun its life long ago as an iron waggon-wheel. "Those "green bits" are leaf celery and beetroot-tops." He tapped the pot with his stick; sparks showered up. "You should remember, Hopkins," he said pointedly with a flash of those too-dark eyes. 'You helped pinch them this morning."

Stanley Hopkins (also a Yarder but far from being as long in the tooth as his supper companion) didn't want to remember. The theft was from a long-abandoned garden but it was still *someone's* private land and policemen—even policemen out of twig[2] were really supposed to be above that sort of thing.

Still, all other considerations failed at the sight of what Lestrade had (with apparent optimism), termed *supper*. He couldn't positively identify what their oven had once been, but it was never meant for culinary practicality. It was thin cast-

---

[1] A garment worn to protect the outer clothing
[2] in disguise or not recognised

iron; he saw that much. Lestrade had arranged the tinfoil-wrapped vegetables in the bed of coals and covered them with ash; after that, the mysterious round metal sheet, and on top, the small cooking-pot. There was something about it that made the young man think of the Great Western Railway. He hoped he was wrong…but he doubted it.

Night crept over Cornwall from behind. Despite the gloom lurking in the celestial backdrop, Hopkins found his attention increasingly drawn to the soft smears of colour tinting the delicate line between ocean and the sky. It was a compelling view and better than the jumbled lumps of dank stone remains across the lonely moor at their backs. They reminded him of alleyway thugs, drunkenly lurching their way to an even drunker victim. Hopkins didn't like the old Neolithic huts at first chalk; with the fading of the day, the place was even worse. Nightmarish. Positively gruesome and disturbing and…
…*threatening* in ways the London rookeries weren't.

He wasn't superstitious; he didn't believe in ghosts, but Hopkins could well believe the land had forgotten to tell the residents that the Ages had moved on without them. Images of wild savages in skins with murderous spears were leaking into the young man's brain. Ghosts would be preferable.

"Hopkins, you've been jittery all day. You've been in disguise before; what is it?"

Hopkins breathed out, grateful that Lestrade only looked puzzled and concerned rather than impatient. "I suppose part of it's because I haven't been out in the open in a few years," he began slowly. "But also, it's quite an ugly case we're on! When was the last time the Home Office had to pull in so many different Inspectors and Sergeants for a single job?"

"1891." Lestrade answered promptly. "Twelve Inspectors, three sergeants, and I believe the total of PCs and Chief

Constables came to …39. I might be wrong about that one…did Bow Street use both of the Irish Twins, or just one?"

"Who's to know?" Hopkins wondered, and for the first time that evening, the two men laughed. Humour in the face of a crawling wet mist wasn't an easy thing to come by. "You're thinking of the Docks Case," Hopkins mused. "Lord, what a mess that was." He sighed and touched his leg with a sudden mischievous expression. "My first true battle-scars."

"Dear me. I couldn't tell you how many I picked up on that one," Lestrade grimaced. "I think I lost count after they stuffed me into that barrel. Some of the details are a blur."

Hopkins shuddered. "I don't mind telling you, I never regret the conclusion of a case, but there are times when we're working on one that I fear we aren't doing any good."

"Get used to that." Lestrade gave the pot a tap. More sparks took wing. "Right. Just a bit longer and we'll have supper…the Great Way Round." (This sadly confirmed Hopkins' reluctant identification as to the scrap metal cookery).[3]

"I suppose what really makes it hard for me is the knowing there're *so many* deaths on this case already." Hopkins sighed and stuffed his hands into the deep pockets of his rag-shop slops. The man he was impersonating had been of the unwashed sort and Lestrade had said bluntly there was no need to don his *exact* clothing unless they were likely to be smelt from the ocean—not when he had to work with him, thank you. "Fourteen poor tinners[4] murdered…all for being in the wrong place in the wrong time. Who would bother killing *miners*, I ask you? Their lifespan is chancy enough!"

---

[3] Great Way Round was one of the affectionate nick-names for the Great Western Rail.

[4] Tin miners

"You're asking the wrong person. Relics and professional degrees mean *this*—!" Lestrade snapped his fingers; it made a cracking sound across the plain, "—against a man's life. I don't care how many years are spent in their education, how many strings they had to pull, favours to cull, patrons to worry. Bone-hunters are a queer lot. They're not murdering each other for *survival*; they're murdering for their *reputation*." Lestrade finished by tapping his forehead to indicate insanity. "When it comes to the landed folk, I swear to you, the lot's barmy as the Queensbury's Third Marquis."

Hopkins shuddered. The cannibal Marquis was not a nice image for one who was all but alone, in unfamiliar territory, with equally unfamiliar nourishment...in front of a cook-fire no less. "Reputation...It's a small thing in the whole scheme." He said thoughtfully. "Too small to be worth triggering a mine's collapse so you don't have to pay some hungry miners a few bob for helping you smuggle out Stone Age treasures!" A part of him was still sour because this was all doomed to wrack and ruin, and they had only been called in because the local police might be lynched if they dared bring the local perpetrators to justice.

"It *is* a small thing." the older Yarder agreed as he threw in a lump of soft-coal he'd harvested at the shoreline. Sparks fountained into the night. Wisps of oily smoke curled up around the edges and Lestrade wiped his hand fastidiously on the damp grass. Bituminous was like that; it put a layer of grime on you before and after it was burnt. "You'd be surprised how many people have been murdered here, Hopkins. Not just for silly potsherds and stone bits and pretty stones. I would say this has been going on since before the Romans."

"How can you be so sure?" Hopkins wondered, more curious than challenging. That was his great strength although he wasn't aware of it. His burning need to know touched the hardened oldsters at the Yard—even the Bow Street crowd, who remembered something of their young selves in the newcomer. "There's not that many records after the Romans left, and most of those are mouldering church records."

Lestrade merely shrugged. "First of all," he began, drawing orange letters in the air with the glowing end of his stick: ONE. "This is *Cornwall*. People have been mining it since they found out about bronze. Tin was valued, so naturally no one was just going to up and tell the powerful trading partners across the seas where they were and how they were doing. If your teachers were anything as brutal as mine, they would have mentioned something about the role of tin in the Roman Invasion." He shrugged. "The Greeks believed in a mythical Cassiterides—Tin Islands—west of Europe, so this place is as good as any to be a point of mythological misdirection."

Hopkins made a musing sound and picked up his tiny teapot. "I remember my teachers saying the Tin Islands had to exist somewhere in the ocean, or they wouldn't be called *islands*."

"Academics." Lestrade scoffed. "No comparison to honest work. Islands *also* mean lumps of earth that rise up…I learnt that from a *real* teacher, name of Mortimer.[5] A tin seam *is* an island, Hopkins. Mines are just the means to extract the stuff hiding in the ground. And as long as there's something worth having, the neighbour sees it as something worth getting." He took his own cup and knocked half the portion down. "Been that way a long, long time."

Hopkins was thinking back. "Most people don't refer to the Romans as invaders," he pointed out. "More like improvers. Saviours of culture and all that." He stopped

---

[5] Mortimer of THE HOUND OF THE BASKERVILLES

talking as Lestrade's too-dark eyes sank into his chest, threatening to rip the heart-roots right out of the ribs.

But the little man only smiled; his sharp, swarthy Briton features bent in that way that Hopkins never—quite—accepted without a little shiver. "So they don't. I tend to forget some small details from time to time..." His lignite-coloured eyes reflected the fire-light. Lestrade's mark had been a man close to his size and colouring...but with a sense of dress best described as Gipsyish. A loose rag draped about his neck the same bright blue as the patches at his elbows. From across the flames, Hopkins thought his normally fastidious officer-in-charge looked like one of the little Tinkers they were frequently running off Hyde Park. The small man's uncombed hair and grease-smeared face only added to the sense of an altered reality.

Hopkins sighed and held out his battered tin bowl with good grace. Lestrade dropped a ladleful of smoking broth inside. At least he could identify the bacon—he had brought it along. The rest was a mangel-wurzel[6] of admirable size. Lestrade had briskly alleviated the abandoned garden of its presence, briskly trimming it for the pot and burying the incriminating evidence with a casual skill that still worried his companion.

"How much longer until time?" Now that the sunset had vanished in the western gloom, Hopkins was beginning to stir with the restless worry of doing his job.

"Just a moment..." Lestrade fished in the folds of ragged scarf and pulled out an iron chain. "Where'd that blessed Pole Star get to?" He muttered to himself.

Hopkins grinned; it was most unlikely the Axis had gone anywhere. He watched as Lestrade set the tiny nocturnal dial on the month, and eyed the little metal disk until it lined up

---

[6] Large stock beet

with Polaris. Unlike the fixed arm of a sundial, a star dial had to move. Lestrade adjusted it until the arm lined up with the uppermost star of the Big Dipper. "Half-hour." He pronounced, and popped the dial back around his neck.

"Half an hour's all my nerves have left." Hopkins muttered.

"You'll do fine." Lestrade was drinking the broth out of his bowl first. "Granted, I'm sure you'd have more of an exciting time with Mr. Holmes right now, but let's stick to the plan, shall we?"

"I doubt Mr. Holmes wants to see much of me anyway." Hopkins grunted.

Lestrade only laughed. "You're in a large club, Hopkins. The Holmes Club. No weekly fees required. Don't let it worry you."

"Things were fine for a long time, and then I made those mistakes." Hopkins persisted. "It was like…I'd disappointed him beyond measure." The hurt still echoed a bit, despite his shame.

Lestrade lifted his eyebrows. "He's not like us, Hopkins. He's not one of us. Don't think of him as anything less than an amateur. I know that seems like it's an insult, but *we're* the professionals. We take the lumps and we take the blame for a bad job. Mr. Holmes is a private detective because he's good at what he does, and he doesn't have to follow our rules." He shook his head. "We can't be like him. He doesn't work all the way within the law and that's not something we can just *do*." Lestrade freshened his tea. "Professionals are career-men; amateurs are in for it because they love their craft. He can pick and choose his cases; we can't. There's a world of difference between the two and we can't imitate his daft ways of solving cases."

"I know," Hopkins admitted. "And I understand that. But I swear to you, every time I work with him, we have to…re-affirm some rule of behaviour."

Lestrade barked. "Too true! You should have seen him before Watson. The doctor is a calming sort." He laughed again at the expression on the other's face. "Just because Watson can shoot the eye out of a bloody crow at a hundred yards and is usually the first one to hit the scene of an attack doesn't mean he's not a stable sort. I'll trust his gun any day; Mr. Holmes rarely if ever touches the things, which is just as well. Everyone needs some sort of limitation." He started into his dinner with hasty enthusiasm, dunking it with some of the rock-hard bread the miners kept in their pockets. "As hard as he is on you, Hopkins, he's even harder on himself. He's a smart one, and that's true. But there's no room in his life for error. That in itself leads to error. Do you understand what I'm saying?"

Hopkins sighed. "Which is why we're out in the centre of nowhere, waiting to catch coded signals from a half-witted gang of academic murderers whilst Mr. Holmes traps the ringleaders in the village?"

"Oh, it's not exactly the centre of nowhere…it was probably even a lively little burgh a few thousand years ago." Lestrade said wryly. "Any time you have to sweep a campsite for sharp arrowheads is a clue to its usefulness in the past…but back to the starting point: we're the back-up in case something else goes wrong."

It was Hopkins' turn to lift an eyebrow. "Just the way you said that implies to me you believe it will."

Lestrade shrugged. "Call me a nervous sort…but Mr. Holmes is as angry as I've never seen him, and it's just as well you and I are out of it. This gang is half-witted, make no mistake. Mr. Holmes would have never known this lot was even about if their messenger hadn't stabbed Watson."

"But Watson put him in the hospital." Hopkins protested. "Why is he that upset? I've seen the man shrug off a bullet wound without a blink!"

"Because it's *Watson*," Lestrade said patiently. "You never worked with Holmes when Watson was with him until that...what was that case? Brackenstall murder? Holmes doesn't care tuppence and a gin-shot for his own welfare, but if someone even *pokes* Watson, it's a giant bear on the loose!"

Hopkins shivered. "Well they shouldn't have tried to kill him. Did anyone ever find out why they tried such a stupid thing?"

"I'm afraid Watson's features are so commonplace they mistook him for a rival in the field. They'll live to rue the day. Mr. Holmes will see to that." The little man didn't sound very upset at the notion of vendetta. If anything, the prospect appeared to be a cheerful one. "Late in life, I've actually come to learn to appreciate irony. Watson wouldn't have been injured in the first place if he hadn't gone on vacation without Mr. Holmes. I was there when they were arguing at the station. Holmes just couldn't put down a petty forgery case long enough to hie to the coast." The chuckle was low and amused. "It'll be a cold day on the sun when Mr. Holmes lets him go on vacation without him after this." He turned his head, eyes sharpening as a flicker of fire caught on the rim of the ocean. "Hah!"

Hopkins was already lunging for his tiny notebook and lead pencil. "Ready!"

"N...W..." Lestrade counted the flashes on the encroaching smuggling ship. "C...V...--*Northwest Cove*--"

Some instinct made Hopkins look up as he wrote. "Lestrade!" He hissed.

"Not now, Hopkins...12 D. L..."

"I think that's Mr. Holmes running across that old Neolithic village!"

"...*Twelve degrees larboard*...probably is, Hopkins...hmn...*two degrees North..?*"

"Lestrade!" Hopkins protested. "I think he's going after those pothunters!"

"Probably." Lestrade was unruffled.

"Shouldn't we do anything?"

"Isn't Gregson with him?"

"Uh...W...I suppose that's Gregson chasing after him."

"He'll be fine. G...R...T...B...--*'Great Boulder,'* or I'm a ruddy slide ruler. Are you getting this down?"

Hopkins scribbled frantically. "It's the two of them in that awful place, Lestrade!"

"You think?" Lestrade drawled. "F...R...S...T...hmn...I think he dropped his lantern on that one..."

A gunshot rippled through the air from the other side of the village.

Hopkins jumped. Lestrade didn't.

"Lestrade!" Hopkins groaned.

"What did I tell you about Dr. Watson, Hopkins?"

"W--He's still in a hospital's bed!"

"You have a lot to learn about Dr. Watson, Stanley. It was only a glancing wound and that is one tough veteran." Lestrade casually lit his pipe off a twig, eyes still on the coastline. "F-R-S-T-S-T...R...M...*First Stream*...that's got to be the little freshet that drains into the Cove..."

"He lied?" Transcribing Morse code whilst following an indubitably thrilling event in a Neolithic village across the field, and holding up his end of a strange conversation, Hopkins had never done so many different things at once.

"Mr. Holmes is an amateur, Hopkins." Lestrade was smiling around the stem of his pipe as he spoke. Hopkins could hear it. "Not a man who works well in teams, he. He still trusts Dr. Watson not to lie to him…and Dr. Watson's pulled some whoppers to save his skinny neck in the past." Lestrade was still smiling. "Not that that's not the most interesting thing about those fellows. I could tell you some stories about them, Stanley…*oh, I could tell you stories…*"

Devil's Milk

Montague Street:

It might have been the lateness of the hour, but the long rows of humble buildings and splintering ghost-stalls looked...faded. The more fanciful policemen walked this part of their twenty-mile quickly and without lingering. There was something about the presence of the fog (which always came with the night), that slid more-than-oily shapes and shadows over the old burial yards and the poor-houses.

Crime was this street's friend, but people did live here. It was just that two different species lived arm-and-arm in the poorer sections of the city. By day it was a clogged swarm of man, beasts, and vendors. At night most of these were gone to parts unknown, but their night-sighted cousins now wandered, plying their own trades, and like their daytime counterparts...tried to avoid the police.

A small man paused just outside a muddy pool of light. His clothing was tailored to fit which set him apart from the majority of Montague's nocturnal population. But he was not a customer nor a purveyor of the goods being offered; those tailored cuts of wool and linen were too sober and not likely to catch the eye. He most certainly did not wish to catch anyone's eye. Not here, not at this staggeringly late hour.

Still awkward in his new robes of office, Mr. Lestrade paused and tried to take in the view of a street he hadn't felt under his feet in nearly a year.

It looked much better in the light of day.

'An expert in these things,' Dr. Roanoke had told the policeman. *'He lives close to the Mortuary....calls it convenient.'*

'And he'd be awake at this hour?' Lestrade had blinked, baffled at the older man.

The old surgeon chose to smile. *'Awake? Man, I daresay he's more likely to be awake than he is to be asleep.'*

Lestrade circled around the nimbus of the street-lamp's watery glow and ignored the faint rumble of carts behind his back. The last to pass was a dead-cart, its driver clad in a chemical mask against fumes. Somewhere in these grey-green buildings, a couple screamed out their differences over something that had to do with Regent's Canal—it was impressive that they could cut the thick fog with their lungs.

The Inspector listened with half an ear. Were it a married dispute, he would be more concerned, but there was more Yiddish than English in the fussing, and everyone knew the Jewish population was rarely violent.[7]

The topic of the shouting finally came clear to his ears, and the little man shook his head. Fighting over an open window? Someone out to be more grateful. An open window here was usually a window ventilated with a brick.

Montague Street was full of moments like this—and considering the sheer unfashionable reputation of Camden...that was almost a compliment. Times had slipped to a poorer state even since *A Christmas Carol*—Lestrade couldn't possibly imagine the Cratchit family being so cheerful and fearless in this day and age. Now one's worries would be much worse than an ailing Tiny Tim and a daughter who couldn't get home to spend a day with her parents. They'd be worried about that same

---

[7] Despite the plentiful derogatory judgments on these immigrants, the police (often puzzled over their customs) noticed a much lower rate of domestic violence and murder than felt typical of the London poor. (From p. 19-20 POLICING THE GHETTO: JEWISH EAST LONDON, 1880-1920 DAVID ENGLANDER

daughter getting home at all, or what their children might be doing to bring home survival money. And fifteen bob a week? People killed for much less than that these days!

In the darkness, a huddled man was coughing the last of his days out with emphysema. The sounds were clarion-clear. The fog was still rolling slowly in...the night would be another battle for this man in the open night, against the dampness of the stinking puddles.

Lestrade picked his way across the gleaming black pot-holes and scraps of garbage too far gone for vermin. Rheumy red and blue eyes stared back at him, defiant and silent. Lestrade courteously avoided eye contact. It would not be appreciated or wanted. The wind blew up a reek: rotting garbage and offal and human filth...they both moved quickly: Lestrade to the other side of the street, and the homeless man to the dubious shelter of the snicket between a small shop and the very building Lestrade was about to enter.

Fruit, the policeman realised. *There must be a fruit-monger's stall and he threw the spoilt parts in the street...* Perhaps the poverty was not so dire here, for in some parts of the city, even a stinking-rotten cabbage would be ripped apart and eaten by a beggar. He'd seen it too many times. He'd seen two men nearly kill themselves with their knives over that rotten cabbage. And yet they had fought the policeman, for better starve than gaol...

A small black shape flitted across his path; its mate ran directly over his shoe. He swallowed an oath. Rats were a part of London...moreso the closer to the water. He didn't miss that part of his early days along the banks, where the feel of those tiny paws over his heavy shoes was a regular occurrence.

He was never partial to animals...and rats least of all.

High time he got this over with.

He took a deep breath. The door-knocker was of the old-fashioned, solid sort, a conglomeration of iron and brass and it was of such an unpleasant *mien* he doubted even a starving man would nick it for the scrap. Jacob Marley's ghost over the ring wouldn't have been as bad as this contraption meant to resemble a Chinese dog with an African lion in its ancestry.

I haven't read Dickens in years...something must be the matter with me...

And in the meantime, the fog was rolling its way to him. Lestrade grimaced at the enemy's latest approach and lifted the knocker, glad for his gloves. Through the thin leather he felt the clammy bite of weeping metal.

The landlady who answered was of the frightening stamp of womanhood that sought control as a right of birth, not merit. The hard, small eyes scoured him like carbolic acid once, twice, even three times before it paused to think that he might desire admittance. His badge, Lestrade was amused to note, took no more than a moment's consideration.

"He's inside tonight." The old dragon said of the hand-drawn image in his hand. "Has he done something, then?"

Lestrade caught the underlying eagerness in the dirty woman, and something contrary and obstinate rose to the challenge. "Not at all. An assistant to a case, if you get my meaning."

Oh, she loved the implication that one of her lodgers in this dirty town and filthy street might have seen something. With a grin shy of three teeth (all on the bottom), she paid a kick to one of the doors in the hallway, and stood aside when that same door was torn open with enough force to send its hinge shrieking.

"Mrs. Wexler?" The high voice belonged to a man who was either upset beyond all comprehension, or had not finished settling his vocal gifts. Lestrade's hopes sank as he watched the drama unfold: a dismayingly young-looking man bent over the landlady like a serpent over a bird. "I trust you have a reason for this interruption?"

"Not I, Mr. Holmes!" Her sniff was *fantastic*. "Your guest."

"Guest?"

Lestrade's heart had still been in the process of sinking at the proof of youth upon that lean face. Then the head with black hair turned, and eyes grey as a spring cloud fastened upon him. *Not so very young, then. Just moves like a young man!...*

"Mr. Lestrade," a voice rolled forth. That swiftly, the impression of youth and inexperience had rolled away like a holed carpet. "You have not yet recovered from your duties upon the London Particular[8] that struck us in '77."

Something about that voice—or perhaps the way he was being looked at up and down like something that was on the other side of the zoo-bars...hackled.

"If someone's been telling stories about my competency, sir, I would like to know about it!"

The young man chuckled. "Not at all," he responded with a swiftness that made the other's head spin. "You are slightly underweight—else your clothing is cut slightly too large for your form, and with your eye to dress that would be most unlikely. A man who spends his limited pay on the better footwear would hardly ignore the cut of his coat when a tailor charges by how much cloth he must cut." A long, nearly skeletal finger dipped in the air between them, and before Lestrade could finish enduring the unpleasantness of his face warming under embarrassment—

"You are an unhealthy colour, even for someone who serves his life among the streets of London. A yellowish tinge such as that would suggest a blow to the liver, but you are obviously not of that sort. Nor do you reek of the noxious chemicals that labour in a factory would bring..." With complete unconsciousness, the

---

[8] A particularly unpleasant and deadly fog.

other hand waved at the startled detective—it still had a tarry pipe between the fingers. "You may have a jaundiced view, Inspector, but you are certainly not jaundiced of the liver."

"I-I beg your pardon?"

"So. We have a man that for some reason, has been putting his health at risk by spending far too much time in London when he should be resting in the countryside away from the fogs. Why is he not? Smoke is a common cause—possibly the leading such cause—for such a dry, sallow complexion...but he can hardly separate himself from the cause of his illness if he leaves the city, for that is his livelihood."

The stem of the awful pipe went to those thin lips; smoke poured out. "Poor diet, exhaustion, stress, and one's blood are the leading causes of sallow skin.

"Despite your efforts to be discreet, Inspector, you have a truncheon at your waist underneath your coat. However, it is not of the usual and more common-place oaken colour model the average Constable clips to his belt. It is a much older style, unique to the Special Constables appointed to deal with the many regrettable riots during the early portion of the Queen's reign—which, if I may, was before you were even born. Your truncheon is smoothed down and painted black. A crude crown is scratched into the paint along with two interesting initials: CID which might in itself mean Criminal Investigations Department, but for the GL beneath. There was a rather famous example of the Metropolitan Police by the title of Chief Constable Davids, "the Wonderful Welshman" who personally appointed a Constable G. Lestrade from his walk along the Thames to the offices of Scotland Yard. He died without heirs, I am told, but there must have been some warmth to you for he passed along his truncheon."

The air seemed thin...or his lungs had shrunk in the hallway.

The man was standing there, smoking, and that damned smile was still hovering over his face. Lestrade struggled to breathe in a way that wouldn't be any worse than it was now.

"Really, Hiatt needs to rethink the pattern of the single-locking handcuffs." *He wasn't finished.* "The non-adjustable grips can cause more problems than they solve."

Lestrade had one of the least-proudest moments in his life: He'd forgotten why he'd come to see this lunatic.

"Have a drink."

That quickly, Holmes turned his back and went inside his room. Lestrade took a step inside, not being told otherwise.

Books littered the walls and floor in stacks, piles, and almost-neat shelving construed of whatever furniture would do the service. Lestrade had the feeling that were it only possible, Mr. Holmes would have put his books on the ceiling in a similar fashion and then completely ignored the danger to his head.

Books weren't the half of it in the dirty-looking light. Glass chemistry bits speckled here and there like discarded Christmas ornaments. A few of them Lestrade was positive he had never seen before, and he'd been haunting the laboratories of late. The largest piece was a glass cone with the tip missing...he was almost certain it was some sort of condensing extractor, but he'd never before seen one that size.

A stack of odd-sized papers teetered in a corner, and only the boldness of the hand made it legible in the gloom: A time-table for the Mortuary.

There were bullet holes in the wall.

Bullet holes spelling out... V-I-C–(cluster of holes)-R.

The little man felt positively dwarfed in the face of so much disaster. A flicker of unexpected sympathy for the man's landlady showed itself.

"Whisky and soda," Holmes was saying, "on the shelf. I did have cigars but I fear they did not survive my latest guest." He gave a sniff that somehow made Lestrade completely forget about the mess. "Aesthetics who smoke to curb their appetite are an unscientific lot." He turned swift as a dancer, bent over a glass bowl, and struck the bottom of his pipe so the unused dottles popped out like a cork upon an impressive collection. The tiny red light of a last gleed expired on the spot. "One ought to smoke for better reasons," the last was said under his breath.

Lestrade was wondering what madhouse--and who could he blame for this sort of joke? Someone must have set Dr. Roanoke up to this.

"Why Lestrade?"

Lestrade nearly jumped out of his skin, caught guilty in having a thought. Holmes was standing up against the undersized and pitifully small fireplace, a freshly-loaded pipe for disaster already lighting in his fingers.

"I beg your pardon?"

"Why Lestrade?"

"I...that is...my name is Lestrade." Lestrade stammered. At least his back was to the door if this turned into a case for the Black Maria. The possibility of this being a joke was swelling like dough on a warm day.

"No, no." Holmes waved his hand so quickly the smoke went flying in all directions. *He really is lean as a scarecrow*, the detective realised. "You failed to react when I mis-pronounced your surname, my good fellow. Thus you are either so used to the common pronunciation, or you chose that form deliberately. I was merely curious as to its motive." He paused and added swiftly: "Although I have encountered a family of Basques and a single Occitan rootling who place the emphasis on the second syllable, you have not the look of that particular branch of Iberian bloodstock. Western Peninsula for you, with your small stature, dark hair and round eyes, in which case one might argue you merely returned to the land of your forefathers.

Still, the matter of the surname is only for my personal curiosity."

Lestrade grimaced. This man appeared to take all forms of curiosity as personal! "How someone uses my name is not a thing I can control."

"You could correct someone as soon as they made their error."

"Harming a person's pride is not a good idea."

"So you allow them to attack yours? There is a price in that form of courtesy."

Had he just been scolded? Lestrade fought for control again. Want to ensure a short, scandalous and ugly career in the Met? Tell your Chief he's got your name wrong. "My name is mispronounced, perhaps, to you. It is not to me."

"Hah!" The bark of laughter was short and sharp…and loud as a gunpowder snapper. "Better the Cockney form than the French? You are in a large company. The drinks are below the glasses."

"Thank you, but no. I am not here to drink." At least, he wasn't before he came here… *Being French has nothing to do with this, sir…*

Mr. Holmes tilted his head to one side like a curious bird of prey. The nose only helped that impression.

"Dr. Roanoke, of Scotland Yard, requested me to detain you what he called a "pretty problem."

The reaction was so extreme Lestrade nearly took a step backwards. The grey eyes went silver as mercury, and a flush traveled up that bony face. Lestrade was shocked that this took some illusion of years off the man—he was in well grown, surely, but his sheer thinness and the impression that his brow was overgrowing his head made one think he was much taller and older than he really was.

Just how old is this madman? Does his mother know he's spending his education on squalid rooms in Montague Street?

"By all means, present the problem to me, and I shall assist."

Relieved that this much was over, Lestrade pulled out the tiny money-bag and placed it on the table. Neither man looked at it for the move would have given offense. Consultants were always jealous of their value.

"A dead man under Dr. Roanoke's attention was a suspected poisoner. When the investigation grew too close, it would appear that he took his own wares to prevent the hands of British Law."

"Ah, so you've finally caught up with the good Mr. Frogge." Holmes responded with a touch of sarcasm. "I warned the Yard some time ago that his life was drawing to the end of the thread."

"That may be, but I was not made aware of that, Mr. Holmes."

"Continue."

"Very well." Lestrade ignored the slight slur against his profession. "Dr. Roanoke is stumped at a piece of paper found in his pockets. It would appear to be from a diary, but the wording is peculiar. Three words in particular are puzzling him: "Milk," goes the first word, and then beneath it, under an indentation, are two more words separated by a comma: "Devil's and Wolf's."

Holmes threw himself backwards into a chair (ignoring a book in the back), his eyes glowing like unholy little lamps as he pressed his fingertips together. Lestrade encountered his most unsettling sensation yet, for the man was thinking, to the point that Lestrade could *feel* him thinking. Just a bit harder, and he would hear those cogs grinding.

"Mr. Frogge, for all his commonality, was a Continental of the first water," Holmes mused. "And he came from a distinguished family of proud chemists, some of who developed or assisted in the development of many drugs we use today." His thin lips twitched. "My expertise comes from a natural interest in organic chemistry, you see. It was inevitable that we would meet one day on the battlefield."

"I take it there was no love lost." Lestrade guessed with no effort.

"Perhaps in a way." Holmes' smile grew wider, and it resembled a silent snigger. "He did feel flattered enough at my attention that he promised to find a way to poison me personally. I'm sure he would have, were he not so caught up in a contract with Merck."

"Did you speak to the Yard over that?" Lestrade was shocked.

"No proof, Mr. Lestrade. No proof—no bother."

Lestrade stared as the threat of premature death merely washed over the young man.

"Back to your little paper...it was mostly likely a diary page. The man kept a log of his more intriguing compounds. But as to what the substances were..." He pursed his lips together thoughtfully. "Frogge kept to the German standards of extracts. Wolf's Milk is the English translation for Solomon's Seal. The plant is graceful yet otherwise unremarkable...but the small rhizomes have a sweetish flavour when tasted, and the German peasant still holds the belief that a wolf will dig up the root and eat it when he suffers damage in battle."

"Solomon's...seal?" Lestrade pulled out his notebook and wrote it down, thinking that he had earned his own fee for tonight.

"Devil's Milk, I fear, will give you more trouble. It is a generic word for several different plants in the *Euphorbia* name, commonly known as spurge, all marked with the ability to week an acrid and thick white sap or latex when wounded. What the Devil has to do with it, I'm certain I have no idea, but I should like to find out some day." He puffed slightly, remembering he had a pipe. "None of the plants that I know of that description are meant to be taken internally. Dandelion has been called Devil's Milk on occasion, but no one hears of a dandelion poisoning. No, if this is a case for poisoning, look to the bottle of *Euphorbia* on his cabinet. If it is a case of a general tonic, I would say go no further than the patch of dandelion in his salad-bed. Either way you shall come to a conclusion."

His pipe recalled, Mr. Holmes regarded its stem. "Frogge was attached to the plants that could kill as easily as they could heal. If he was using *Euphorbia*, then I would suggest one should look at the clients who were being treated for skin-cancers. The sap's use in dissolving the blemishes are well known. He may have even treated them successfully, assuming they never roused his unpredictable temper and led him to throw his terrible additives into his potions." Grey eyes flitted over Lestrade again. "He was a man of his pride, our late Mr. Frogge. To his peculiar way of thinking, death by using a man's own medicine against him was in truth the Hand of Justice."

Dazed beyond the grip of speech, Lestrade found himself standing under a street-lamp like a common loiterer. He was actually sweating.

What had just happened? He was a policeman, an Inspector…and if anyone was supposed to be upset and off-balance it shouldn't be him!

No wonder Roanoke sent him in his place. This Holmes character—and a man who was overly blessed with *character* if there ever was one—was like no one in his life. He flushed again to remember the little ways he'd been embarrassed by the man. His clothing, his ill appearance, his own name…

And yet the man—or youth—or some muddled-up combination of the two—had figured out what had taken

Roanoke hours. *That quickly* he'd put it in his mind, and his mind had tossed out the answers.

"Take this to Mr. Sherlock Holmes of Montague Street, but don't tell him what I suspect. If he comes to the same conclusion, then we'll know I'm right."

Lestrade rubbed the back of his neck, thinking. They had all sorts of consultants working for the Yard, but damned if he'd ever seen one like this.

Well, he was rude even if he was smart, but Lestrade could notice things too. All that mental showing-off had to have been from all that reading scattered about the room…and it was clear that given a choice between a book and a meal, the book would win.

Aesthetic, was it? People starved themselves for different reasons. He didn't completely respect those who had the means for food and didn't take care of themselves. But the way that man nipped about, there was a chance he actually forgot to eat once that brain took over.

Plants that heal, plants that kill. He wasn't so unfamiliar with them…Good Lord. England was crawling with poisonous plants. But that idea that something that could kill could also heal was familiar too.

Something bitter could be something sweet in the long run, if it helped cure an unpleasant condition.

The thought came to him then, in that weak puddle of light, and he started laughing whilst the homeless man in the gutter wondered if he should call for a Bobby.

A bitter substance for a sweet outcome.

One might as well describe Mr. Sherlock Holmes.

An Ordinary Meeting
1881:

It would be years before Sherlock Holmes condescended to refer to Lestrade as 'the best of professionals' and for now the real crown was bestowed upon Gregson for being the smartest of the Yarders. This honour would be as digestible (and chewable) as a cocklebur salad were it not for the fact that Holmes was only speaking the truth. Truth, as the lowliest policeman knew, had a habit of being nasty, and even if they didn't know from Mr. Holmes' observations…Gregson would be sure to remind them of their inferiority against his brain.

Lestrade also believed without evidence that Gregson's enviable solve-rate had to do with the fact that most people took one look at the flinty-eyed boulder in a suit, the jaw that sought exercise by testing the strength of an oncoming fist, and his own fists, which, when compressed together, looked like a bony football…and decided to co-operate with everything the man wanted in terms of a confession. Some were *so* helpful, they were willing to make things up as they told their side of the story.

Despite the charm of the pin-striped package that was Gregson, Lestrade was passionately annoyed at his rival for other reasons. Mostly…Gregson really *was* smarter. By quite a lot.

He was even smarter than the Chief, but proving again how smart he was, he never let slip this interesting fact. As opposed to Lestrade, who seemed to get in trouble with the

Chief on a daily-to-weekly-to-monthly basis without using any of his smarts at all.

There were days when Lestrade hated them both.

He felt like a tiny cairn terrier up against Gregson—and often acted like it because if anything was guaranteed to make his temper hare off without him, it was too-smart, too-smug visages dripping with worthless compliments and even more worthless bits of 'advice.'

Gregson knew this.

And flaunted it lavishly.

"Still moping over the forgery case?"

Lestrade stopped eating his fish long enough to tilt his head up, sewing his mouth shut against any foolish words that might want to come out. It was just habit. And oh, joys, Gregson caught him in a private moment with supper in *the Elegant Barley*. "Not moping so much as annoyed." He admitted to the big man. "What are the odds of *both* experts on type dropping dead in the same week?"

"In a city of millions?" Gregson decided to pretend Lestrade was actually asking him. "Not too bad, actually. And since they were father and son?" Not too bad on top of that. Add a cracked well-casing too close to the street renovations downhill from the new sewage culvert—and the odds seem bettable to me."

So. Gregson knew about it. "Is that even a word?" He asked waspishly.

Gregson smirked. "Try reading once in a while. You'd be amazed at what happens when your eye goes over all those little black shapes on paper." He paused, just as Lestrade was mentally corking his impulses with a chunk of fried haddock. "And don't tell me you don't have time to read, Lestrade. If you move your eyes really quick, you can catch some of a news-story before the oil bleeds through."

Lestrade thought of throwing his supper in his rival's face, but damned if he was going to name his termination of service after Gregson.

Because, annoying as Gregson could be (and he was tops), he still had to keep something in storage for when he consulted with Sherlock Holmes.

After Holmes moved to his admittedly better rooms on Baker Street, Lestrade's first reaction was to give a private little groan. He still ached from the Break-bone fever[9] that had wasted a good third of the Force, and it was too early to be back on his feet. Holmes' old lodgings *at least* had the convenience of a respectable tavern where he could pause afterwards and wash the taste of being outdone by the amateur in about eight gills[10] of the best Grozet in London. His mother had always sworn by a regular dose of Grozet[11] to chase away the plagues in the arteries—she wouldn't have thought it would be her son's salvation as an ulcer preventative. But—Baker Street being in the opposite direction from the *Malmsey Keg[12]*-- Lestrade had a very soldierly attitude to the lots life had thrown to him.

He would just have to find another, equally comfortable shift in his life. And so he paid his calls to Sherlock Holmes, private consulting detective and bona fide slight madman.

His resolution that was assured the first time he met the housekeeper. She was a stamp above the last, slightly gin-perfumed matron of Montague Street. A proper lady, Lestrade

---

[9] Influenza

[10] Two pints; a gill is traditionally half a cup.

[11] Deriv. from *Groseid*, a gooseberry ale of antiquity.

[12] Malmsy is a sweet wine from the *Malvasia* family of grape.

was glad to doff his hat to someone who could pay him the respect of looking him in the eye—and he had a feeling *her* cooking would be trusted (Mr. Holmes' refusal to notice food might have kept him alive more often than not when he was at her address).

"Mind you to always knock before you go up, sir." She told him kindly. This was indeed a change from the last housekeeper, who operated under the hope that someday the Suspicious Mr. Lestrade would take her difficult lodger off her hands with a pair of Derbies. "Mr. Holmes is an excitable enough fellow."

"You don't say, Mrs. Hudson." Lestrade's acting skills were largely underappreciated.

"And then of course, there's the poor doctor."

Lestrade's arm locked up in the act of hanging his hat on the coat-tree. For a moment his own expression (sallow and ill from the epidemics), goggled back at him in the mercury-backed mirror. *He's completely gone mad*, then? Was his first thought-- *Holmes has finally finished due process of mental law.*

"Yes, a good young man, and a decent lodger, but his nerves have been shattered, Inspector." Mrs. Hudson skewered him with her eyebrows. "Maiwand."

Lestrade was shocked. "Maiwand?" He breathed.

"Aye, sir. Wounded badly enough to be sent back to us, and took the fever on the way. Do be so kind and do nothing that would upset him." Mrs. Hudson took his coat with the casual efficiency of those who know their own business better than anyone else's. "Shall I bring up a cup of tea?"

"Well...thank you; that would be most kind." Lestrade's thoughts swirled like dry leaves in the gutter as he ascended the steps. *Dear me, Sherlock Holmes sharing rooms—with a war veteran at that?* He didn't know which portion was more unbelievable.

He paused at the open door and saw the long legs propped on the ottoman before the rest of him. He knew at a glance this was not Holmes' whipcord, skeletal energy. A step further and the man glanced up from his reading with a pleasant smile illuminating the pallor of long illness. Despite the blue-tinged pallor and the hollowed cheeks, he was completely ordinary looking; Lestrade was relieved, as if someone had to have some tangible abnormality to prove their desire to spend more than two hours with Sherlock Holmes. *Come to think of it, that's the most ordinary-looking man I've ever seen. He's all shades of brown--hair, eyes, skin, shoes and clothes! He could be a model for the everyman in the* Strand.

"Good-afternoon." The man asked in a pleasant enough voice; it was trained and modulated to affect a variety of tones for the occasion, but there was something under the 'r' that spoke of the soft, low burr of the Queen's Scots. "May I help you, sir?"

"Good-afternoon, sir." (When in doubt...touch your brow, his father would say...but Lestrade was made of sterner stuff, and lifted his hand on the premise of doffing off his hat for the second time in as many minutes.) "Mr. Lestrade. I am here to see Sherlock Holmes."

The man quirked up a thick eyebrow like a gun cocking back.

Yes, *Scottish.* Lestrade thought. *No other race in the world can do...that.*

"I'm afraid he's stepped out for a bit, but he might come back soon. Would you like a cup of tea whilst you wait?"

"Thank you, your housekeeper has already offered." Lestrade took a glance in the room and noted the walls ruefully. "Well, it didn't take him long..." He muttered under his breath.

The man had heard. "I can't imagine what his rooms were like off Montague Street." He put his book aside and leaned forward to offer his hand. "Dr. John Watson at your service, Mr. Lestrade."

"And I at yours." The hand was bone-thin but firm, a short-lived strength until he recovered his natural reserves. *This man is terribly ill*, the copper noted. Lestrade knew for himself that particular leanness was unnatural. This body should be bigger and broader; he didn't carry himself with the power of a small man had. Though the face was friendly enough, open as a bowl, it was because of force of will and a defiant confidence, not from a vapid lack of character.

There was a look to his eyes, though, that a man on the Force would recognise: Eyes of a veteran. Eyes of nightmares and walking ghosts.

The recognition went both ways, Watson seeing Lestrade knew, and knowing Lestrade was similar in mind. It drove Lestrade to look away and around the walls again. "I say, did he leave you any room for your belongings?

Watson threw back his head with a laugh.

"I came with little enough," He chuckled. "Save my life and *some* of my health." Humour glittered in those dark brown eyes--the liveliest part of him. "And a few insignificant vices, to which I reserve for my full attention once I'm back on my figurative feet."

Lestrade chuckled softly. "I do understand. I'm still labouring under the latest epidemic of London. A part of me can barely believe I'm out and about."

"Are you certain you should be?" Watson tilted his head to one side thoughtfully. His eyes were bald and scorching with their simple cut-to-the-core gaze. "If you don't mind my saying so, though you are an *improvement* over my own self."

"That's a fine way of putting it, but yes. My work makes no allowance for such things as a three-week holiday."

"Ah." Watson's face was rueful. "If it weren't for the wound pension holding penury at bay, I'd be saying the same." He shrugged, both knowing the wound pension was a daub in the eye as far as keeping poverty at bay. "Not that there's much call for an ill physician!" He lifted that wry eyebrow again. "I used to teach the finer points of handguns to men going into Infantry... somehow I think *that* would not inspire confidence in my abilities as a surgeon either." He accepted it philosophically.

Scot without a doubt. They're as eloquently ironic as the Irish, but--thankfully—stoic as the figurative stone. I don't think I could bear an Irishman in the same room as Holmes.

"Well if you must be about, keep drinking fluids. Water if you trust in its cleanliness; broth, juice—stay away from milk in all forms. That could just make it worse." Watson had found Ship's tobacco and began packing away a methodical blackthorn pipe.

"I thought milk was supposed to be good for what ailed." Lestrade blinked, thinking of the milky hot teas of his childish days.

Watson winced slightly as he put the tobacco on the table-- or perhaps it was the strain on a stiff shoulder as he pushed aside a small box of bullets? "The last thing a sick man needs is more mucus."

"Well, I'm not going to argue with that—unless you tell me I have to foreswear my evening pint. Then we'll have words and I'll take back my fee."

Watson grinned at him, and despite the fact Lestrade thought he was dreadfully young to be a doctor, he was struck by the core of strength glimpsed inside. "Be sensible in your pints, sir. Elderberry ale would be best in your condition."

"Never heard of it." Lestrade confessed. "I'm a Grozet man myself."

"Then you should have no sacrifice of your morals." Watson blew smoke—not easy to do because he was still smiling. "It's a heather brew of elderberry fruit and flower. There's nothing better for getting the immune system going— naturally I'd recommend a tincture or syrup, but I've found ale goes down a bit fairer." His lips twitched. "And it's one-twentieth the price."

Lestrade's first experience with Dr. Watson was hardly memorable—but then, most beginnings are ordinary.

Scotland Yard:

"Feet hurt?"

Lestrade glared up at his much-larger rival without his usual strength. "Yes. Yes they do hurt, Tobias. I've recovered from the very same illness you have, and I happen to still be hurting *all over*, but I'm glad you remembered *my feet*."

Tobias Gregson chuckled and folded up his newspaper, ignoring the jostling going back and forth as files were transferred from office to storeroom.

"What the devil has you in such a good mood anyway?" Lestrade asked suspiciously.

"Funniest thing you heard all week." Gregson promised.

Lestrade had his instant doubts: for one thing, Gregson might be smarter than Lestrade, but his sense of humour was oft a wholly different language to Lestrade's. There were things that set Gregson off that Lestrade couldn't even fathom. And, there were times when Lestrade comprehended Gregson's humour-- and disagreed with it. "What is?"

Gregson cleared his throat and looked both ways. Of course everyone in the Yard stopped pretending not to listen and angled in.

"Sherlock Holmes has a room-mate!"

Lestrade's overtaxed nerves cringed at the roar of laughter that washed over the cold walls like a wave against Cornwall.

"Oh, sweet Marigolds in June!" Bradstreet wiped his eyes as he struggled for his breath. "That's the ripest—"He sputtered into laughter again.

"I know! Where in God's name did he find him?" Gregson was leaning on the desk for strength. "*How* in God's name did he find him?"

"You can't be serious, sir!" Constable Alfreds was appalled at the thought. "Sherlock Holmes likes people about as much as Martin Luther liked women!"

"I think *Luther* liked women more than Holmes does!" A wag chipped in. "But didn't he have boils?"

Lestrade shook his head and resolutely tried to concentrate on his reading. The problem with being on a forgery case—you inevitably started looking for forgery in everything, and that included the newspaper type you were reading. Mr. Holmes called it "being in a fog" but Lestrade suspected the truth was closer to his chasing hares.

"...your turn, Lestrade!"

Lestrade scowled at the finger Gregson had poked into him. "My turn for what?" He stared suspiciously at the hat full of loose coins.

"We're opening the betting pool on Holmes." Bayard said simply. "Most of us are giving him a month to drive the doctor out."

"A month?" Lestrade repeated. He wasn't certain he'd heard correctly. "Are you mad?"

"Well, we've thought it out." Bradstreet added. "It's not like the doctor can just pick up and move because he feels like it. He's got to find another place to live first."

"He's new to London, that's certain." Gregson pointed out with that cool, infuriating way he had—it reminded Lestrade in some way of Holmes, but worse—Lestrade didn't *have* to see Holmes every day of the week; Gregson he *did*. "The man got rooked by a cabbie because he didn't know the straightaway from 'Bart's."

Lestrade watched, amazed as the points were ticked off on fingers: Dr. Watson was a veteran and couldn't stand excitement. He was crippled and surely couldn't get around well. He was *clearly* ignorant and innocent of the kind of monster Holmes was, and he *wouldn't* have roomed with him had he known.

Lestrade took it all in with silence, and wondered why that familiar feeling in his gut was coming back. Holmes could take all the teasing and mockery six ways from Sunday—he didn't need defending. *Because they're selling the other man short*, Lestrade realised. *They're judging him by association. Now how many times have I scolded them for that? Sloppy detective work for certain!* Lestrade's blood was far from boiling, but it was threatening to simmer. "Where there's smoke there's fire" was all good enough when one was a fire-fighter, but not when one was trying to untangle the knots of human nature. Assumptions and their consequence.

He stabbed his papers down on the desk and stood up, the violence of his move startling the others. He reached into his pockets. 'All right, I'm in. Who's in charge of the points?"

"Charlie."

"Charlie, put me down that Dr. Watson is going to stay with Holmes."

"Gorblimey." Charlie shook his head in wonder but dutifully chalked the lines in. "How much are you in for?"

"One pound." Lestrade snapped. It was worth it, he thought in mean satisfaction—to see their reactions. Gregson looked ready to swallow his cigar.

"Shouldn't you be back in bed?" Gregson demanded.

Lestrade knew he shouldn't, but he couldn't resist smirking at him. "Perhaps I know something you don't."

Gregson scowled. "And what would that be?"

"It just so happens, I've met the good doctor just yesterday." He sought out the entire contents of his pockets. "And Dr. Watson," he dropped the last handful of half-crowns into the hat, "keeps a loaded firearm."

A Study in Brown
1881:

It was Gregson who found the little notebook under his desk—plain brown and unadorned, his first thought had been a comrade's lost possessions. One look at the acres of neat writing within the pages, and he knew differently. This was an educated man's script. The wonder of the writing itself—clean as an ink-pen but in pencil—faded almost instantly in the light of truth. Within a short period of time a gleeful transcriber had copies throughout the Yard.

"And *you* gave him *your notes*." Gregson accused. There was yet some way he could blame Lestrade for this.

Lestrade wearily looked up from his desk. He was hungry, tired, and he'd been dealing with Gregson for most of the day—a new record. "You know this is like eaves-dropping. I say we give it back to him as soon as possible."

"I'll give it back to him all-righty. In neat little pieces." Gregson threw himself into Lestrade's guest-chair (knowing neither Lestrade's chair nor its owner could handle him very well), and set the back of it against the wall, *thud*. "Looks like he's writing a book."

"Then he's a braver man than you or I…perhaps foolhardy." Lestrade willed the last six minutes of his shift to hurry up. He poured a last cup of watery tea and nursed it in both hands.

"We let him along on this case, and this is some fine thanks we get… *'Sallow and rat-faced.'* he sneered. "Well at least we know his pen can peg a man."

Sgt. Briggs gave a wry look up as he rescued a thin avalanche of blank warrants off the floor. "He sure'nuff knows how to write about London, though. When I brought my Anna here, she cried a fortnight."

Lestrade was briefly distracted from his looming tragedy by a new one. "That's terrible, Briggs. Is she any better?"

"Oh, yes." Briggs was pleased to report. "She only cries on Easter and Christmas."

"Oh..." Lestrade stared at his peer in uniform, slowly realising the boy was telling the truth. He wondered if Christmas included all twelve excruciating days of it in the Briggs household. It might explain why he never grumbled to be on duty on any of the major holidays... Still, it was better than nonstop crying every day, wasn't it?

Scotland Yard settled with its back to the wind, facing each copied page of Watson's observations with emotions various and sundry. Lestrade knew in his bones that in the case of anyone but himself, Gregson and Murcher it was all delight. More than once the unmistakable sounds of muffled guffaws drifted up from the stairwells. He had a terrible foreboding that a great many pages were being collected by his comrades in arms.

As deeply annoyed as Lestrade was about the whole mess, he had to admit Watson spared no one, not even himself. Reading Watson's first, stubbornly incredulous reaction to Holmes' deductive abilities was like reading his own first experience—but, mercifully, Holmes hadn't shredded *him* apart as badly as he'd done the poor doctor. That in itself was worth the time of the reading.

"I think we needs file that one." Bradstreet offered. He stood apart from the rest in his peaked cap and frogged coat, but no one would ever think of making fun of him. Bradstreet's cubic capacity was an advantage in his rougher sides of London. "We should make the reading of it mandatory to the new'uns coming in."

"Oh, I don't know about that," Lestrade protested. "Tradition was good enough for us, wasn't it? Send the poor wretches off all unknowing to their fates, just as we were done ourselves."

"Cruel, Geoffrey. Cruel..."

"That quack'd best have a solicitor!"

Gregson stamped past at a blessed minute to the hour. "I'll have him in court, by-God. If he thinks he saw it bad in *Afghanistan*, I'll give him something to dot-and-carry-on about!"[13] Instead of his usual pause to gloat about his rival's resemblance to rodents, Gregson had clearly discovered the part on which Lestrade had been snickering.

"I agree." Lestrade said blandly. "Your hands are hardly *fat*, Tobias. Perhaps a little on the Euclidian Square side...and the plumpness of your musculature could bring about a false impression..."

Gregson whirled. "By God, he's got his nerve! I don't care if he's a soldier or not! This was uncalled for!"

"On the contrary." Lestrade said icily. "We don't like each other, Gregson—there's no point in pretending otherwise. But we could at least be civil and respect each other's barriers in the line of duty." Lestrade slapped the loose pages down on the rail and folded his arms across his chest. "And if you think we have it rough, for God's sake, why don't you actually read these accounts and see how *Holmes* is portrayed."

Possibly Gregson was just too astonished to pick Lestrade up and toss him out the nearest window. Or Bradstreet's presence was an influence. Lestrade made a mental note that once he got home to write on his calendar the historic occasion of cutting his rival adrift: (*Have witnessed phenomena referred to as 'speechless'*).

---

[13] A reference to Watson's unsteady gait from his injury. 'Dot and carry one' often meant the stride of men with unevenly matched legs or even a wooden leg.

"Don't you even care?" Gregson finally demanded.

"Yes I very much *do* care, thank you. But can you prove Dr. Watson is spreading falsehood?" Lestrade tapped the papers with his fingertips. "And again, I submit to you as if we were in court: Who would you rather be in this particular story, Inspector—yourself, or Sherlock Holmes?"

Gregson's silence was awkward. He was not used to being faced with a question that required that kind of thought.

Lestrade inwardly sweated. *He* was not used to being on the obverse of Gregson's attitude. Gregson was smarter than Lestrade by far—it was the common knowledge that Gregson never let him forget. But Lestrade's willingness to get out and plod through the streets had gotten him to Gregson's level. The Bobbies called him "The Concrete and Clay Inspector" for good reason, and for the most part Lestrade was satisfied with his reputation.

The worst part of his job was that he had to know his own limits better than his rivals. Gregson could always be counted on to throw some intellectual problem at him and make him look like a fool, just to get even with a half-point Lestrade had scored on him a week ago. Ergo, Lestrade had learnt early on it was best to take his lumps and move on before the indignities' rates could gather interest. He took it from Gregson, but damned if he would take it from that amateur Holmes.

"Read it all through, gents." Bradstreet said quietly. "The doctor tells the truth. And he *certainly* told the truth in that the two of you could band together in a common cause. Now that's something none of us ever thought'd happen." He shrugged his massive shoulders. "The case needed Mr. Holmes, that's true, but when the two of you combined your talents, we had the man inside four-and-twenty hours."

Talents? Bradstreet meant well, but that was a *sad* choice of a word. Gregson would never apply 'talent' to Lestrade. Lestrade decided he had no choice but to take his slim lead and finish with it.

"Gregson, it looks like Dr. Watson is writing a book. People are always asking us to our faces how we feel about the latest write-up. We can lie, or we can tell them the truth. *Or* we can completely save our faces and take the third method: We can say this is being done with our complete permission."

"You can*not* possibly be serious!" Gregson roared. "After the way he wrote about us?"

Now it's us? Lestrade gritted his teeth. "We cannot stop Dr. Watson from writing unless he prints an utter falsehood. Now, can you find one?"

Gregson's face was close to violet, but he shook his head. "He shouldn't write about us in such a disrespectful manner."

"Disrespectful? Tobias Gregson, *this is nothing*! The day when we could see another Inspector Cuff[14] is over. When was the last time you saw a print of us that had both the good and bad together? That's going to give Watson's pen even more credulity. And if I'm to believe my street-vendors, it'll make us look a bit more human to their eyes. Do you *not* remember the time *Punch* wrote us up?"

Gregson and Bradstreet, both to a man, flinched at Lestrade's verbal slap. *Punch* had written about the Yard almost three years ago, but the memory still lingered like septic infection. Bradstreet once confessed the caricatures still flashed in front of his eyelids at night when he was feeling most vulnerable. No Yarder had bought a subscription or used the paper for more than a game of darts since. Well, there was Jones, who insisted they were the thing for lining the bottom of his rabbit cages...

---

[14] Wilkie Collins' *The Moonstone*

"*Punch* also accused us of being selfish glory-hunters who refused to work together in the 'Defective Department.' Now it's true we do work together, but we only do it when we have to. I for one am content with you working on your side and me to mine. But if the Yard gives everyone the impression that we know about Dr. Watson's writings, and aren't upset…it will go better for our reputations in the long run."

"You want us to take away a martyr." Gregson's eyes narrowed shrewdly. "Well done, you." This was bitter praise indeed.

Lestrade hadn't thought that far. He didn't deny it—it was simpler. "It's a sensation novel[15] for certain. If we act like its important enough for an upset, people who wouldn't have looked at it otherwise are going to think we're hiding something." He gnashed his bile down his throat, pretending he was stepping down on the now-knowing leer on his rival's face. This was the worst case of eating crow Lestrade had ever put himself through, worse than any of the times the Old Man dressed him down in front of the whole Yard. Gregson wouldn't leave voluntarily without a verbal evisceration, and Lestrade couldn't handle that on top of all the bitter honesty he'd just spewed. Besides, it was the end of the day. He opted for a dramatic exit with Watson's notebook. Four more hours, and he'd be on holiday. He could last that long.

Thirteen minutes of concrete and clay later, Inspector Lestrade had promoted his mood over Dr. Watson from "reigned-in furious" to "dully annoyed"--Mothers and clergy who counseled to turn the other cheek either had thick cheeks or thicker beards. Watson's notes simply rankled with him because it cut too close to the bone.

---

[15] Early precursor to the mystery genre

Lestrade had passed the day when he made no more than a ditch digger, but he wasn't making so *much* more that he could gloat about his pay. Being promoted up from second-class Inspector had cemented Gregson's sense of animosity (*rivalry* was the polite gentleman's word), but the slight wage increase had been a relief. The difference in bob was enough to keep put leftover bulls[16] into the bank. Solving cases helped; grateful clients and the finder's reward could make a year's difference in how one met the finances.[17]

It helped but didn't cure the condition, and wages were deliberately kept low on the reasoning that more money would attract people who wanted the job for the income, not as a desire to be an enforcer of the law. Lestrade not that sort, but he was cynical on the attitude. Many, many of his comrades were policemen because of the promise of a pension—too few jobs had that luxury.

Somehow it made things worse that the author of all this criticism was completely sophisticated, well-written...and *a year short of his thirtieth birthday*. The central character was an amateur *two years younger*. Lestrade in contrast was thirty-eight, had laboured since his fifth birthday, and (despite twenty proud years of service), still struggled with occasional words, needed his dictionaries, and was fully sympathetic to people who complained of having younger, smarter siblings in a household. If London was the four million-person-household, then Sherlock Holmes was surely its most infuriatingly precocious scion.

---

[16] Five shillings

[17] Inspector Jones had a right to be glum when he and Sam Brown lost the tenner reward in SIGN. That would have paid his taxes...and kept his house in vegetables for twelve months.

Lestrade did *not* like defending that work of the written word to Gregson. It still made him slightly ill to recollect the arguing points. On the other hand, no one could accuse him of trying to coddle up to the press now! That (so far) was Lestrade's one sunbeam in the cloud.

But Bradstreet was *right*.

And since Lestrade could afford to be wholly honest with himself (in the privacy of his own mind), there was something about Watson that still impressed him. If Watson was telling the truth, he'd been practicing surgery since his twentieth year. To leap from hospital to war was a bit unusual, especially since he'd returned from his experience a full ranking Infantry Major. That was *seven steps* of rank he'd managed to achieve in a very short time—even allowing for an automatic officer's commission for his skills in surgery. If Maiwand hadn't leveled his fortunes with a timber-saw, he no doubt would have remained in the military the rest of his life.

He'd probably serve again, too. Lestrade thought back to that eerily ordinary looking man. They'd underestimated him; *that* was obvious. He'd placed his bet on Watson simply out of some misplaced sense of contrariness to balance out the careless judgement of his comrades. But Watson had shown the stuff of his being during that Hope case... Following Holmes quietly, keeping his distance, never speaking out of turn—his memory must be phenomenal to string so many details of the crime into logical points. His notes progressed as naturally as beads on a string.

He's a clever one, Lestrade scowled. *For the most part, quiet, showing manners when Holmes forgets his; and then jumping into action without a second to spare. If he hadn't put his part in with Hope, someone would have been sailing out that window! And then when he put his hand on Hope's chest...*Lestrade hadn't expected to feel any of the softer emotions on Hope's behalf. But the look on Watson's face had drawn him close to it. Watson was a soldier who didn't hesitate, but he placed a high enough value on life to regret its impending loss.

I cannot believe he is rooming with Sherlock Holmes…But for how much longer? It was a good thing Lestrade's expenses were paid up for the month; he suddenly didn't hold hope that he'd win his pound back on the 30th.

Lestrade lived in in one of the small flats carved out of a still-dignified if threadbare stone Regency rectangle just off Paddington Station. He could just barely claim "Paddington Street" as his address; his trod was a narrow road built over a derelict rail-line used to freight goods to the now-abandoned warehouse two buildings down. It had been part of the Station's original territory for a very brief period in the city's history.

His Paddington Street was a small, barely-mapped artery connected to the beating heart of the Station, one of the busiest places in the entire city. Lestrade liked being so close to a place where the old blended with the new, and there was still a schoolboy's glee at living by the world's first underground railway. He never quite lost his thrill at travelling *under* the city. To be honest, he also liked being in one of those many places in London that was old yet overlooked by most cartographers.

Once in his flat he paused and put his back against the door with a sigh. The hubbub of London muffled against the walls, an underwater sound mixed with the upstairs stench of the Elder-Johnson's linseed oil and paints (if only he could accept the less obnoxious water-colours of Johnson-the Son, but artists seemed to be a quarrelsome lot even within their family).

A wet-linen coil of steam from the Harpers crept out of the basement at his side. Home, sweet home.

He really lived a fair trot from Number Four Whitehall, but the rooms were too decent to give up. He had his bedroom *and* a study, and Mrs. Collins provided supper and the promise he was not disturbed by the other tenants. A shame no one ever thought of recruiting feisty old widows for law enforcement. Then again, her stern moral vertebrae probably *prevented* more up and coming young careers in mischief than he would ever arrest.

The Inspector groaned to himself and pulled his shoes off, replacing them with his indoor shoes (slippers were for people who were never called out of the house at a second's notice). One more hour and he was certain of blisters. *Off* went his jacket and *loose* went the tie. His collar, stiff with starch that morning was now stiff with sweat and soot. He pulled it off with a shudder of relief and let it join the growing stack of the week's wash (Harper's of course).

No evening for Grozet. Very well. Now that Gregson wasn't around to prod his conscience—Lestrade could not bring himself to agree to *everything* that fat-handed, flaxen-haired man said or did—he could do a little detective work on his own. It wasn't as though it would be the first time he'd brought his work home.

Some minutes later he was ensconced in his study with a pot of cock-a-leekie cooling by increments at the one window. Mrs. Collins' ratter trotted in, found no rodents for killing, and settled down on top of his feet with a self-important sigh. Lestrade automatically moved the small stack of papers out of the terrier's way as he lit a cigarette. At his wrist was a pad of paper and several pencils. *Time to get to it. Watson himself admitted I took accurate notes. We'll see if he has cause to rue that observation.*

1) Sherlock Holmes
2) Dr. Watson
3) T.G.
4) G.L.

Less than an hour and three sheets of foolscap later, Lestrade had come to the following points:

One: Sherlock Holmes was written about, for good or ill, more than anyone; Holmes had by far the longest and most elabourate list of sins. The Yard detectives were portrayed as petty and jealous and barely educated at their worst, but that didn't *exactly* compare to the horror of a mental image of a grown adult sulking in a chair wreathed in tobacco smoke and complaining about bizarre mental phenomenon...*beating the corpses with a stick?*

Two: Anyone doubting Holmes' mental balance was out of true would just have to read this out and see for themselves. His destiny was clearly written on the madhouse. Mrs. Hudson must be getting more than the usual rent on her lodgers. Sherlock Holmes was without a doubt the worst roomer in God's Grey London.

That last point went far in re-establishing some of Lestrade's original sense of sympathy for the doctor. He could well imagine the spiritual and psychic agony of being forced to invalid inaction in a small room with a man who *scraped his bow across his violin*—a perfectly good Strad—as he thought.

He and Gregson were a bit tougher, but Watson seemed to have made even points with them. For everything disparaging against them (and the Yard) Holmes would slip some inadvertent comment that could be taken as back-handed praise. *I wonder if Holmes was educated by nuns...?* The thought was an attractive one.

As supper steamed to a palatable level, he figured out some of what bothered him. It was Watson's own self-portrayal. Lestrade easily recalled his experience with the man, and whilst he couldn't *sense* the doctor was lying about himself, there was still something greatly off-tune about it.

'The campaign brought honours and promotion to many, but for me it had nothing but misfortune and disaster.'

Now why does that statement strike off? Lestrade scowled, trying to reconcile that compound sentence with his impression of the man. Granted, he didn't really know him outside of that first meeting, and then there was the actual case, but...

But I was paying attention to him; Lestrade's abashed enlightenment went down about as well as a mouthful of spoiled Darjeeling. *I was watching him as well as Holmes. But if you look at this...Watson barely existed when we were talking... Sloppy detective work.*

Lestrade tapped his way down the list.

"Gregson is the smartest of the Scotland Yarders,... he and Lestrade are the pick of a bad lot. They are both quick and energetic, but conventional -- shockingly so. They have their knives into one another, too. They are as jealous as a pair of professional beauties. There will be some fun over this case if they are both put upon the scent."

No, that wasn't flattering by a *long* chalk, but the implications did not escape Lestrade—at least not this time. Holmes was dead-on accurate, and Watson recorded it neatly.

The pick of a bad lot. There were good men outside the usual rings of corruption, but...Lestrade's head throbbed. It was a pleasant change from that feeling in his gut. *We'll never live down the Turf Scandal...*

Holmes is portrayed by Holmes' own words, and by his room-mate's own words. I swear, I never thought of Holmes being vain, but he has the right of it. He's also right that Holmes has mixed feelings about notoriety.

And Watson...Watson writes from the perspective of a ghost. That is queer. For some time Lestrade pondered the list he'd written out, his pencil tapping on the paper. Solutions failed to present. There were too many pieces left separate, like looking at a jigsaw puzzle badly scattered and trying to see the theme of the assembled piece.

Finally, he got up and made his way to the shelf for something to drink with the soup. *But first...*Lestrade put his pencil to the calendar. *"Today Gregson learned what speechless felt like."*

Lestrade took his holiday with mixed feelings. The Yard was still up in arms—and when was it not--although not for the usual reasons involving crime, malcontents, public disturbances and that extremely large but well used category known as "vice." A three-day weekend meant one thing to Lestrade's mind. *Rest.* After weeks of running himself about, he could finally lie down and sleep until his own body wanted to wake up.

His plan worked until two cab drivers decided to quarrel over the same fare at the top of their lungs under his window. Lestrade fumbled for his watch and blearily peered at the numbers. Finally, he closed one eye and focused on the facing. *Six?* He groaned and pulled the covers off his shoulders.

The air was warm but Lestrade knew better than to trust it. The smell of the Thames echoed the movements of the weather over the water. It would not be a perfect day forever. He donned his heavy coat but left it open for the sun and yawned his way down the street. Street urchins scattered like quail; he ignored them, knowing the lot on Paddington Street was fairly well-behaved—at least they were to him. There were several streets where his small size translated to "fair game" to the future dissatisfied residents of London.

"Morning, Inspector!" Constable Perkins lifted a hand the size of a coracle paddle in greeting. Lestrade was amused to note that whilst the Paddington urchins flew before him like small insects, they flowed *around* Perkins as though the policeman was a large and rather tough boulder. "Are you headed to 'Bart's then?"

Lestrade slowed his step, hands in his pockets (off duty after all). "'Bart's?" He repeated slowly. "Wasn't planning on it. Why, is something happening? *If Holmes is trying to tattoo the corpses again I don't want to know about it...*

Perkins blanched. "I'm sorry, sir, I thought someone would have let you know." Up close the dark smears of sleeplessness were clear under his pale blue eyes. "Constable Lions was injured in the line of duty."

"Lions?" Lestrade sucked in his breath. Lions had been assisting Bradstreet on a notorious baby-farm practice.

"Yes, sir. They were storming the building where the bodies were hid, sir, and it was quite old and run-down. Lions was last in line; they think his weight was what did it after everyone else's, and he went right through, into that wretched basement. Cut himself open on a broken billhook, sir. Doctors aren't sure if he'll have the use of his leg back."

Lestrade closed his eyes for a moment. Lions was young but coolheaded. He was calmer than even many of the old-timers at the Yard. He did not know if the man could face debility with the same attitude. He also did not want to think of Lions suffocating or breaking his own spine in a convulsion of lockjaw.

"Thank you for telling me, Constable." Lestrade said finally. "I'll pass on to him that you were concerned."

Perkins flushed, awkward at praise. "Not at all, sir. We stick together."

"Yes..." Lestrade thought of Gregson. "That we do, Constable."

Lestrade grabbed up a sausage roll from a vendor and as an afterthought, stuffed another into his coat. He ate the one on his way to "Bart's, his mood not improved by the fate of another Constable.

Why didn't *Punch* talk about how *dangerous* it was to be a policeman?

Punch was popular because of its reputation for sticking to "inoffensive" material, but the truth was, there was no such thing as a gentle ribbing when it came to such a serious matter. Policemen, plain or uniformed, were at risk as soon as they stepped into the street, and that risk did not go away when they went home. They weren't paid enough to put up with half the lot they did, and on top of the people who were *willfully* trying to cause them harm, there was the problem of London itself.

London was not safe.

That great cesspool, Watson had called it. *True, that.* He shuddered to think of what would happen to that 'cesspool' analogy once the Thames started warming up and people conducted housecleaning on everything from garbage to dead animals and even churches were known to toss unwanted bodies into the river to make room for the more affluent. The Wharves were pulsing, malignant organisms, and people disappeared every night—men, women and children. They also disappeared in both directions. Gregson was killing himself trying to prove the resurgence of the shanghai trade off the East side, but so far it was going no further than the slave market over on Bethnel Green.

Lestrade didn't bother with wondering at Lions' 'accident' as it was *no* accident. Buildings that sheltered crime were deliberately kept squalid, and a Bobby could face getting hit by a tripwire, snare, or doctored-up pitfall as fast as a bomb laced with poison. Fifty years ago, entire portions of London had been populated with nothing but criminals. It had caused a level of crime to match the last time England had been invaded by the enemy. Those desperate hours had created Sir Peel's MPF, but the problem had only subverted, going from brazen to subtle to controlled and intelligent. It had taken years whilst even the magistrates had held the Peelers in contempt, but they had *done the job*, and made Charing Cross safe.

Well…as safe as any part of London.

No, there was precious little in the way of assistance for the police. If there was, they wouldn't have to resort to consulting with people like Holmes.

And he does help, but Great Heavens he is arrogant with it! Lestrade caught himself fuming, and controlled it with a grimace. *Enough.* He would be visiting a comrade. Lions was married, wasn't he? Lestrade turned the possibility over in his mind. His wife—Marianna?—she'd be worried. He set his steps eastward.

'Bart's had been in practice since around 1137, but Lestrade doubted a single family who stretched that far back would be so friendly. He passed a placard in the hallway advertising the local clinics throughout London and the purpose of each—and almost stumbled in his tracks when he saw that the card read *"If you cannot read this, ask someone on duty to read it for you."* It left him a shade more disillusioned than he'd woken with that day. *Must've gotten someone from the Home Office to do it...*

Constable Lions was a big man—should he survive to become a plainclothes Inspector he'd make a formidable figure. Even in a room surrounded by the bed-ridden, he stood out with his bushy black mane and beard. Most nocturnal Constables grew beards to keep warm and prevent 'colds in the throat' as per the wishes of the Department, but Lions' was a proud mane of curly India ink that was only defeated by the crowning glory of an equally lavish collection of locks (Gregson swore he had William Teach in the family). The loss of blood made his skin very white as he sat propped up with a newspaper, and he looked up with pleasure at his visitor.

"Well, good-morning, sir. I hope you aren't here to convalesce too."

"Not at all." Lestrade shook his head at the lump under the blanket. There were obviously a great many bandages underneath the left leg. "But I'm surprised they put you in a room all to yourself." He nodded to the 'walls' of the room, which was nothing more than four hanging white sheets that reeked of one of those hospital ward chemicals—the sort of stuff that would trim out your nostrils. "Have you been promoted?"

Lions blushed at the mild frivolity. "Not at all, sir. It's just that several of the doctors, well...there was a bit of a fuss over me when I came in, and I suppose you could say there was a fight."

"A fight?" Lestrade pulled his coat off and sank into the one chair—obviously brought in for the consulters. "What kind of fight?"

"I'm not really sure, sir. Except I don't mind telling you I'm never playing a game of tug o' war at the family reunions ever again. I know what the rope feels like now." Lions blushed even further. "There was this new doctor, fresh out of surgery from somewhere, trying to say my leg would have to come off. Then this second doctor, he comes in and he's younger than the first one, and he says—pardon me, sir--bloody hell no one's getting amputated on my watch, and they started shouting in the hallways—oh, thank you, sir." Lions took Lestrade's sausage roll.

"Go on, lad, you seem to have had the livelier night." Lestrade leaned forward on his knees. "I take it the argument was resolved for the best?"

Lions chewed and swallowed. "Not in so many words, sir. A new'un came in off the street, still in his walking-clothes and his stick, and took a look at the two fighting, and the mess I was making on the floor, and sent me to the back surgery." Lions suddenly guffawed. "Wish I knew what they looked like when they saw their prize plum had left!"

Lestrade breathed out. "But your leg will be fine?"

"Oh, yes sir. Right as rain, 'e said. First he dug out all the bits of rusted-up metal—that took a while! But first he had to re-open me up as the wound had already started to close…after he finished digging it out he flushed it out with carbolic acid, and then a bottle of silver…" Lions started to lift the sheet to show Lestrade, but the smaller man hurriedly declined the invitation. "And did you know, he even let me watch as he sewed me up. That was right decent of him, I have to allow!" The bushy Constable beamed with pride. "I can now say exactly what it is they did to me—because I saw every bit of it!"

Lestrade did *not* share that kind of sentiment. "I'm pleased for your peace of mind, Lions. I didn't think surgeons would release their jealousy long enough to let us laymen in on their trade secrets."

"Oh, this un, he's a real bene, sir. Soldier, like. Didn't believe in treatin' a grown man like a kitten, but he warned me that if I had to stay on the silver treatment, my skin'd soon go with my uniform!"[18] Lions had half finished his meal. "Said he had a lot of practice back in the war."

"Did he now?" Lestrade felt his brow go up. "By any chance, would you recall his name?"

Lions shook his head. "Never gave it, sir. He was mostly asking me the questions." Another chew and swallow whilst Lestrade idly calculated probabilities. "Nothin out of the ordinary about him, though. No distinguishin' characteristics."

Lestrade felt his other eyebrow slide up. "Now, come on, Lions. Everyone has a distinguishing characteristic or three."

Lions looked doubtful. "Well, nothing that couldn't be proven, sir." He gave the bewildering information. "I mean, he was limping pretty hard on his right side, and his left shoulder was stiff, but you know, that doesn't prove he's injured there."

"Ah, well…you're right about that. But surely you've some way of describing him."

Lions shrugged. "'E could have been any man off the street. Awful thin. Didn't look natcheral."

Lestrade bade Lions goodbye, rubbing his chin as he did so. A nurse was flagged down, and a few polite questions under false pretence sent him outside to the small trod permitted to sight-seers and the convalescing public

He found his quarry down on one knee lifting a small object off the ground for the benefit of a knot of boys that had the hardened look of the Cock Lane gang. The nearest boy took whatever it was he was passing on, and the ragtag children fled like chickens at the sight of the grain pail. Then he rose to his feet, and his lack of balance momentarily surprised the Inspector. Watson needed every inch of his walking stick.

---

[18] Heavy doses of colloidal silver could turn a person blue.

The notebook came to his mind: Watson had admitted he could only travel outside in the best of weather. That weather was passing. Clouds were pulling over what little could be seen of the sky. It was a long walk to Baker Street.

The man had gone from being all shades of brown to brown and white; his face matched his shirt collar and made his dark eyes even starker. With excruciating slowness he sank down into the nearest bench with his bad leg stiff and straight. For a moment he leaned on the end of his cane, head hanging down.

Lestrade frowned to himself, uneasy about walking in on such a moment and also because something niggled at his brain, something he was watching that didn't quite fit. He stayed where he was for the nonce, waiting for the incongruity to reveal itself. Watson would not thank him for trying to help him. Soldiers had their pride.

Watson's tired reverie was interrupted by more company; four dirty ragamuffins dressed in three or four layers of clothing—all they owned, no doubt. They clustred up to the doctor, pelting him with questions in piping voices that Lestrade couldn't make heads or tails of—although he was fairly certain not all the words were in English. They were calling him 'Crow' which was the low word for a doctor, but Watson seemed unable or unaware he could take offence at the word.

Watson lifted his head slowly and smiled with the patience of a man who has had to endure younger, messier, and noisier humans all his life. To their questions he reached into his pocket and pulled out a small brown paper sack, folded neatly and tied off with string.

"All right, no glocky fanning, now." Watson said patiently and the smallest boy jerked his hand back from his discreet search for valuables on the doctor's clothing. "Which of you is good with numbers?" He demanded. Clearly, everyone felt they were. "Well, then, you need four drops per pound of water. Who knows how much that is?" He shook his head at their sudden hush. "A pint of pure water is a pound and a quarter, lads. Say it for me."

"A pint of pure water is a pound and a quarter!"

"Very good. Now you know what happens if you take more than a pint a day?"

"It undoos all the good."

"It will *undo* all the good." Watson corrected without rancor.

Definitely not brought up in Catholic, Lestrade thought.

"Is this enough for Mum?" The oldest asked him in a tone of voice that sounded a bit belligerent.

"It's enough for *all* your family, and I suggest you run it home and start mixing it." Watson leveled his finger at the boy's face. "Send for me if there's no improvement by tomorrow morning."

There was no thank you, no comment to say they'd heard; the doctor was suddenly alone at his bench and rubbing his leg with an impatient scowl whilst two men with a too-familiar stamp on their features swaggered up to him. Lestrade felt his inner voice groan as he calculated just how close they were to the outer district of the opium dens.

"Spare a bit of soft, gov'nor?"

Watson lifted his head slowly, as if the notice of his incoming roll was just beyond his abilities. "I *beg* your pardon?" He asked politely.

Oh, now, *that* was enough. Lestrade couldn't be an accessory to murder—or even a toff-rolling. He began looking for a way he could discreetly sneak up without being seen until it was too late. There was always the chance Watson could handle this by himself. He was not surprised by his new guests…

"Saw you dispensin' charity among the poor there." The larger of the men—wasn't it usually that way—was smirking. The smaller man looked lighter and quicker—he might even be the leader, using his friend as a diversion. "And we were next in line, as it were."

"I assure you, you'll get no more than a few shillings." That eyebrow went up again as that voice dropped to the dry note Lestrade remembered. "And I'm afraid it won't look too well for you the next time you go to the clinic, Mr. Woods."

"We'll just have to live with that, won't we?"

Lestrade was stamping out just as Watson's cane touched the first man's sternum. He barely seemed to tap, but the bruiser stopped dead in his tracks just as he was closing his hand over the doctor's shoulder.

As soon as his fingers touched him there, something flitted across Watson's face like black lightning. He rose up, weight favouring his better leg, and his opposing arm lifted. Lestrade saw the flash of gnashed white teeth in a white face with dark eyes and a terrific impact sent the would-be assailant on a short journey through the air. The standing man backed away, kneeling down to his comrade's side in a show of loyalty—his only admirable action.

"I'm not sure you need me, doctor."

Watson whirled, his face open to Lestrade's and for a moment it was a terrible thing, like a violent wave cresting. Just before it could crash, the look was smoothed over and replaced by tired regret.

"I know them." He said softly. "When the hunger for their drug comes, they'd commit whatever crime is required."

"Yes, I recognise the breed." Lestrade agreed. A single glare was enough to freeze the would-be thieves. "You aren't going to go anywhere, are you? Thought not." He pulled out his police whistle and blew; Watson flinched at each blast but held himself in check very well. "You might as well sit down, doctor. It can wait for the Bobbies. This is Holder's beat; he won't be long."

"Holder," Watson breathed out slowly, collecting his nerve. "Didn't he play cricket at one time?"

"W-well, why, the very same." Lestrade blinked. "Do you play cricket?"

"At one time I did." Watson passed a gallows-grin to the smaller man. "But I gave it all up for rugby."

Lestrade forced his embarrassment down his throat. If Watson was looking for pity he would have done so in better ways. As it was, Lestrade sensed the doctor was just stating a fact because he was trying to face a bitter truth about himself.

And at that moment, the puzzle pieces that were Watson jigsawed together with a sharp *click* in Lestrade's mind.

Watson wrote about himself in a distant voice in the details of his past. He ironically seemed *more* alive pre-London than he did *in* it. In the present he was showing himself as struggling and failing to understand the genius of his fellow lodger. He concentrated on his failure to comprehend that mind—a struggle everyone at the Yard could sympathize with. Watson might describe others in unflatteringly honest lights, but those were outside observations, notes on how people were behaving, talking, and how they projected themselves. When it came to the *inward* rationale, he kept the frustrations, the inadequacies, and the incomprehension in his own viewpoint...and thus, was hardest on himself.

'The campaign brought honours and promotion to many, but for me it had nothing but misfortune and disaster.'

Watson was in transit between the young man who had been in the prime of his life and fortune, and the shattered, useless soldier who somehow survived Maiwand. Instead of serving the Crown he was now dependent on Her benefice. The two ill-matched facets had not yet melded. It all fit on him like a shoe that hadn't been broken in. He was a stranger to himself.

'I had neither kith nor kin in England...' '...be it remembered how objectless was my life...' '...My health forbade me from venturing out unless the weather was exceptionally genial, and I had no friends who would call upon me and break the monotony of my daily existence.'

The man was trapped inside his lodgings more days than not with no one to see day in and out but that half-mad detective.

Oh, dear Lord. He is a ghost. He doesn't see himself as real yet. That's why he writes the way he does. That's why Holmes' attitude doesn't really bother him. It's the admitting that he exists at all that's important!

Lestrade kept his composure cool on the outside of this face for the longest three seconds of his life as he and Watson regarded each other with polite masks of civility.

And he is right. We don't give Holmes full credit. It's our habit. We've convinced ourselves it's our right because he only offers advice...it's our careers, and we put our lives on the line every day, and that gives us our sense of entitlement. We want our merits to prove our worth, but how does a private consulting detective prove his worth?

That was a question Lestrade was could not answer. *Holmes puts himself at risk too...just not as often. But either way, dead is dead.*

Lestrade found himself wondering what Holmes thought of Watson. If there was a god, perhaps he simply thought of him as no worse than the other mere mortals in his life. Hopefully no less.

"His name is Carl Masters." Watson cleared his throat. "The other fellow is his brother-in-law, Charlie Woods. They are both opium addicts." The doctor leaned on his stick, a peculiar mix of emotions on his face. "Carl has cancer of the lymph nodes. He does not have long to live."

Carl was groaning; Lestrade discreetly stepped on his right forearm to prevent any further mischief. Watson was looking at them the same way he had looked upon big, dangerous Jefferson Hope.

"Dr. Watson...you are sorry for them? They could have cracked your skull easy as glass."

Watson blinked as if puzzled at the question. "No." He said simply. "But, I regret what led to this."

Lestrade wasn't certain he understood, but unless he was wrong, Watson could be trusted as a man who would not fight just for the sake of fighting.

"Well." There was a slight awkward silence. Lestrade put his hands in his pockets and pulled out the notebook. Watson's eyes went wide and his cheeks pinked before paling. "I believe you dropped this..."

"Yes...that I did."

"Next time you may want to put your name upon it somewhere. Saves the trouble of a man reading another man's writing." Lestrade cleared his throat. "So tell me." He cleared his throat. "And be honest now."

Watson tilted his head to one side, growing red. "Yes?"

"Now that I've gained back four pounds, do I still look sallow and ratfaced?"

"Oh, no." Watson's lips twitched. "I soon promote you to lean and ferrety. Finish gaining the rest of your weight back, and you'll be sleek and satisfied."

The rest of his weight? "What about Gregson?"

"Gregson shouldn't gain any more weight." Watson made a face at the thought.

Lestrade thought his holiday was looking much brighter.

A Well-Read Ghost

The little bookseller died at dawn.

It was Murcher's beat; the big man got a little stuffed-up in his voice when he relayed the news. No fault to him. Hardly anyone could remember not seeing the wizened-up little figure scuttling back and forth the busy streets of London.

"Plato!" He would insist upon a poor, bewildered student from the University. With his rough, croaking voice he might have been a black-clad frog hopping around the tall, young, straight and unwary quarry. "The Classics must be appreciated by such a fine gentleman such as yourself!" Or, upon spying a tired-looking cutter coming out of 'Bart's... *"Galen!* Surely you cannot pretend to be a student of your Art, sir, your Medical Art, without learning of your forefathers!" And despite the fact that a cutter's chance for advancement was rife against his station...the man would find himself buying the book in trade for a moment's peace. And who was to say how he didn't profit? The old man had an instinct for knowing the secret hungers that walked around him.

Lestrade had fallen victim himself, once or twice. Unlike Gregson (who could be cozened into a fancy dictionary), Lestrade merely wanted to know more of the law and its changing nature. Some of the titles were still unfinished; heavy, hearty stuff with pithy contents needing the attention of one chapter a night. But he had bought them, and, buyer beware, Lestrade had never allowed himself to regret his side of the bargain.

They all knew he was poor. He had a stall, if one could call it that; a costermonger's little get-up and painted with so many layers of mahogany varnish it must have been proof against the thought of rain or snow and wind...he took better care of his little cart than he did himself; he was always cleaning it when he was on the kerb, muttering to himself in sing-song little snatches of foreign languages. He was a familiar sight to nearly everyone throughout London.

Lestrade was picking his way down one of London's older and close-set streets at the sound of Murcher's whistle. That quickly, his breakfast was diverted and he was one of the people drawing to the big Constable...the difference being he was supposed to be there. His heart began to sink at the little glimpses of shrunken black form through the crowd Murcher was swatting back like horseflies. The corner of the little portable stall protruded from behind his blue coat-tails. At the hunched-over little form inside his battered black frock-coat, with the blue veins shrunken into his dry hands, Lestrade felt the descent complete.

"He seemed fine enough when I walked past him," Murcher nodded and touched his thick fingers to the brim of his helmet. The crowd took the cue and scattered. The policemen ignored how they moved slowly, as if to prove they weren't intimidated. "Just a little tired. I asked how he 'uz, and he croaked, "sufficient today is the evil thereof."

"Sounds just like him." Lestrade knelt carefully on the rim of the street, and tilted the slumped head that was resting on the hollow chest. What he saw was all too-familiar, even if he hadn't seen the dark, glimmering track of death through the thin white hair running down and behind the stained collar. The frail old head, scarcely more than the three pounds or so it was supposed to weigh, was even heavier in death as it wobbled on the neck. The light grey eyes were already clouding over.

Atheists were strange folk, the Inspector thought not for the first time. How could anyone witness the change from life to death, especially in the eyes, and not believe in a soul?

"Looks like a burst vessel, straight enough..." The quickness of the death was offset by the appearance one left behind. The Inspector quietly leaned the head back and with

Murcher's help, stretched the old man's body upon its back. The pooling blood had already suffused the face behind and around the white side-whiskers with a plum-like tint and made a slight swelling where the wrinkles sunk into the face. It was difficult to make the body rest supine; perhaps the rumors were true, and he really had broken his back in the past. (Lestrade doubted he really had handicapped himself in a coal-mine. Miners didn't have time to read.)

There was nothing in the way of dead-filth, just the usual filth of the living upon the clothing. Lestrade wondered how many rag-shop vendors had given the old man the clothing he wore. It was nosy and he felt like a peeping Tom, but it was inevitable to wonder. The cream-coloured shirt had once been beautiful silk. The collar atop the shirt belonged to an earlier age. The cuffs were too large for those thin wrists. The cufflinks were cunningly fashioned of tiny polished acorns. What the Inspector could see of the waistcoat was a rusty wool, only barely dark enough to match the street-battered black wool.

"Wonder when he last et?" Murcher was asking.

Lestrade shrugged. "He always went to Brucie's for bread and tea in the evening. Someone ought to tell him…where was he seen last?"

"He was sniggling eels by the Bridge yesterday."

"I'm betting you that's where he set up for the night."

"Lord, I hope not, sir. The wind coming off the Thames was fierce last night."

"It usually is, this time of year, but two old men would choose it if it meant less chance of being preyed on."

It always took long enough for the dead-cart. Lestrade folded the scrawny hands across the chest. No sense wasting time. He didn't know if there were provisions set aside, or anything in the way of possessions outside the cart. Brucie ought to be told. Another harmless old soul that even the cutthroats ignored out of whatever decency they might possess...or perhaps even they knew there was nothing worth killing for inside those old coats.

Another piece of London just died, he thought. He'd seen the old bookseller for years—even in his early days on the beat and he'd looked old even then. His white, wild hair bobbing like grass tufts as scuttled across the city with his cart and his books strapped to his shoulders. When a building was about to be demolished, he was there. When something crumbled and was thrown out into the rubbish...he was there too. He ignored the brass fixtures, the antique brick, anything else of value...it had been the books he wanted. It was the books he pulled out of the rubbish, lovingly dusted them off, and repaired their pages well as he could. He read every book he sold, and recited large bits from his memory when persuading a sot to buy. He took pricier volumes to antique and reliquary shops, persuaded them of the use of his time, and walked off (if temporary in his wealth), better than he'd been earlier.

No different from the mudlarks and street-Arabs who knew a good deal in the tip when they saw it...and how many times did the respectable establishments rely on these bitterly poor people to find a crowning piece for their display?

Lestrade once (in his salad days) took him for some sort of beggar trying to nick a few coins on the pretext of a book. But Old Leathersides, the wags off Lambeth said, Old Leathersides had loved his books too much. When he saw someone worthy of his wares, he pressed upon them and harried them with his good intentions until they crumbled to soggy sand and took up the book.

"He's blinkered Mr. Holmes a time or two," Gregson had commented once. Years later his voice was still hushed in respect for one of the Modern Wonders of London. "Then again, maybe he didn't. Holmes is a queer enough bird...could be he can find sense in spending money on a book written in a language England's never seen, and bound in a country we can't even spell."

Can't even spell...

Lestrade thought of that then, without knowing why. It seemed very wrong for someone to master more languages...and not be given honours...at least a soft bed and a good meal once a day. What use was education if it wasn't respected? Old Leathersides had conversed to him in what he'd said was Hebrew, Greek, Latin...once he'd sputtered out a string of Guernsey-talk, the shock of which had nearly sent the little policeman into a gutter. Even more strangely, he spoke of books the Inspector hadn't imagination to conjure by himself. He hadn't belonged on the streets of the homeless any more than the rest. Who had taught him?

Murcher was clearing his throat as Lestrade quietly went through his pockets. A pawn-ticket for a bottle of preservative oils. A silk handkerchief, given better care than the rest of his clothing. A broken watch with an ivory back and a deer leaping across a carved wood. A single piece of jewelry hung at his watch-chain: A finely carved cameo of polished sea-coal, of a young woman with eyes too large and haunting to be healthy.

"A city of millions...*millions*...with millions of those dedicated to crime...and he manages to die of natural causes."

"Seems to me, sir...any death in London is a natural cause." Murcher answered softly-and with not a small grain of truth to his observation.

Lestrade looked up at that, and decades later, he still didn't know what he was about to say to the man—something stern yet encouraging, something a superior would say to bolster up a man in a gruff, no-frills way...but all that went to pieces at the sight of a tall, thin man striding through the crowd with his walking-stick out like a third arm.

One look at the look on Mr. Holmes' thin face, and Lestrade felt his heart sink to a new depth below his ribs.

"Lestrade," Mr. Holmes began with a high, quick catch to his voice (usually so capable of slicing a man through with a single look, a single eyeball, or the lift of a nostril...even the way that starving amateur could put his pipe to his lips could be an insult or condemnation)...

"Good-morning, Mr. Holmes." Lestrade slowly rose to his feet; he'd stayed put for too long, and his left foot ached like a living thing was in his shoe...with teeth that wanted sharpening on the thick bone under his arch. "I'm afraid Mr. Leathersides passed away just now."

"I can see that, Lestrade."

Too late, Lestrade realised he had accidentally caused insult. Of course that man, who had loved books (especially books of every method of murder or suicide known), would be able to see at a glance the bookseller had died on his own.

There was nothing for it now. An apology would mean little to Holmes, assuming he would even be paying attention.

With a single swoop (birdlike, he could be, and bloodhoundish at a puzzle), Holmes dropped to his knees with far less concern for his trousers than Lestrade...but to be fair, Holmes didn't have to worry about his superior's censure...Holmes acknowledged no superiors.

The horses were pulling up the dead-cart now. Lestrade knew he was being old-fashioned, but he still couldn't call it anything but that. Carts for the dead; carriages were for the living.

"He had some books for me..."

Lestrade didn't like seeing Mr. Holmes shaken up and taken aback. He far preferred the man to be what he was supposed to be: annoying, arrogant, and smug and vague and everything a policeman wasn't supposed to be. Not a man who had a foundation shaken before he was ready.

"If you can recognize them in the stack, Mr. Holmes, I'm sure he wouldn't have minded..."

Those unsettling grey eyes. Lestrade has never gotten used to them.

"And to whom the payment, Inspector?"

The voice is cutting as always. Thank God. Holmes wanted things back to normal as much as he.

"He was a mate of the old rag-man Brucie under the Bridge...He had no kin that I was aware of, Mr. Holmes..."

"Nor did he. I'm quite certain of the fact."

Holmes straightened by inches, his tall, skinny form like a lost lighthouse in the swarm of the street. "Again, to whom should the payment go? I can give Bruce something easily enough, but what of Mr. McDaniel? He never wanted a burial. Not even in a potter's field."

Lestrade didn't bother asking how Holmes knew his real name or his desires. Book-lovers were their own breed; they spoke in their own private tongue.

"I can't say, Mr. Holmes. Except perhaps that if you truly knew him, you'll be able to think of some way to commemorate him."

Again, Lestrade struck a nerve without meaning it, but this time it didn't seem to be painful.

Lestrade and Murcher waited, respectfully silent, as Mr. Holmes slowly and quietly paged through the meagre supply of battered books and just as silently...pulled three out.

"What will happen to his personal effects, Inspector?"

"They'll be put up if no heirs respond in the usual matter of time." Lestrade assured him. Holmes had to be upset if he'd forgotten one of the most basic of London's laws with the poor and deceased.

Holmes nodded at that…and pulled out a handful of coin that his Montague-Street-dragon would prefer to see in her own apron. There was a sadness to the way the young man put the money down, as if he was trying to say how heavy it was and how light was life…but before Lestrade could ponder the oddness of his own thoughts, Holmes had turned his back and left them to the business of putting up the husk of a quiet, meek, and harmless man of books.

Lestrade let events slip from his mind—a necessary quality for an Inspector who must carry many tasks at once. Standing fast was one thing; standing fast in a current would drown a man quick.

But not long after, he stepped to the sausage-cart on his way to work and nearly spat out the mouthful of breakfast into the cold London air.

Old Leathersides was scuttling across the kerb.

The Inspector stared shamelessly, almost horrified at his own paralysis. But the vision failed to vanish. It flitted like a bat throughout the crowd, the pile of books belted to one stooped shoulder, a satchel at his waist.

"Dante!" The high, piping and cracked voice exults like the priest on Sundays. "The fine Italian of the Empire! Dear Sir, you cannot say your collection of the classics is complete without The Divine Comedy!"

Lestrade stared until his eye hurt, but Mr. Holmes was already gone, and his target was struggling to say no.

He would give in. The Inspector knew that.

Mr. Holmes would grind him down as surely as Old Leathersides. Would inveigle his way to the man's house and there he would find…what? Proof of what crime? Or confirmation of what innocence? The old Bookseller would go off, and whoever had hired Mr. Holmes (perhaps someone even in the Yard, like Gregson)…would get a note on their desk.

He shook his head, admiring and unable to truly disapprove.

Mr. Holmes had been good to his word. He had found a way to remember the old man.

And it was a fitting form of tribute, too.

Mr. Holmes had discovered the perfect disguise.

Men see what they want to see.

No one wants to see a ghost.

You Buy Bones:
A Novella
You buy land, you buy stones; you buy meat, you buy bones.
--17th-century English proverb

1: You Buy Bones

February, 1882:

Despite opinions to the contrary, Scotland Yard *did* pay attention to minutiae:

- Time of death
- Coroner's reports
- Factors in weather
- Annoyances of one's co-workers
- Social events
- Annual fluctuations in murder
- Statistics
- Etc.

The problem with all of them was that the minutiae never-ended and there was precious little chance for rest and reflection.

Despite the usual depression that came with this daily remainder, Lestrade was feeling good that morning. Mrs. Collins had suffered one of her wild hares in the kitchen and her long-standing gratitude for having an Inspector as a boarder (guaranteeing a shield from all but the worst kinds of interference on Paddington Street), had led her to stuff a large parcel in his hands as he made for the door, umbrella in hand.

A typical February day in London is soggy with snow, slimy with the addition of the soot-soaked fog, and made raucous with the special kinds of traffic disasters that result from poor brakes, invisible ice, and people rushing far too quickly to get from a warm and dry place to the next warm and dry place. A steaming hot bundle in one's icy hands can only be an improvement.

On his way out, Inspector Bradstreet opened the door for Lestrade. He sniffed and stepped back inside. *"Package from Mrs. Collins!"*

Before Lestrade could say or do anything, the big man ducked his head directly over the cloth and inhaled loudly.

"Hah!" He said smugly. "Beef tongue with potato and leek!" A puzzled look crossed his face and he sniffed again. "Hang about. Why are you bringing in cooking from your landlady, Geoffrey? The future Mrs. Lestrade should be doing this."

Lestrade simply *looked* at the other man. His old friend was overdoing the good cheer, but with the mourning-black on, Bradstreet was in deep need of something to make merry with. "There is no 'future Mrs. Lestrade,' and remind me *again* why you and your nose weren't placed on the Bakery case, Bradstreet?"

Bradstreet grinned as he straightened; Lestrade tried to ignore how the jet tiepin at his throat glittered back like a single beady eye. "I love my food, Lestrade...I don't take it to work with me. If I started investigating into what I ate, I'd be skinnier than Watson."

"*God forbid.*" Lestrade commented. "But I think he's starting to look a *bit* more natural. Ran into him at the Tavern the other day." Lestrade struggled to manoeuvre the obstacle of eager detectives. "All right!" He lifted his voice. "Didn't *any* of you eat breakfast?!"

"I didn't." Barnes popped in.

"Barnes, you *never* eat breakfast. And if you did, I'd worry about you."

Barnes' walk was in one of the worst digs of London during the cat-eye shift. He seemed to have more than his fair share of lounging corpses as a result. Dumping one's murder victim into the middle of the train tracks might be a fundamentally bad idea in the light of day, but in the gin soaked moonlit nights, it was *almost* a reasonable notion to the criminal mind. Barnes hadn't eaten red meat in a year.

Lestrade struggled to his office with a full burden, aware that Bradstreet was ploughing through with his own brand of assistance. He set the basket down with a gasp of relief once he was in his office. "All right, then. Now what?" He stared at the stack of papers on his desk. "And people say spontaneous creation is rot." He muttered under his breath. "*I'll show them spontaneous*—here now, what are you doing with that? My caseload's full up!"

Bradstreet held up a folder. "You asked for this last week."

"*That was six cases ago!*" Lestrade blustered. "Where was it then?"

"First ordered, first served." Bradstreet said pitilessly as he set the papers down. "It takes *time* to interview madmen. Pass it on to Jones if you're feeling a bit spread thin."

Lestrade's annoyance threatened to metastasize. "Why Jones?"

"Oh, he's still working with Holmes here and there, you know. Those loose ends about the pick-pocketing gang off Court Street."

Lestrade shuddered. "*There's* a story or five," was his verdict. "I prefer to stick with the ordinary, wholesome London criminal—once they cross the Thames or Hadrian's Wall I'd just as soon leave them to my betters."

"What about the Forty Elephants? Wouldn't you rather deal with foreign criminals than the Forty Elephants?"

"When it comes down to it, Bradstreet, most of us will never see *that* particular elephant."[19]

"Amen." Bradstreet made a face at his friend's scorching wit. Lestrade sank down in his chair and began fishing for a moderately-long pencil. "Ugh. Save me some of that tongue, would you? I've got to deal with a missing husband case this morning."

"Good luck with *that* one, Bradstreet." Lestrade said with feeling.

"Is that all you can say?" Bradstreet sniffed.

Lestrade tilted his head, considering. "Missing husband?" He repeated.

"Aye."

"Was he philandering?"

---

[19] The Forty Elephants was a legendary gang of women; 'seeing the elephant' was a contemporary American phrase for seeing something that turns out to be disappointing.

"Most definitely."

"Check under the floorboards."

"Aren't you the wag today?" Bradstreet walked away, shaking his head and muttering dire Border imprecations under his beard. The little Inspector grinned at his retreating (and very broad) back. He reached for the top paper on his desk purely by default. It was a request for a summary on a recent rash of stabbings involving...*coney butchers*? Lestrade groaned out loud.

Three hours later he had completely lost his appetite—not to the sorrow of his cohorts, who were willing to do his landlady's cooking justice. Sadly, they added to his distraction by their long-running speculations on how the marvellous (and mythical) Mrs. Lestrade would be cooking once Lestrade saw fit to let her make an honest man of him. Gregson had been particularly ungrateful for his free meal with discussing a large *Euclidian algorithm* that he swore would calculate Lestrade's geometric shape from "rectangle" to "square" with a fortnight of decent cooking. By the time the door to his office opened again to show one of the clerks, Lestrade was ready to crumple his papers until they were promoted from a two to a three-dimensional form, and file them into the dustbin. "What *is* it, Matt?"

"Message for you, Inspector." The boy produced a yellow square. "Dr. Watson inquires if you can meet him for an early supper at your favourite tavern."

Lestrade realised Watson meant the '*Keg*. "Hang about, lad..." Lestrade scrawled a hasty answer on the cheap paper. "Send it right back to him, I can break free early today, seeing as how I'm missing a..." He caught the boy's eye to the desk. "Go on, help yourself." He sighed.

Montague Street:

Watson was in the process of passing coin to a street urchin Lestrade recognised from Baker Street. "*And tell her there isn't a bit of horse in this*!" The inspector heard the doctor's parting shot as the boy took off with a rope of sausage.

"Do I want to know what that was about?" Lestrade asked as he came up behind the other man.

Watson started slightly, but quickly relaxed. "I assume you have a strong constitution." He retorted. "The usual rumours of horse in the pork sausage. Mrs. Hudson insists I give her order an inspection if I'm to have any peace at the breakfast table tomorrow."

Lestrade folded his arms and roared. "And surprised she didn't ask Mr. Holmes? Wouldn't it be just like him to be on something like the Epping Sausage Forgery?"[20]

Watson looked skyward to the sooty clouds. "I'm afraid I accidentally let slip to Mrs. Hudson that I ate a cavalry mount during the War." He said grimly. "If Holmes has experience with horsemeat, it isn't on a culinary level."

"Goodness. Did you like it?" They fell into step. Lestrade's shorter stride could match Watson's limp easily, but the little detective remembered when he had to slow down for the doctor's pace. If his strength grew back in those long legs, Watson would be the one slowing for *his* stride someday.

"Not at all disagreeable." Watson was honest. "Sweeter than one would be accustomed to in a red meat. Very lean, but *tough*. The camp-cook made a passing cake out of the fat as well." He lifted the tip of his walking-stick to gently push a wandering dog out of the way. Only long experience restrained

---

[20] Counterfeit food

75

Lestrade from blowing his whistle to report the stray; it wasn't his responsibility to do the job for the beat Constable.[21]

"At any rate, Holmes must be *interested* in food to get involved." Watson's wry tone made Lestrade snort.

"He's been queer about food since I've known him." The little man noted with a long-standing expression by rolling the eyes upwards.

Watson flicked him a look to the sides of his gaze but said nothing. Whilst they'd known each other less than a full year, Watson still seemed on uncertain ground; he didn't like criticism of Holmes in any shape or form, but the Yard had heard him stand up for himself many a time when Holmes was being particularly...*Holmes-ish*.

In a way, Watson acted a bit like a brother more than a friend because of that particular division in loyalties; brothers never hesitated to criticize one another, but woe behold the outsider who joined in! Since coming to that realisation, Lestrade had refused to mould his behaviours in any way, but he *understood* better. Watson was still annoyed that the Yard wasn't getting more accommodating with his much-smarter friend, but he also accepted they all had different ways of working.

"I started my day out with tongue under a crust, and now I'm planning haddock and Grozet." Lestrade ducked quickly to avoid a wave of slush coming off the cab wheels. "Is that agreeable?"

"Rather much. Anything hot would be welcome." Watson said softly. His limp was still pronounced, but it had gotten so that in the rare perfect days, one barely saw it. Lestrade knew for a fact it didn't interfere with his ability to chase down someone who deserved a rugger's tackle.

---

[21] Policemen were expected to carry string at all times in the hopes of securing stray dogs—which were an ever-present problem for London.

The *Malmsey Keg* was unchanged during Lestrade's month-long hiatus, and the Inspector was glad for it. There were too few places in London where one could have a quiet meal and a drink and the usual Policeman's post, *The Elegant Barley*, was too far away in the opposite direction.[22] He suspected that was also one of the draws for Watson, as he'd seen the man here by himself on occasion, ordering one of the cook's spicy Indian, or simply sitting with a drink in his hands and listening to humanity as it flowed about him. Lestrade had never met a man so content with simply watching and listening. It was as if the common man were something he was still trying to understand, and he was enjoying the study.

"I didn't expect to hear from you, actually." Lestrade lifted his hand to indicate he wanted his plate of fried fish (Watson opted for the 'Day's Delight'). "As miserable as this weather is, decent men are staying in."

Watson shook his head. "I was at a medical convention."

"I trust it was informative." Lestrade said carefully. Watson looked like he was about to confess to something that required no less than a discreet execution and a burial in an unmarked grave.

"Oh…it was informative." Watson said in a strained voice. "It is why I am here."

"If this is business, then do go on. I'm available at any time, you know that." They paused in silence as their food arrived, and Watson put his pay down without noticing he was over the mark. Lestrade made note to be certain the balance returned.

Watson took a deep breath. "Inspector, I'm going to ask you a difficult question."

"Go on." Lestrade prompted whilst swirling a forkful of fish in horseradish. "It can't be any worse than what Mr. Holmes has asked of me in the past."

Watson sighed. "Does Bradstreet have any missing relatives?"

Lestrade felt the words dry up in his mouth. He parted his lips, but failed to bring up any words. He closed his mouth and watched as Dr. Watson's face grew progressively glummer from across the table. He cleared his throat. "Yes." He said thinly. "Yes, I'm afraid he does." He cleared his throat again, and a maelstrom of thoughts suddenly clotted in his mind. "Have you heard anything?" He lowered his voice although Bradstreet could have hardly heard from inside the station. "Have you *seen* anything?" He hissed.

"Lestrade…I want to be wrong." Watson's face was as grim and cold as Lestrade had ever seen. Against a desert-tanned face, the ice-white chill of voice was a terrible contrast. "I can't speak to him until I've exhausted all possibilities." The doctor set his drink down and leaned back, toying with his cufflink. It was the manner of a man who is suddenly indecisive; something Lestrade had never associated with the doctor. He thought fast and decided things easily without the slightest self-doubt. "Does Mr. Bradstreet have or had in the past, a younger female relative with six fingers on both hands, vestigial extra toes, probably webbing between said digits, and a spine that was slightly bent forward due to an eighth vertebrae?"

Lestrade watched the toneless, awful way Watson was speaking and began to feel sick. "She's dead, isn't she?" He whispered.

Watson nodded.

"Her name is—," He stopped, catching himself just in time. "--*was* Elspeth Bradstreet." Lestrade supplied flatly.

"She was his baby sister...they were farming-brokers...the family moved from Lerwick under a...cloud...when Bradstreet was no more than an infant..." Lestrade picked up his Grozet and swallowed for something to do. Even though he dearly wished to explain that 'cloud' to Watson, it wasn't his story and he'd already said too much. "She vanished about ten years ago...they were visiting family at the islands for an extended holiday, and during the parade...she was...simply gone. They near ripped the place to pieces, and he hasn't been back since."

"I see." Watson had his hand over his mouth in an expression of troubled thought.

"Doctor...what *have* you and Mr. Holmes stumbled into?"

"Holmes has nothing to do with this."

Watson couldn't have shocked Lestrade more if he had suddenly announced a membership to the Hellfire Club.[23] "It is something I...stumbled upon at my medical convention." The doctor had been leaning forward; catching himself with his bad manners of posture, he leaned back, but the slowly reforming muscles of his broad shoulders were bunched under his jacket (the wounded shoulder was still smaller). Watson looked very much like he wanted to find someone and use them for bullet-practice.

"I'm sure, Inspector, you are not unfamiliar with cases involving body thieves." Watson began slowly, and wet his lips with his tongue. Lestrade had never seen the man so unnerved, and that unnerved *him*. "And I am sure you are prescient enough to stay abreast of crime as you can. The medical field is rife with its possibilities..."

---

[23] There are many Hellfire Clubs, most united in an anarchist approach to having a good time. Pagan worship and orgies are the most common charges, and "Do what thou wilt" is the unofficial motto of all the clubs.

He suddenly breathed out, a quick sound. "I came across a skeleton that was being exhibited by a man I am ashamed to say I know." He looked ready to spew at having to use the word. "This man was a fancier of the traces of physiology and pathology in folklore. He went at some length at our dinner about the existence of a subspecies of humans—for lack of better term—that were known as *selkies*. Half-man, half-seal. This man held that mythological stories of a supernatural slant were merely the ability of the human imagination to account for different physiological attributes."

The doctor suddenly took a large drink, disgust painting every word that followed. "Lestrade, there are a great many stories involving selkies among the Orkneys and Shetland isles and the coast of Scotland. A human is marked as having selkie blood by webbed fingers and or webbed toes, and sometimes, extra fingers and toes. This is nothing more than an afterthought of development in the womb, but the tendency does run in the family. There are times when a bit of Highland blood mixes with the Lowland strain, and the result is a slightly hunched back due to an extra vertebrae, or worse, an extra half-vertebrae which causes scoliosis of the spine."

Lestrade was gnawing on his lip. He stopped himself. "Dr. Watson, I sense you have yet to tell me the worst part."

"The man finished his lecture with a human skeleton." Watson repeated himself although it threatened to choke him.

"But..." Lestrade forced himself to eat a few bites, thinking hard. "Doctor...where does Miss Bradstreet come into this?"

"There was a single scoring mark on the neck vertebrae." Watson drew his finger across an imaginary line at his jugular. "Exactly where one would commit murder. I asked where such an amazing specimen was collected, and my 'colleague' grew uncharacteristically vague for the first time that evening. I answered him with enthusiasm, professing such a fine skeleton would no doubt be the envy of any college, and after some minutes he warmed to my naivety—" Watson's voice turned sardonic—"and he admitted to purchasing the remains "somewhere up north." I remembered Bradstreet mentioned that his mother was a Roane, and that is a common Shetland name...*Ron* is Gaelic for seal." He swallowed hard. "So you see, I hope to be proven wrong."

"But how did you know *Bradstreet* had a missing female relative?" Lestrade forgot his manners—*hang* his manners—and leaned forward, drink in a death grip. "What tipped you off, doctor?"

Watson was very pale as he stared at Lestrade across the table. "Some people," he whispered, "have the ability to look at a skull...and see the face that it once wore." He did not blink. "The face looked like a younger, feminine version of Bradstreet."

"Doctor Watson," Lestrade said without thinking, "that is the most damned talent I have ever heard of." He could have crawled under the table in his following embarrassment.

Watson merely looked sad. "It is not one I would have chosen for myself."

"I can't imagine you would." His cheeks were still on fire. Lestrade topped his drink and signaled for another. His head swam with thoughts, all of them dark and polluted. *I will never, ever underestimate this man again*, Lestrade vowed. *Naivety, indeed*. "How do you think he came about the...the skeleton?"

"How?" Watson glared as he forked up rice. "The child was murdered. If you knew half the stories I heard when I was a student about what an ambitious, ruthless man who *claimed* to be a physician was willing to do in the name of his research or status..." He chewed grimly, too much a soldier to sacrifice nourishment when he had no idea what the next day would bring. "I've been party to many a perusal of a murder victim, and I fear quite a few were in the army. My term in India was most informative. Cutting a throat is simple--after practice." Watson's eyes narrowed, a portion of his mind pulling back and dredging up memory. "People go missing every day, Inspector. I for one can't think of a better place to hide a corpse than where the corpses are normally kept."

"I think, at the very least, we can get your...cohort...for obfuscation of the law." Lestrade thought hard. "But...as I recall, the worst bodysnatching ended at 1854 when unclaimed corpses were turned over for the use of the medical students." Lestrade had been about...eleven years old? He still remembered the horror and how the people had talked.

"I know." Watson said darkly. "It was the *medical profession* that supported this ghoulish business...it was the *medical profession* that made men and even women steal remains and sell them like so much merchandise. From the perspective of a *medical man*, Inspector, if I were to tell you how much the *medical profession* protested the law of 1854, you'd think me mad."

"Why...would they protest it?"

"They were afraid of their...brokers, for lack of better term, not being able to secure the bodies they *really* wanted." Watson's calm, stony voice stunned the Inspector. "A respectable man had to have his own skeleton. That was the least of it. As for an ordinary corpse for the students to study on, but for specialists and researchers who desired fame and fortune...well, not just *any* dead man or woman would do." His expression did not waver. "My profession still has much to answer for, Inspector." He stopped and took his drink as if washing out his words with the soft ale.

Lestrade thought that if Watson could sit and eat, he could too. He took another drink first. "Right. We'll go in from as many directions as we can. The first problem is proving your colleague's role in either murder, or accessory to murder, and to prove it was Eslpeth Roane Bradstreet who was the murder victim." He couldn't believe he was being so calm and collected about this. A part of him was screaming inside the caverns of his skull, wanting to turn over the tables and run for the Home Office, foaming at the mouth for justice. "How would one go about doing that?"

Watson stabbed a potato. "Reconstructing faces from what lies beneath is such a new science it isn't even systemised yet. It was only last year that anyone attempted to write a decent study on the subject. Man by the name of Welcker…There are a few others in the study, but I'd be surprised if we see anything definite by the end of this century."[24] Watson stabbed another potato. *Clink.* The heavy oaken table rattled. "The problem is there are *so many* possible factors. You can reconstruct a face by looking at what soft tissues remain, and that is absurdly simple compared to reconstructing from a plain skeleton."

Lestrade sincerely doubted it would be "simple" to figure out a face from mummified flesh, but medicine was not his field. "This wouldn't be a case for Sherlock Holmes?" He cleared his throat. "It seems that he would be…" He shut his mouth at the look Watson was giving him.

"If this can be solved," Watson kept his grim, quiet voice, "without *another single human being* learning of this, I'd be overjoyed." He said quietly. "Holmes is *personally* as discreet as the grave, but his *everyday personality* is anything but. He stands out like a…like a lighthouse in the desert!" He seemed gratified when Lestrade choked on his drink at the description. "You've seen him work, Inspector. If someone refuses to cooperate with him, they have very good cause to regret that later. The medical profession is *not* where a person makes

---

[24] The first real work was in 1895

enemies. Politics and career sabotages and betrayals aside, there's also the volatile subject matter itself: The last time there was a scandal involving murder victims and body thieving, a riot led to the death of some promising young students, a college was fire-bombed to the ground, the religious factions had a field day with a prime reason for keeping impressionable young minds *out* of school, and innocent men were forced to leave the country merely to save their honour at being accidentally associated with the perpetrators of such a heinous crime." He held Lestrade's gaze sternly.

"That was considered one of the *smaller* riots. I don't care that it happened in another country where morals aren't supposed to compare with English law. A killer resurrectionist can easily escape by inciting a ravening mob."

And, just in case Lestrade hadn't gotten the point, Watson moved in for the kill: "This is a matter of honour for the Medical Community, and I do not want Holmes to be the victim of its pride. *He knows no fear.*"

Silence descended like crepe over the table. Watson allowed Lestrade time to think it over.

Lestrade didn't need much time to agree with the Doctor. Holmes had demonstrated no fear of anything on this planet; his outspoken honesty rang like silver against dross, and infuriated as many people as he soothed.

And Mr. Holmes had always been very public in his statements about professionals who perverted their hallowed trust in office, Queen, and country. What would he say of a corrupted man of medicine? Everything true...and nothing good.

Policemen learnt early in their walking-days it could be easier to accuse a Peer of the Realm of a crime than a man of medicine. The field was usually highborn, influential, capable of subtle manoeuvres, and terribly efficient at dispensing with opposition. And most men of medicine, if they weren't higher-born, were higher-connected. Their connections had connections. They were for the most part untouchable.

A man as passionate for the truth as Sherlock Holmes would sweep through those dark fields like the Reaper himself, cutting down all tender pretentions in his way. And in the face of his unflinching honesty, the entire nation of medicine could rise up against him, ignoring that Holmes was right, just seeing how Holmes had insulted them by daring suggest one of their own was less than perfect.

And he wouldn't care, Lestrade shivered inside his coat. *He wouldn't care at all because the truth is all he sees. He'd be eaten alive...*

Holmes' career was just beginning to rise from Consultant to something more active. It was more workmanlike in that he was leaving his padded arm-chair for information gleaned upon the streets and first-person. Lestrade had always respected the young man for having smarts and gifts, but it was clear to any wag at the Yard that Holmes was on his way up; men didn't change their patterns when their old ways worked unless they were aiming for something.

Oh, dear.

"Mmn...." Lestrade tapped his fingers on the table thoughtfully. "I can too easily see the picture you paint." He rubbed at his chin, feeling the new outgrowth of hair coming in for the evening. "Is there a way we can get our hands on this skeleton? Would it help our investigation in any way?"

"It would." Watson said firmly. "As to getting the skeleton...I debated on whether or not I should try to collect it for myself before I contacted you, but I wasn't sure if you were disposed to listen to me from gaol."

"You would have gotten my attention." Lestrade admitted. "But it would have guaranteed Mr. Holmes would have gotten involved."

"Again, I'd rather it not come to this. Bad enough he'll know I had dinner with you."

"Careful." Lestrade smiled for the first time. "Scotland Yard sees that as the opening chance to nab a poor victim for their own ranks...Police surgeons are few and far between. We're always on the prowl for an unsuspecting addition."

"I'm afraid you'll have to wait until my life is a bit more destitute than it is now."

Lestrade laughed very softly. "Very well; I have a few of the smaller cases I can offer to the newcomers...basic, straightforward stuff that'll let the lads cut their teeth...This is something that requires nothing less than full focus." He sobered and took a deep breath. "And we need to have a meeting with Bradstreet as soon as possible." He hesitated. "This is a hard case, and a harder manner, but I know for a fact we can trust him to be nothing more than a professional."

"I had that impression. I came to you because you've known him longer, and if it were me, I would need another person with me on such a nightmare." Watson suddenly remembered his mug and drained it dry. "But I would like to be very clear on this if we are to go further."

"Speak freely, then."

"First, do not mention yet how I divined the possible identity of this skeleton." Watson's eyes were utterly flat. "I know I am right, but there is no scientific means by which I can prove I am right. Avoid this if we can. We can stick with the physical characteristics that the poor girl was famous for, but let us leave her face out of this. It will be enough if we can prove the murder, or at least his part in it."

"Completely understandable." Lestrade agreed with feeling.

"Finally, do what you wish to this monster." Watson's face was shadowed in the tavern, and Lestrade was suddenly glad. "But when this is finished and he is behind the bars that own him, *I want to speak to him.*"

Lestrade swallowed hard. "Easy enough to arrange." He held out his hand, and the other man shook it. "But if I may inquire upon one small detail?"

"Ask away."

"Is there a particular reason why you asked *me* to assist you?" Lestrade had reason to look dubious; he knew better than most that Watson's notes about the Yard were less than flattering—and the depictions of himself were least of all.

"You worked on a similar case in the past." Watson said at last. "One of my patients was related to a person who died at the hands of a man you arrested some years ago...you were hailed as being 'discreet' and 'sensitive' even when it went against the wishes of your officiating Inspector on the job...Carney Ambisinister."

Lestrade flinched as if struck. In a way, he had been. "Th-that's an awful business," he confessed. "For all our efforts, his hand still remains at large. It's probably in someone's private Black Mass now."

Watson was surprised. "I thought you had found the stolen hand."

"We did...the first time. The *second* time...the hand was stolen straight out of the Black Museum. Some terrible work of cultists." He looked down. "We keep a false lure at the Black Museum...hoping someone will grow overconfident and...make a mistake."

"I see." Watson let it pass. "When working with such a corrupt mentality, Mr. Lestrade, anything might be possible."

"Yes," Lestrade agreed. "…And I'll speak to Bradstreet. I'm not wholly pleased about the timing of this…" He took a deep breath. "His youngest children left their bodies this winter."

Watson nodded, his eyes dark and full of meaning. "I would not disturb a man who is already in mourning, were I not convinced of the evidence of my senses."

"Don't concern yourself on that." Lestrade assured him. "It's…well, it is a personal issue, and it likely will not be a problem." Now if that wasn't a lie. "Rest assured, you have welcome news."

Watson unbent just slightly at that statement, and a cloud broke up in his face. He looked relieved to be listened to…and to be believed.

"Can you give a description of your man?"

"I can do better than that. Look on page 47." Watson reached into his pocket and withdrew a tiny book—the sort sized for personal convenience. "A Gallery of the Bone Specialists of England. 1879."

Lestrade went to the directed page and found himself scowling at the printed image of a gentle-faced old fellow with serene, light eyes and thinning hair on a high brow. On the reverse of the page was titled a 'Quote of Reflection' and it was from Shakespeare:

"This life,
which had been the tomb
of his virtue and of his honour,
is but a walking shadow; a poor player,
that struts and frets his hour upon the stage,
and then is heard no more:
tis a tale told by an idiot,
full of sound and fury,

"Well, *that's* charming." Lestrade muttered.

Watson made an unkind sound. "If read by a cynical eye, it isn't the worst of them." He held up his hand as Lestrade meant to return the book. "Keep it. I have an older copy." He made an unpleasant twist to his mouth. "He was handing these out as part of his lecture, as he was one of the editors and carried his name upon the title. Our copies were affordable but much abridged. He did of course, have the means to sell us a much more thorough edition if we so chose..." The Doctor failed to look impressed. "He told me this one was his own printer's proof, and I was already thinking of contacting you...so...I found myself paying more than I really ought for the ownership just so I could get his image in my hands the faster."

"That's advertising for you." Lestrade looked at the name under the face: "Dr. Jonas Q. Parker," and studied the veritable unchained alphabet running after his name. "He must have a lot of degrees."

"He gathers a new one every other year."

"Well, if you're certain you don't want it back..."

"Very." Watson almost snapped. "Keep it. I don't want it."

Lestrade felt it might be best to conclude the interview. He took one look outside the tavern's small windows, gauged the weather, and announced his intention to split the fare home. Watson agreed quickly.

They rode northeast through London in mixed silence as snow whirled before and after their passage. Lestrade's head was full of conflicting emotions and thoughts as much as was his companion's. Foremost on the small man's mind was the troubling instinct that Watson really wanted to avoid Holmes' involvement out of some sense of…shame.

Shame was not the sort of emotion that belonged on Watson, yet Lestrade didn't think he was wrong. Watson stared blankly through the wrinkled glass of the window and seemed barely aware of their passage, his brown eyes sinking into the details of the floundering city. Street lamps hissed tired light, and hissed again when the heavy flakes of snow struck the thick glass globes and boxes. Children ran but not for play so much as for money: brooms clutched in lean hands they offered to clear paths for the well-dressed worried for the state of their hems and fine leather shoes. Just off the corner from the University of London's prestige and glamour, Lestrade recognised its absence in the form of one of the old Crawlers huddled in a door-way. Wrapped head to toe in layers of cloth the old cripple waited for the snow to cover his threadbare woollen cloak, and give him an extra layer of warmth with it.

The cab turned west. The dying light was slanting from the grainy black of floating soot to the pearl-grey of dusk; the clouds collected a brown tint, and the cab began to slow as the flakes flurried in an eye-stinging spray like the ocean. It reminded the little professional a little too much like the ocean, and he spoke to break out of his thoughts, trying to keep the homesickness away before it returned.

"I'll wire Bradstreet and see if I can't meet with him early in the morning before his regular work-hours." The steam from his breath hovered slowly in the cool air.

Watson shifted slightly in the terrible light; the street-lamps added to the lack of visibility, as the illumination was now catching such a blaze of snow one could barely see through the curtain of grey glare. He was relieved when the cab slowed, even if it was worse for his shoulder.

"I am at 'Bart's every day if you require a meeting. My morning is mostly the rounds; I usually save the evening for research. You can find me easily enough; the secretary who sits by that large potted pink-lemon tree is my usual contact on where I am and what I shall be doing."

"That should be easy enough to remember." Lestrade glanced upward out of habit as the cab slowed. "And here you are…" He slid aside to give Watson room. The doctor stepped out as if his legs had forgotten how to move, clutching the edge of the door with his free hand. Lestrade was relieved when he made it safely out. "Tomorrow, doctor."

Watson waited, leaning on his stick as the cab clopped northwest. His shoulder injury was doing his legs no favours, as it took conscious effort to correct his imbalance when he walked. When his attention wandered, he caught himself walking without proper posture to reduce the vibration of his step into his clavicle. And that, of course, led to an aching, already pained leg on top of an aching shoulder. Vicious circle.

The snow chilled through his shoes. Less than a quarter-hour had passed and half an inch of the lacy stuff had drifted up. Without thinking anything of it, he looked both ways to see if any of those poor Irregulars were running about, but it would appear they had the sense or the means to burrow indoors on a night like this. That felt better. The night was only going to get worse, and even though the boys were a living refutation of the Germ Theory, he still didn't want them out. There was always the chance Holmes had them out running some kind of godforsaken errand, but he devoutly hoped not.

Holmes really had a lot in common with those children, he mused with a half-smile under his mustache as he crossed the street—walking on eggshells for the lumps of ice he could feel under the snow. If the Irregulars were but a single organism, they would mirror Holmes in so many ways: frantic energy slipping through the worst parts of London; immune to hardship...Watson supposed the only real differences were minor: Holmes donned filth as a disguise that was natural to the boys, and he missed meals because he forgot food, whilst they usually didn't have a meal to miss in the first place. Otherwise, the two sides were masters in their specialised field of education, and there was a *strong* possibility that both learned from each other as much as possible.

Watson suspected his friend's intellect was attracted to the Irregulars for their burning anarchy and ability to be everywhere at once and remain invisible. They were an Army, and he was their King.

A shriek floated up from an alley and Watson realised how very tired he was when his start caused his balance to falter. He slid hard and gnashed his teeth as his knee landed with perfect aim on the top of a cobble. As always, the pain provoked an automatic reaction of blind fury; he pushed himself back up to both feet, leaning a moment on his stick, and listened hard over the pounding of his heart in his ears.

The shriek resounded, and Watson was astonished out of temper to see a rabbit take off from the depths of the alley, a small mongrel hot on its heels. The doctor shook his head in silent wonder. Nothing did quite sound like a frightened hare. What in the world it was doing loose in London was beyond explanation.

London was beyond *him*.

Calm, now. The middle of the road was no place for such questions. He stepped cautiously, his jaw aching now from the effort of control as now he could claim soreness for three out of four limbs. "*Fill all thy bones with aches,*" he quoted the Bard sardonically, and breathed easy when he made it to the door of 221B. The anger was melting like the white caps off his shoulders. Another gift from war, to face pain with rage. A full year had passed since his return…

…why was it taking so long to heal?

221B:

Kitchen-smells struck Watson full in the face and he stopped for a moment in the middle of the foyer, breathing in scents that were far from horror: corned beef and beetroots simmered salty sweet odours in the air with sweet-spicy breads. He closed his eyes, reminding himself that the wet, gritty snap of London was now on the other side of the door.

"Oh, there you are, doctor," Mrs. Hudson emerged with the slightest bit of flour on her hands. That it was there at all was astonishing. "I'll have supper ready soon. There's a longer wait on the dessert. This time of year, it's terrible to wait on the yeast, but I do admit the rising is superior when it is slow."

Watson breathed in deeply through his nose. "I am perfectly pleased with the wait, if the end result is a portion of what I can smell." The first of a genuine smile came to his face as he was helped out of his coat. "Mrs. Hudson, you are remarkable."

"Tush." She responded with her usual alacrity. "You may thank me tomorrow morning if you are still satisfied."

He climbed the steps slowly, but at the landing he paused. The sitting-room was much closer than his bedroom, and he would have to come back downstairs anyway. The small dish of curry had burned itself out of him in the cold weather—weather that was growing ever more icy. Yellow light slipped through the door-frame, and he found himself turning the knob.

His fellow lodger was lying with an outward lassitude upon the settee by the fire, a long-stemmed pipe between his lips. Watson looked for the violin, found it safely in its case with the latch open, and felt the disappointment of missed music. Reams of newsprint had fluttered to the floor as sadly as a flock of broken-winged birds. And, worst of all, the tang of some harsh and scorching exotic chemicals touched the back of the doctor's brain.

A pipe, a Stradivarius, newspapers and chemicals all within a few hours were hardly a reassuring sign as to the mood of the man.

Holmes' eyes were slipped all but shut, confirming Watson's suspicion that he had found the outside world wanting, and had reacted by a retreat to the inward one. The way he pulled on the cherrywood resembled too closely the contemplative, sensual and short-sighted pleasures of the opium dens. He must have begun his nicotinic ritual whilst dissatisfied—it appeared to be passing now, by whatever method. Watson glanced at the chemistry table, noting the number of carefully-collected dottles and unburned bits of his day's pipes. The pre-breakfast smoke was going to be thick tomorrow.

"A pleasant evening with the good Inspector, Watson?" Holmes drawled. "I do hope you'll take advantage of something besides the curried mutton at the *Malmsey Keg* someday, my dear fellow. They are quite renowned for their hearty dish of Country Captain,[25] and their spoon bread is all the rage amongst our returning soldiers."

Watson's exhausted mind churned through several possible responses, but he knew from experience that whilst Holmes *appeared* to be generous with his insights, the least discouragement could keep him from talking for well a week.

---

[25] West Indies chicken dish.

Watson liked the idea of rooming with a statue as much as the next man. "Holmes, I promise you if I was not so utterly exhausted, I would be accusing you of following me about London in the guise of Wiggins! Or was it truly Wiggins I gave the sausage to at noon?" He rubbed bloodshot eyes until the burning sensation faded; and Holmes began laughing around his pipe. Billows of smoke erupted from the corners of his mouth like the seams off a locomotive.

"Ah, you give me credit for my disguises that falls within the fantastic. Not that I've never wished for the ability to change my height! If there was some way to surmount that particular problem, I *assure* you I would be taking advantage of it on a daily basis." Holmes paused to add another injection of smoke into the room. Watson couldn't help but notice the haze around the table lamp. "Not a difficult deduction at all...You have brought back a sack of Grozet for your consumption...Inspector Lestrade's addiction to gooseberry ale is almost a legend among Scotland Yard. The only Grozet that is not guaranteed to send a customer blind, deaf, or dumb—if not temporarily witless—is to be had off Montague Street. Before I found our rooms here, Lestrade would top off his consultations with me by detouring to the *Malmsey Keg* and washing his annoyances down with at least two pints." Holmes detached his lips off the pipe long enough to exhale the ghosts of harsh shag. "But I am not privy to all your thoughts, my dear fellow. I for one have no idea what would inspire your collabouration with Lestrade."

Watson's mind latched on the nearest available truth. "Lestrade intimated that the Yard is always in need of a police surgeon." He admitted, and a small part of his psyche was gratified to see Holmes' eyebrows pop up whilst a frown tightened his chin down—the impression lengthened his entire face. "I am flattered, and I have promised I would look into it…but at this point in life, I confess I don't feel very capable of fulfilling such a post." He nodded downward to his truly-aching shoulder, and honesty coloured his voice.

"My shoulder is still weak; my leg still hurts. A reliable income is always appreciated, but I'd be a liability no matter how they paint it."

"My dear fellow, your talents would be put to waste at Scotland Yard." Holmes waved off the whole mess with a flick of his pale wrist, bending his head to his pipe again. Despite the languid—dreamy, even—demeanor, Watson had the distinct impression that Holmes was annoyed straight down to bedrock. "I've met the usual lot who stands in for Police Surgeon. If you think *Lestrade and Gregson* are limited in their intelligence, I submit to you, all thoughts of logical conjecture are starved out in the autopsy rooms.

"And the coroner's trials? If there is one thing on which I *must* agree with Gregson and Lestrade, it is the observation that the judges who oversee these trials are pulled out of a most remarkable pool of mediocrity and pedantic intellect. One would have to go to the House of Lords to encounter such deliberate examples of oxygen-starved brain cells."

Holmes stopped long enough to blow a geometrically graceful smoke ring whilst Watson mourned the fact that Holmes at his verbal best was completely unprintable, unless they both wanted to move to some wretched outpost of the Empire. "Watson, you are better off with a private practice; *you know this*."

"Sometimes, I do *not* know." Watson wondered that he could deflect Holmes' attention on to himself by scraping his every last nerve raw on the exposure of his insecurities. But, in a way, Holmes was an excellent conduit for the voice in his head he did not want to listen to. "May I remind you, London is still an unfathomable wilderness to me?"

"As it should be to anyone with common sense." Holmes dismissed that with *another* flick of his wrist. "It is fatally dangerous at worst, and at best…chaotic and illogical. One may only cope by creating an oasis of reason and logic within the city…a depot of commonsense connected by other depots, by which sane people travel."

"Holmes, how on earth do you do that?"

"Do what, my dear fellow?"

"Manage to…vivisect human nature in such a way. Are you positively certain you never tried your hand at fictional writing?"

Holmes' snort of feigned outrage was so pure it only made Watson's amusement grow; by perfect timing Mrs. Hudson emerged with a very heavy tray of hot food against the growing freeze. "Ah, Mrs. Hudson's famous Red Flannel." Holmes announced. "Most excellent."

Watson paused to wonder if Holmes was being so pleasant about his meal because he was trying to jolly his roommate out of his mood. *That* was a slightly uncomfortable thought, but not one that was easily dismissed. Normally the roles were reversed. And Holmes could say what he would about Scotland Yard; the doctor was aware that the detectives were astonished that it was the nightmare-plagued war veteran with chronic wounds that carried the *nurturing* role in 221B, and not the man who was still whole-cloth.

As much as he's smoked today, I'm surprised he even has an appetite; Watson passed the butter to Holmes and searched for the pepper. *Perhaps that is a factor to his ignorance of regular meals…I should look into that possibility. If everything I ate tasted of tar and nicotine, I'd hardly want to eat myself…*

Holmes was not finished with his new favourite topic. "I would be horrified if you went to work for Scotland Yard." He informed the other man whilst he poured the hot lemon-water.

"Not that the Yard could help but improve by your presence, but the cost would be your mental demotion."[26]

Watson drew on the reserves of patience he cultivated *specifically* for Sherlock Holmes—reserves that seemed to grow the more he stretched them. "I promised I would consider the matter." He pointed out. "For my own peace of mind, I must think of alternatives." *It isn't as though I'll get rich with writing my small articles!*

Holmes grunted and poured an unhealthy amount of honey into the lemon-water. "That is a bad lot." He repeated.

"My impression is the men are decent enough." Watson was beginning to feel his patience stretch to the tearing point.

"Oh, they are decent enough—within their training which is inconsistent in quality and ranges from the abhorrent to the exemplary! Outside of the usual incompetent, one has to be mindful of the unflattering example that is supplementing his meagre income with the usual street-bribes or worse, a palm-greasing for passing information to the higher class of criminal who has the desire and ability to cause genuine harm in London." Holmes had forgotten his drink in favour of the beef. "Corruption is no more than it is anywhere else, and I assure you, no Inspector who has something to hide comes to *me* for consultation! I made that very clear when I first started.

"But the lot is bad, Watson. They are bound up in the chains and strait-waistcoats of the system they are sworn to serve, and the rate of losses against justice is simply too high—no, it is not acceptable. For Scotland Yard to stop being a bad lot, it must improve itself from within."

"Holmes, have you contemplated the possibility you are simply ahead of your time?" Watson wanted nothing more than to savour a stupendous meal, but Holmes had, as usual,

---

[26] Holmes is concerned at the lower status a surgeon has compared to the higher-grade of rank as a physician.

grabbed their conversation by the horns and was now driving it bawling down a road with a stick and Watson was along for the show. "Prophecy is often little more than drawing sensible conclusions and solutions to a problem—but just because the solution can be seen does not mean it can be met."

Holmes grunted. "My dear fellow, logic should be the *simplest* of all disciplines to master. That no one takes the time to do so in childhood means the human race must inevitably suffer."

This from a man who didn't see a reason to try to understand the world around him with a logical, systemic approach in proven sciences like calculus, astronomy, and basic language.

He doesn't want to know who Thomas Carlyle is...and understanding the man gives one insight to the criminal motive...If I told him one of my own classmates was murdered over a literary scholarship, would he even know what I was talking about? Watson kept his opinion to himself only by a large force of will and a larger forkful of beef. Food made an effective gag. It was easier to keep quiet when he ate. *He doesn't know or care that the earth revolves around the sun...I wish he'd patrol 'Bart's with me during the nights of the waxing moon...he'd see for himself the number of births and deaths increase—as well as the shows of mental illness. He might find it a small influencing factor in some of his murder cases...I know I would. There's a reason why* lunacy *and* mania *and* moon-struck *and* moon-calf *are all words in the medical dictionary...*

Holmes had subsided for the moment inside his vegetables—not that Watson was fooled by this temporary retreat-by-omission. Holmes reminded him of Colonel Hayter in moments like this...he softened one up with the main argument, allowed the enemy to defend themselves, riposted, and promptly withdrew his forces to regroup for the oncoming attack.

I wonder what would happen if I arranged for those two to meet? The thought was undeniably alarming, but also attractive.

2: The Disclosure of a Skeleton
"Never be surprised at the crumbling of an idol or the disclosure of a skeleton"
--John Emerich E. Dalberg

Watson was too worn down from his day to devote attention to both meal and company. Holmes wasn't in possession of a high level of pride at himself for pressing such an awkward issue when his fellow lodger (or victim) was so low in spirits, but as usual his impulses were at war with his slower-acting caution.

Holmes had seen that look before, when the doctor was tightly gripping to focus on the world around him. When his plate was scoured clean, he rose and went upstairs to change-- quite a departure from his normal routine. It was easy to deduce Watson had been at the end of his strength and needed to rest in the sitting room before he went upstairs to actually sleep.

Holmes finished his own dinner with a continuing sense of discomfort and poured out the brandy by the chemistry table. By the time Watson returned, he would have reason to sit by the fire and thaw the freeze that still slowed his movements.

Holmes knew full well what broken bones felt like—and Watson's bones had been shattered during the war, and it was a poor way to acquire a barometre.

Soon enough, Watson returned looking a bit more human. He blinked in initial surprise as Holmes held the glass out, and then took it with a grateful murmur.

"Not at all." Holmes waved that off, feeling his ever-present impatience bubble up. Did Watson think he was so self-withdrawn that he would not notice his fellow lodger was dead on his feet and worn to the bone?

Not that, he reminded himself. Watson's long-term presence was slowly reminding Holmes of the many differences between the way *he* saw the world, and the way the world *thought it worked*. In a way it was distraction, but it was instructive. It pulled him outside of the simple intellectual boundaries of his mind and into a much murkier realm of emotion.

He sank back down in his favourite chair, for now not returning to his pipe. Watson had taken the couch, the better to adjust his aching shoulder and a clearly complaining blow to his leg and was half-asleep before the flames.

There was no great intellectual algorithm to that knee; Watson's balance was not the best with the roads being what they were. It would have been polite to say something, but in the matter of Watson's recovery, Holmes was resolutely out of his depth. He had never thought of the body as something to use, but the doctor had was a natural athlete; the kind of man who enjoyed pushing his physical limits. Holmes somewhat understood that drive, though for him it was the thrill of seeing how far his mind could control his body. Afghanistan had tragically left Watson with a frame he barely recognised, and he was still making mistakes in depth and perception.

Holmes had little use for any deep emotions, and these had him troubled on a level on which he did not often see; the Biblical admonition, *'if thy eye offendeth thee, pluck it out'* reminded him of how Watson sometimes stared down at his stiff arm, or rested his hand on his knee, as if the genuine articles had been stolen whilst he slept and he wondered where the originals were hiding.

Watson had not lied about his nerves, but the greatest enemies are those inside one's own brain. Holmes had often witnessed the moments of self-castigation in his friend, and the emotion was not far from devout loathing. Whatever had happened in Afghanistan had been the propelling force in his deliberate uprooting of his personal identity. No one simply chose to place themselves in *London* for the mere sake of it; no, Watson had quit the world he had owned before the military.

Holmes had caught on long ago that Watson's body was broken, but that was the smaller portion of the problem. Inside that broken body huddled a spirit with something large and precious missing. The clues were as subtle as they were unmistakable; the way the doctor hesitated sometimes, as if something had triggered a memory against his will; there were moments when a thought would occur to him and sever his existing mood. The worst times were when Holmes was a reluctant witness; Holmes would spy Watson in unguarded expressions when the doctor had no suspicion he was being watched.

Who is it he searches for in London? The question alternately flared and smouldered in Holmes' brain. *Why does he not seek them out? It is someone he both needs and dreads.*

The silent and painful hope in those brown eyes stymied Holmes, for those thoughts should not be anyone's business but Watson's. Watson made no attempts to seek this person out by means of mail, newspaper, Scotland Yard or even the nearest consulting detective who sat at him across the breakfast-table every morning.

He was grateful that they had never needed to speak amongst each other merely for the sake of it; Watson had that rare quality of silence, and days could pass when he barely initiated conversation at all. It was all part of his nature, and Holmes found it a simple thing to live with—his own habits, he was certain, were far stranger and irritating.

There was a price in seeing too much.

"My apologies, Watson."

Watson had nearly fallen asleep. He lifted his head slightly, drowsy puzzlement tinting his eyes. "Whatever for, Holmes?"

"You are in a low mood and I should not be pressing my opinions on you." Holmes felt his awkwardness grow, and with it, a converse desire to snap his impatience to the world. "It is clear your day has been as bad as it can get."

Watson shook them both with a gallows-laugh. "Oh, dear fellow, one *never* uses those words around a physician. A day can *always* get worse." He realised he was in danger of dropping his glass and finished it quickly. "Any day one can walk away can't possibly be a complete disaster."

"I feel I prefer your every-day displays of optimism as opposed to that one," Holmes mused. "But then, most emotions are outside my realm, not just the softer ones."

Watson opened one eye again, and this time the look was of patient tolerance. "Holmes, it hardly matters. You've got a soul and that's what matters the most."

Holmes sniggered. "I am often accused otherwise, my dear fellow. I believe it was the Assizes who commented that my curiosity in crime must have been spurned by the grievous theft of my soul as a child, henceforth I dabble in shadows, hoping to find the thief."

Watson chuckled too, impressed at his wit. "I'm afraid I can't speak for your childhood. But I can say with confidence you have a soul. Through it your emotions are expressed." Weariness thickened his voice; with the brandy and the warmth of the fire, he was sliding fast to Morpheus.

"Of course, you had to purchase it first…"

"Purchase it? My dear doctor, I shall have to examine that brandy for foreign agents. "One does not have the ability to purchase a soul."

"I couldn't disagree more…" Watson riposted drowsily. "If it's available from a Tottingham Court Road peddler for fifty-five shillings."[27]

By the time Holmes had recovered enough to say something, Watson was asleep.

***

221B Baker Street:

"You won't find any answers there, my friend."

Watson slowly released his gaze from his plate to look at his breakfast companion. "I'm sorry; I was woolgathering, Holmes. What did you just say?"

Holmes nodded at the plate. "I was saying you won't find any answers there—well, at least you won't find too many.

---

[27] Holmes' Stradivarius! Holmes revealed in *The Adventure of the Cardboard Box* his Strad was worth at least 500 guineas, but he had purchased it from a "Jew Broker" off Tottingham for 55s. A guinea is worth 1 pound + 1 shilling, and used for tipping; a gentleman's coin. A tradesman like a shoemaker was paid in pounds, but a guinea was used to pay an artist. At the same time, it was a mark of a true gentleman to pay with guineas. A shilling is 5 pence or a 'bob". Holmes had a reason to be smug!!

Other than the fact that Mrs. Hudson's way with sausages are to be commended. They accompany her hand for coddled eggs and toast."

Watson snorted softly and returned to his fork. "Very true." He admitted.

Holmes did not quite sigh, but his eyes glittered. "Was the Convention *that* dreadful?"

Watson's response was to put down the fork and rest his head in his hands. (Holmes committed himself to an heroic act of will and forced his lips shut) "In some ways, going to that convention was one of the worst mistakes I've made in my life." The doctor confessed.

"And you've had the opportunity to make *so many* mistakes in your advanced years." Holmes observed.

Watson lifted his head and managed to skewer his room-mate. "In the course of things, Holmes, one doesn't need to make *many* mistakes. *One* is all that's required."

"Whilst I've often said as much in tracking criminals from those very mistakes, my dear Watson, it is upsetting in the extreme to hear such a philosophy from *your* lips." Holmes' concern, when he was able to express it, could be difficult to combat. "Pessimism does not become you, Watson."

"You are the philosopher among us, Holmes." Watson regarded his plate and finally began cutting his food. "*I'm* the frustrated writer."

"Better frustrated than frustrating, and that you never are." Holmes' sudden desire for neatness led to his using the toast to clean up what remained on his plate.

Watson almost laughed, but it was not the kind of laugh anyone wanted to hear. "What would you say to a doctor who is blood-sick, Holmes?"

Holmes would never admit it to anyone but himself, but Watson had a gift for flattening others with the sheer intensity of his gaze. This was one of those times.

"I would say it is a rare physician who never feels that way." Holmes picked his words with care; a chasm had yawed open between them, and he was not certain of his path. "One of the finest painters I know cannot bear the sight or smell of his art five months out of the year; an accountant is prone to the silence of a stone two-thirds of his waking day in balance of what he refers to as 'the chatter of mathematics' in his head...you have seen for yourself how stale I become when the mood overtakes me." Holmes abandoned his clean plate for a teacup. "The contradiction of your profession, Watson, is that you as a physician are sworn to uphold life, and yet that oath requires you to be constantly exposed to death and miasma. You would astonish me if you were immune to it."

Watson appeared to be *slightly* mollified by Holmes' observations. "That convention was full of death." The words were nearly blurted out. "Edinburgh medicine is no light thing, Holmes. It has been holding its own ground among its peers since before it was established in the eyes of the world. I was witness to the most brilliant minds of our time, and I heard their thoughts; saw their demonstrations; came out of it intellectually inspired and encouraged...but that was only the *intellectual* aspect.

"Perhaps it is because we are still in the wake of war and its strains...but...for every living man there, I *swear* there was a skeleton, or something that was once alive preserved in jars. The dissections had never been so hateful to my eye, and I witnessed enough tasteless jokes levity to last a lifetime!" He rubbed at his forehead against the tight band that had appeared. "I don't remember this when I was a student...can a war change views to such an extent? Where was the reverence?" He finally whispered. "Why was it so rare?"

The doctor had closed his eyes. Holmes could see how his eyes still moved behind the lids, seeing things that had passed. "I can stand being a locum." He said at last. "I can build on my practice in a year or two, enough that I can purchase something around Paddington or even Kensington...but I tell you Holmes, I see more respect for the dead when I'm with you, or in the cool-room at Scotland Yard."

***

Paddington Street:

Bradstreet took the news well, all things considering.

Lestrade had slept as poorly as Watson; every few hours he would catch himself lying wide awake in bed, staring at the black of the ceiling. He would force himself to relax and drift into a doze—but then the enormity of his task would rise up again and undo all the good of the light rest. Bradstreet had commented on it as soon as he'd knocked on the door, as snowmelt evaporated off his blackcloth-broad shoulders like dirty mist.

For all their similarities, Lestrade was not capable of mourning longer than a short period of time. His people were hard-cut children of the Channel Isles and it went against their grain—not to mention their faith—to wear grief heavily. Grief held the dead back from their rightful passage to Heaven. Excessive grief meant their loved ones had to carry heavy buckets slopping over with coal-black tears. At the same time, he understood that Bradstreet's people weren't his people, and it stood to reason they'd think and see things differently.

Mourning was a necessity, and one that Lestrade understood even if his own people recoiled from its demonstration. More than expression, Bradstreet was silently advertising that the loss existed. It told people how to act when they were around him—no overt levity, no jokes within a certain frame, nothing that would be inappropriate.

Bradstreet was a large, gentle man for all that he was fierce in a fight, but Lestrade wished his friend had not had to wear the black *so very much*. First his sister, then his parents, then an infant...and now his two youngest down from the same fevers and his wife had very nearly followed.

In all but the first case, the passings at least had the comfort of the impartial hand of death. The first one, Bradstreet's only sister and his closest flesh and blood...had been of willful violence. That was not anything like knowing disease and old age had come calling. It was much worse.

The big man listened in perfect silence, dark eyes intent, never once asking a question. Lestrade was glad when he could finally finish, and the silence steamed between them as Lestrade served up some of Mrs. Collins' hot coffee and raspberry scones.

Bradstreet chewed through two of those scones, his face wrapped in the deepest concentration Lestrade had ever seen in him. His thoughts were so absorbed he couldn't even let his emotions out; his eyes clicked like cogs, making Lestrade recall Mr. Holmes was when he was body and soul into a case.

"We had thought of that." Bradstreet finally said. His mourning-jet cufflinks were dulled with too much recent use; they scraped against the table linen. Lestrade shivered, relieved that the silence was shattered. "There had been a few people who were curious in her...from a... *medical viewpoint.*" Bradstreet spoke to the top of his coffee, which was muddy and milky and speckled with tiny grounds as if those minute flecks held all the secrets normally revealed by tea leaves. He did not speak to Lestrade. It was easier that way. The years made his face ancient around the lower-mask of his moustache. "I still have the list of names of those who were willing to pay our parents for the honour of examining her."

"Dr. Watson said he was collating the names of them who were the most outwardly involved." Lestrade pushed the jam pot to Bradstreet, mostly to give his hands a task.

"Watson has family up there, doesn't he?"

"I have no idea." Lestrade confessed. "Why?"

"Well, he's a *Watson*." Bradstreet said as if that explained everything. At Lestrade's utter blank helplessness, the thinnest smile touched his lips. "Watsons were first registered up there in Edinburgh. Some four hundred years or so…it's a war-name. Battle commanders. They're about the worst family you'd ever want to trace, I think there's about *fifty* different septs and the Edinburgh strain suddenly vanishes as if it never existed around the first part of our century.

"But as much as the Crown lavishes on its wounded soldiers," Bradstreet's second emotion of the day was sarcasm, "I can't imagine he would have gone up there and paid for a place to stay when there was family to stay *with*." He rapped his fingers on the table. "And if he's so determined to be in on this, I'd say we avoid the fantods for his sake. *Anything* Watson does for us up there could still cause a backwash to any kith or kin."

"I hadn't thought of that." Lestrade muttered.

"I daresay most your procedural thoughts fled at his news." Bradstreet said softly.

"Would you rather stay out of this?" Lestrade blurted.

Bradstreet looked amazed. "I am dead until I find my sister."

"Forgive me, Roger." Lestrade hated himself.

"Geoffrey…" Bradstreet suddenly looked awkward. He cleared his throat. "Forgive *me* for asking this…and you don't have to answer…"

"No, do go on." Lestrade couldn't imagine refusing Bradstreet in view of what was happening.

"This could be very dangerous…a doctor who kills for his own glory can do it again. Are you certain *you* want to be a part of this?"

"Roger, for God's sake. How could I not be?" Lestrade's face flared at his embarrassment.

Bradstreet only grunted. "On that sentence…Have *you* made peace with *your* kinfolk yet?" He probed.

Lestrade felt words dry in his mouth. It was his turn to speak to the coffee cup. "There doesn't seem to be much point in my trying any longer." He said at last. "A rope is a final argument."

Bradstreet did not compound his confession with words of sympathy. There was no need.

***

221B Baker Street:

Watson had never before known guilt for poking through Holmes' papers. *Holmes* certainly never cared—his only confidential writings were locked up in a trunk half the size of his own bed, and Watson would never touch *that*. Even if the mercenary urge had come to him, he had every faith it was its own level of organizational Waterloo. But this was the first time he was actually employing Holmes' own research for a personal matter and it felt vaguely like exploitation.

Just because Holmes had neither rhyme nor reason to his creative filing system, and just because he could *never* find a blessed thing without covering the carpet in four inches of tossed foolscap, didn't mean Holmes wouldn't have a sudden attack of genius on something that was different from the day before. Watson eased the leather binder off the shelf and gave it a stern glare before opening it up.

He sighed hopelessly. Holmes was a neat and hygienic creature when it came to his own skin, but when it came to the way he ordered his life and notabilia…obviously the detective had been smashing *all* notes under the 'B' category in these pages, in no alphabetical order at all, until some sporadic fit of common sense seized him and then he would put everything in order with the paste-pot.

Watson reminded himself that the next time he was trapped inside their apartment he had a new option with which to creatively whittle away his time. He gingerly leafed through two inches of paper, seeking particular names.

The word 'body-thief' illuminated itself across his eyes like a cannon's flare. In another second, he realised he was on the right track. He glanced at the clock. A few more hours before he would be expected at St. 'Bart's. If he was careful it would be plenty of time.

He settled down and began to read.

3: Carry a Bone

A dog that will fetch a bone will carry a bone.
--proverb

<u>"Body-thieves"</u>

"*...market exists for human remains in part or in whole; market depends on the immoveable factors of 1) an unscrupulous buyer and 2) an equally unscrupulous dealer who is thus in contact with 3) the actual enactors of the crime. The latter is normally among the lowest ranks of London's social order, somewhat akin to the Celtic sin-eater, and their emotional state is against the hope of redemption. For all their gruesome work, there is a pitiable element to these creatures; they are firmly convinced they exist for Hellfire.*

'The dealer is perhaps the most unscrupulous of the three. It is he that arranges for profit the actions between 1 and 3. He feeds upon the weakness of the buyer, convinces him of the necessity of his law-breaking and his departure from his moral code. His financial stability depends on this skill; you will find him a deceptive fellow, who dresses and acts inside a broad social definition, all the better to blend in with as many different circles as possible. To the buyer, he is deferential and politely subservient; to the hapless body snatcher he is a cold and sadistic bully. The German word <u>schadenfreude</u>, *for one who takes pleasure in another's pain could hardly be more apt...*"

(Scrawled in the margins as an afterthought): "<u>Radfahrer</u>: *Ger. word for one who browbeats subordinates and flatters superiors...*"

Watson lifted his eyes from the fat book and watched tiny grey ice-balls throw themselves against the window-glass. It was a depressing day; he regretted every glance out the window. His subject content did not help his mood or the throb in his knee, which had grown from red and angry to sullen and purple.

His respect for Holmes grew the deeper he worked into the mystery of body-thieves and their world. Holmes had more than the ability to observe the world around him; always he was seeking motive for the actions he noted. There truly was a deep need in him to prove the world was *not* as nonsensical, random, and illegal as it was often seen. Everywhere he wrote there was an effort to see the underlying cause, the beginning.

Holmes scorned literature, and professed to be ignorant about it even when obscure verse floated trippingly off his tongue to seal a surgical comment upon the conclusion of a case. Watson wondered if he had simply not yet drawn the proper conjecture, for there was the stirring of a true artist in these hasty lines. The overall mood was as evocative as it was gently cautious, informing and warning at the same time. It reminded him a great deal of Rossetti's *Goblin Market*, where a young girl tried in vain to warn her sister from the seductions of the freely offered, yet venomous fruits (a greater allegory for the sweetness of danger could scarce be imagined):

> *"We must not look at goblin men,*
> *We must not buy their fruits:*
> *Who knows upon what soil they fed*
> *Their hungry thirsty roots?"*

And yet, for the sensible Lizzie's efforts, the goblins continued to sing,

He wondered how much time the detective had taken to research the reams of paperwork before him—and how slow had his hand been in recording his lightning swift thoughts? Holmes' hand was not the neatest; the letters often segued into each other in an effort to save time and space on the paper. "Inartistic" a scholar would have decreed, but Holmes was one of the greatest artists Watson had ever hoped to meet.

The doctor rose with a wince, and limped severely to the table where the teapot steamed warm. Holmes would be back within the next two hours. He was well-settled in his task, off on whatever goals his restless mind had driven him to meeting. God alone knew what *that* would be. Previous experience warned the doctor that his services might be required when he did return—hopefully for mundane purposes, such as a salve against the chafing of a filthy wool disguise, and not the profound, like last month's split knuckles (Watson had removed a fragment of the foolish attacker's tooth out of the ring finger). There were times when the faintest perfume of the Jago lingered upon his person but Holmes was too clean to keep a disguise longer than needed, and he scrupulously gave his business to the nearest bath-house when his work in the disease-ridden areas was done. Mrs. Hudson was, of course, quite grateful for the courtesy.

Surely the government would have snapped up his talents had they known of him! His ability to mark people with the objective interest of a chess master would have been invaluable to the military minds and certainly to the political deciders of Britain. What would his life have been then?

No doubt he would have risen quickly to be as famous as a Wellington or Nelson...but goodness knows he would have had to employ a flotilla of secretaries to keep up with him! Watson shuddered at the vivid image in his mind of Holmes with a long-suffering aide-de-camp following in his wake, determining the particulars of battle and then pulling a secret surprise out at the last moment, saving Queen and country.

Watson sighed. When thoughts like *that* came to his mind, the only cure was a large pot of *coffee*. He rang the bell and politely requested it of Mrs. Hudson, who, in the light of his room-mate's routine of bizarre requests, never turned a hair. Tonight he would be at his usual rounds on at the hospital, and caffeine was not normally advised on the onset of a full shift's labours. But even pretending to rest when he didn't know of Holmes' whereabouts was ridiculous. It was easier to rest with a nervous system full of stimulant, knowing Holmes was finally safe, than lie awake ignorant.

St. Bartholomew's Hospital:

Scotland Yard knew the military man—they'd been led by Colonels and Majors throughout various points in the history of their office. At any given time at least one man in ten had retired from the red uniform to don the blue. It didn't mean they were *like* the other men on the force; they had a high drop-out rate; they had ways about them. Ways that were not easily explained, but had to be tolerated.

If forced to explain, everyone would admit resolve and sleeplessness was their greatest common factor.

"Inspectors…"

Lestrade wondered at the look on Watson's face as he limped down the hallway, folding up a long no-longer white coat marred with terrible looking stains.

"Forgive me," he said by way of greeting, "we had a terrible mishap at the tracks at dawn."

"That looks like mud, blood, grass, and...well I'm not sure what *that* is on you, Watson." Bradstreet cocked his head to one side and looked the younger man up and down.

"It looks like chalk." Lestrade guessed slowly. "The cheap kind...like the earth pulled out of Plymouth and used by children."

"Exactly." Watson looked down at his clothing. The coat had protected with minimal results. "To be precise, proof that someone was trying to sneak a dark horse in under a pale identity...Are you a fan of the races?"

"Er..." Lestrade was unsure how to proceed. "My family once cherished a fond notion that their son would bring about fame as a jockey."

"I've noticed your hand with horses. Was that the motive?"

"Well, that and the fact that for some time it looked as though I'd never see an inch over five feet." Lestrade shrugged, suddenly awkward. "I was never so glad as to gain six inches over the mark in my entire life."

"Couldn't have made a jockey with your weight anyway, Geoffrey." Bradstreet rumbled with a grin. He whacked Lestrade on the shoulder with terrific force; the small man barely moved, long used to his larger friend's ways. "Of course, it means he can't *run* as fast as most of us..."

"Can't have everything, and it's a small price to pay for not smelling horses all my life." Lestrade snapped testily.

"I thought you liked the horses?"

"Not that well." Lestrade muttered. "And I can't enjoy the races much anymore. I keep thinking of all the criminals that are in the crowds."

"My greatest crime is an irrational weakness for the underdog at the tracks. It ensures I win no more than one out of six times." Watson had signaled to an orderly behind Bradstreet. "If you gentlemen have a moment, there is a meeting-room we can use; it's quite private."

"By all means lead the way." Lestrade agreed.

Watson took them to a small room lit with an amazingly ineffectual little fireplace and a stained-glass window made up like a clustre of rosemary, heavy with blue blooms. The murky winter light cast only the palest stripes of colour on the dark paneled wood of the walls and seemed to be at war with the small lamps. Watson picked up a dried wreath of rosemary and placed it on the outer door-knob. A smell reminiscent of roasted lamb or hair-rinse or Christmas floated up.

"A signal," he explained to their eyebrows. "To anyone else on the floor that a private consultation is taking place and we are not to be disturbed." He lifted his eyebrows to underscore the point. "Consultation of the bereaved."

"'Rosemary, that's for remembrance.'" Bradstreet quoted the Bard.

Watson chuckled. "Exactly. Nothing short of a fire or an attack by drunken Dynamiters will disturb us now."

"Neatly done." Bradstreet heaved himself into the closest chair and let his head fall back with a short puff of breath. "Lestrade's filled me in on all the details y'gave to him, Watson."

"I've been trying to work a little research into my time," Watson pulled out his Oxford Street cigarettes, and lit one with great relief. "I confess I've been nerve-wracked." Anyone looking at him would have no trouble believing that; his cheeks were dark with hollows that pulled shadows around his dark eyes. "It somewhat helps a bit that some folk are planning out the first anniversary of the disaster of Maiwand. Everyone seems to look at me and draw their own conclusions for my appearance." His matter-of-fact statement was a little off the usual demeanor they were used to witnessing.

"Have you found anything new?" Bradstreet opened his eyes and leveled the uncomfortable doctor with a look. "I can understand your unease, doctor. Please understand, I mourned for my sister years ago. I have *always* known she was dead, but it was the *details* I never knew. We are not discussing *her*; we are discussing her mortal remains, which were the *least* of her."

Bradstreet would have made a good soldier. Watson pulled hard on his cigarette. "I learned there were a few men who were willing to make a study of your sister's condition. One was purely from the nature of a folklorist; the second was from his own work in familial history..." Watson had managed to pull half the cigarette dry in five breaths. "One man had both interests, and a fourth was curious from a private project that studied pathological disease."

"Disease?" Bradstreet repeated sharply. "She was hardly diseased."

"Forgive me for not clarifying a point." Watson stared at his smoke, and then defiantly rose to stand by the chilly little fireplace. A single flame snapped, weak as a wisp. "There are very few causes of polysyndactyly such as your sister's. The first and most well-known cause is simple inheritance; family traits handed down. All the other causes for this condition tend to be by the influence of rare syndromes or diseases; Mongoloid children, for example, can have the tendency." He shrugged slightly. "I suspect it is simply inheritance in your family, but I do not have that proof."

Bradstreet nodded. "It happens in the Roane side of the family off and on. Not so much as one would think, but it's a bit like...well, a bit like twins popping up. You know it can happen." He lifted one of his big, normal hands up. "I don't have a single trait, but let me tell you, I was certain to tell my future Mrs. Bradstreet all about it." He spread his fingers wide apart. "Luckily she seemed to feel that not a problem, but then she was from the *other* Roanes."

Despite the circumstances of the meeting, Watson was privately amused to see how Lestrade (safely behind Bradstreet's shoulder) grimaced like a monkey at this reminder of complicated Celtic lineages. He was reminded (again) that no Royal House could hope to impress the intricate knotwork of kith and kin from the tribes of Britain.

"But modern medicine is capable of dealing with…some of the webbing, is it not?" Lestrade wondered. "Not like in the past."

Watson winced. "That very much depends on the case. The webbing can be surgically split between the digits to allow freedom of movement. There are some disadvantages to this; the scar tissue builds up and becomes awkward. The webbing will try to return. Superfluous digits can be surgically removed, but best that be done when the patient is as young as possible." Smoking had calmed the doctor somewhat. He looked less like the burnt-to-the-bone young man they had met in the hallway. They knew Watson was at least nine or ten years' Lestrade's junior, but here he looked much younger than that; like a new student struck down by influenza.

Watson tossed his spent Bradley's[28] into a pillar of sand and reached for a new victim in the same motion. He paused only to light on a tiny gas-jet perched over the mantle (which was for show and a pacing man's elbow more than practicality). After a moment he exhaled fresh smoke through his nose.

---

[28] *"…for when I see the stub of a cigarette marked Bradley, Oxford Street, I know that my friend Watson is in the neighbourhood."*—Holmes to Watson, HOUN.

"Part of the problem with research is finding all pre-existing sources. Since our earliest days, polysyndactylys were sent to the famous courts of Europe. It was a mark of status to have a fully equipped Court, complete with not just the oddities such as dwarfs and merged twins, but folk such as albinos and the extra-fingered were a subject of study by the most learned minds of the time. Scientists congregated not just to Royalty because they were funding all the discoveries; they were going to Court because that was where all the proper studies took place." For a moment, a very strange expression flittered over his face, as if some unique thought had occurred, and he discreetly buried it.

"I've been working peculiar research," Watson looked chagrined at his admission. "There have been a few..." He hesitated, not knowing what to say. "Criminals that took Holmes' attention in the matter of...unethical medicine."

Bradstreet's nearly-black eyes were square with tension. "Ye needn't try so hard to spare my feelings, Watson." He rumbled. "I tell you again. It's something I thought of a long time ago, and I thought of it daily, it's just that...well, there was never any *proof*." He leaned sideways to better reach into his coat-pocket, and pulled out his notebook. "I drafted this up on the way over," he leafed through the book and pushed the open pages over to the standing doctor. "There might be some more names; these are who I remember off the top of my head."

"Hmn." Watson's brown eyes skittered down the list; twice they saw his brows go up. "May I make a copy of this?"

"With my blessings." Bradstreet answered.

Watson limped over to a vacant chair, pulling his own notebook out of his jacket.

"I say, doctor, what happened to you?" Lestrade wondered. "You weren't walking like that last night."

"I planted my kneecap into the street right after you left." Watson explained. "I won't blame you if you can't believe this, but a *rabbit* took off running out of an alleyway with the most wretched scream, a terrier-mongrel at its heels, and I was shocked enough to lose my balance. The cry of a wounded rabbit is maddening to hear."[29]

"I'll bet that was someone's planned supper," Lestrade commented. "This time of year, people try to get what they can in the way of a decent meal."

Watson's hand slowed over his transcribing. "Yes…" he murmured. "I can believe that." Holmes had written the winter months had been ideal for body-snatching; weather, low traffic and financial need being all on the side of the ghoulish brokers. He chose to be silent.

"We await your information," Lestrade cleared his throat; he and Bradstreet traded a concerned look. "I assure you, we're not fond of the idea of exposing this…matter…in a way that would punish the innocent."

"Innocent?" Watson muttered; his eyes had slid inward, watching something in another dimension. "I'm not convinced there are innocent parties in this. Not directly. But they have innocent friends and family." He controlled himself with an effort. "Bradstreet, I have a rather unusual request to make of you."

"Name it." Bradstreet grunted.

"There might be another form of proof that would help with this." Watson's voice went soft and quiet. "I…you'll think me mad for this question, I'm sure. But is there anything you possess that would contain your sister's fingerprints or even her handprints?"

Bradstreet leaned backwards in his chair, rubbing his mustaches in thought. "There…there may be." He said at last.

---

[29] Just a small homage to ACD's own observation on the fact…

"I would have to look for myself to see…that would take a bit of time, you understand."

"Yes…" Watson nodded. "I understand." He looked down and rubbed his shoulder absently, completely without thought. The unknowing mention of his wound embarrassed the policemen for reasons they did not understand, as if they had spied him in a private moment. "It would be most important to find any proofs."

"The evil that men do lives after them;
the good is oft interred with their bones"
--Shakespeare

Bow Street:

Bradstreet fumbled with the key to his door. The Bow Street District wasn't the worst place to live in London, but he didn't like his sick wife and young children inside without him. Poor Hazel was still moving slowly after her long illness and the little ones were frightened at the sight of their strong mother weak and pale. He stopped as soon as he was inside, trying to shake the weather off his clothes on the mat and not on the floor itself.

"Hello, Papa." Alice hurried to help him with his coat; Elena a breadth after. The girls had sobered and grown up a bit faster than Roger would have liked. But…in a way it was better than what his sons were doing.

Garrett dealt with the sorrow in the house by throwing himself into his books, and Brian, always nervous, was trying to eat them out of the house. Bradstreet had stopped buying sweets as soon as he realised his son's habits, but too little too late.

"Hello, my girls." Roger bent to kiss them on the tops of their heads. "How are things? Is your mother up?"

"She's reading." Elena said helpfully. "We have her under the blankets by the fire, and lots of red tea."

"Good for you." Bradstreet approved. He shook the cold out of his wind-stiffened hands. "Where are your brothers?"

"Upstairs. I think they're trying to finish that model boat." Alice did not sound hopeful. She carried little faith in brothers on principle. "Papa," she tugged on his sleeve. "Brother Jerome stopped by today." Her large eyes mirrored her sister's. "He sat and talked with Mama a long time."

Jerome was of a different church but a kind man, honestly humble and simple. Bradstreet couldn't imagine the little man causing any sort of strife in an already shadowed house. "What is the matter, sweetheart?"

"He asked if there was anything we would like to donate to charity." Alice dug her toe into the floor. Her voice was still and small. "She said he could take the cradle."

Bradstreet swallowed hard. His eyes threatened to fill up for a moment and his gaze slipped over his daughters' smooth heads. "I'm glad of it," he said roughly. "Somewhere, there's some little'uns sleeping warm tonight, eh?" He smiled through a brick wall of hurt and patted them both on their narrow shoulders. They both took after their mother in looks…thank God. "Ladies, is there any chance of a cup of tea whilst I see to your mum?"

The girls looked at each other, horrified at a slip. A moment later they were scurrying down the hallway to the kitchen. Bradstreet took the moment to wipe his eyes and square his shoulders.

Paddington Street:
Lestrade had gone through a great deal of trouble to check out every book he could find that was pertinent to the nightmare at hand. He told himself he might as well. The

weather was execrable. He was to all purposes, trapped in his rooms unless someone gave him an excuse to go outside—he rather hoped that would not happen.

He lit the small oil lamp at his desk for extra illumination and rubbed at his eyes. His evening had been simple enough: go through Watson's book in the search for any clue as to the ways of a certain Jonas Q. Parker. That endeavour lasted as long as Lestrade's gut could hold up in the face of page after page *after page after page* of printed images that consisted of 1) some sort of medical celebrity, 2) some sort of dead thing to pose with.

Lestrade's fortitude had seen a lot of death—none of it pretty. He was simply not made for the exposure of this sort of…bloodless, sanitised morbidity. After page 23, which was Parker's life in 50 words or less, he had given up and stuffed the book in his most neglected corner. It was high time for some fairy tales. With a shot of *chouchen* to chase away the chill that had crawled under his skin.

He had given up on hopes of avoiding material that delved into the realm of folk and fairy tales. The courts would laugh at him; the prosecutor would find a gold mine of comedy in his testimony if word got out…but…There just wasn't any way of getting around it. Besides, the lure of folklore and oral memory was part of the reason why Elspeth was dead.

Stick to the facts and you can't go wrong. You're not an educated man; you're not a scholar. But if you keep it so simple that anyone can see the truth, they can't argue with it. Roger's sister died because of these tales.

Lestrade's insides gnawed to think of it. Bradstreet shouldn't be forced into this. Not with those little boys just put into the earth. The Inspector's rage at the injustice cut close to his own bones; this was the *third* time they'd had to bury their infants. Why couldn't Bradstreet's family forgive him enough to make their peace? Was it pride? Something worse? *Three infants...*

Lestrade was also estranged from his own family, with a good deal more reason than poor Roger, but he vividly recalled the toll upon his parents when his youngest siblings, two sisters and a brother, died after larking out to catch fish in the Red Tides. His mother had never quite recovered, but she had been a small woman; he favoured her. Childbirth had been a strain on her no matter what. He tried to make himself remember them, but a part of his mind shied at the heresy even though he blamed himself for falling to superstition. His sisters and brother had been innocent. There was no shame in their memory but he tried to respect his parents' ways by not mentioning them. The names of the dead could call them back in the mistaken belief they were needed.

The little detective rubbed his arms against a cold seeping inside his ribs.

Lestrade lined his writing-pencils up, sharpened and ready to go as he thought. The real tragedy was in the rest of the Bradstreets. Roger's wife was distantly related to him (tenth cousins), so the split had reflected upon her as well. Their remaining four children were growing up separate of grandparents, cousins, aunts and uncles.

All because they put him to a task he could not bear. Roger was a big man inside and out; two of Lestrade put together, gentle and generous and willing to walk the extra mile in the freezing rain if that was what it took—or struggle through another yard of paperwork at the office even though he needed a dictionary for half the words he had to write. Perhaps his parents had never thought of him as fallible. If that was the case, then the lesson had come hard to them all.

The Inspector lit a cigarette and held it away from the first book. Clergymen were usually a mixed bag for reliability; ofttimes their reports were coloured to what they were taught they should think or feel. His own experience had taught him to look for their 'telling phrases', such as 'the locals say' or 'reported belief' that would transfer knowledge without giving the impression the priest actually enjoyed the tales.

Case in point, the Rev. James Wallace of 1693 writing of the Orkneys.

The man's approach was as mechanical as a Thoreau pencil:

"Sometime about this country are seen those Men which are called "Finmen"; In the year 1682 one was seen some time sailing, sometime rowing up and down in his little Boat at the south end of the isle of Eda, most of the people of the Isle flocked to see him, and when they adventured to put out a boat with men to see if they could apprehend him, he presently sped away most swiftly: and in the year 1684, another was seen from Westra, and for a time after they got a few or no fishees: for they have this Remark here, that these "Finmen" drive away the fishes from the place to which they come."

Lestrade was finally seeing a pattern after half a night's reading. He prided himself in being a sensible workman, owning no use for fanciful acts of imagination or embellishment. The Shetlands might have some of the more colourful examples of selkies, but the tales started in the Orkneys. Looking at geography, it suggested the beginnings of this human condition was from the Nordic people blended with the bronze-skinned Laplanders. Some of the descriptions of the seal-folk were just fancy descriptions of sealskin-clad travellers, paddling their coracles across water too choppy for any heavier craft.

Of course, Lestrade's Channel Island blood *might* be forcing this perspective, but when the denizens of one island were called 'donkeys' and another 'toads' it wasn't hard to imagine another people called 'finmen' or 'seals'...[30]

He marked the page with a clean scrap of foolscap and set the book aside for later, reaching for the next one down the stack. The latest reference, just put out that year, was from Karl Blind. The book was so new it creaked in his hands.

"In Shetland, and elsewhere in the North, the sometimes animal-shaped creatures of this myth, but who in reality are human in a higher sense, are called Finns... Their transfiguration into seals seems to be more a kind of deception they practice—

Aha.

-- For the males are described as most daring boatmen, with powerful sweep of the oar, who chase foreign vessels on the sea. At the same time they are held to be deeply versed in magic spells and in the healing art, as well as in soothsaying.

Lestrade snorted to himself. Every newcomer down the road was suspected of the same thing. Still, the writer was making an effort to separate fairy tale from truth.

"By means of a "skin" which they possess, the men and women among them are able to change themselves into seals. But on shore, after having taken off their wrappage, they are, and behave like, real human beings.

---

[30] Jersey =Toad; Guernsey=Donkey; Rabbit=Aldernay; Sark=Crows

"Anyone who gets hold of their protecting garment has the Finn in his power. Only by means of the skin can they go back to the water.

"Many a Finn woman has got into the power of a Shetlander and borne children to him; but if a Finn woman succeeded in re-obtaining her sea-skin, or seal-skin, she escaped across the water.

"Among the older generation in the Northern Isles persons are still sometimes heard of who boast of hailing from the Finns; and they attribute to themselves a peculiar luckiness on account of their higher descent."

There was something about that account that…rang…strangely. Lestrade couldn't put his finger on it, but it likened him to being a child again, and being told a story that was edited in a way that made the whole matter fall…flat.

He scowled and pulled more smoke into his lungs. Imagine that murder could be committed over fairy tales, but at the same time, he'd seen worse committed over even less. Was it only last month they'd had to pick up the pieces of a man who had been dismembered by a mad butcher? The excuse for that death had been the man's choice of dress. It didn't even help that the butcher was clearly off to Hanwell.[31] The fact was clothing had been the factor that tipped him to his action.

I'm out of my depth. I know it. So is Roger and I daresay Watson too. But there was a motive for this murder, and we have our own motives for seeing it ended. Lestrade tapped ash absently; it gave his hand something to do. *For whatever reason, Elspeth was murdered because of folklore. Folklore*

---

[31] Full phrase: "Gone off to Hanwell and no return ticket": Gone crazy.

128

started it all. There has to be some clue we can use in ferreting out this case...

Bow Street:

The Princess and the Goblin sprawled under her long fingers, and on the floor, Mark Twain's A Tramp Abroad rested where it had slid off her lap. Hazel Bradstreet slept deeply, but for the first time a blush of colour touched her lips. Her husband smiled to see it, but blinked askance at the third book on the floor, At The Back of the North Wind.[32] He bent over the settee and kissed her cheek. Her skin was still quite pale; her freckles transparent. She smiled to see him and reached up to hold his hand. They shared a silent look of affection.

"How are you, dear?" Hazel asked softly.

"Glad to be home, Coll." He kissed her hand. "Did you rest?"

Hazel managed to laugh, just a bit. "I hadn't any choice. Those girls of yours are tyrants!"

Roger laughed right back. "I wonder where they get it from."

"There's no telling." She moved aside and he circled the couch to sit at her waist. "They said they're making bread. If it works, that'll be our supper tonight."

"Perfect." Roger held her hand inside his big ones. Hazel wasn't a small woman; she was built along the lines of an Amazon should that fierce species choose bright plaids and wear their hair in Repentance Curls. Next to Bradstreet she was willowy.

Her warm eyes sank into his. "Roger, is something wrong? You're wearing your 'work face' again."

---

[32] A rare book of theodicy. One of Samuel Clemens' favourites because his own departed daughter loved it immensely.

He sighed through his nose. "I'm sorry, dear. It's just that..." He took a deep breath. "We may have a clue for Elspeth."

Hazel's face paled even further for a moment, and then her delicate colour quickly flooded back. "Oh..." She said faintly. Her hand rested over her mouth. "Oh, dearest."

"I may have to leave for a bit, to find out the truth." He warned. "Not now, perhaps not for a few days. I'm just...letting you know." He wasn't going to tell her Watson's account. Lord, no.

Her fingers gripped his painfully. "I don't want you to get your hopes up, Roger. But...if this is so...then...then it can only be for the good."

Roger was mute, gripping his wife's now-weakened hand inside his. The house had been his inheritance from his father, who had died before Elspeth. They took in roomers in summer to deal with the expenses, and he knew every long fitted plank in the floor, every inch of wall-paper and the smell of soft-coal with polish and soda. The house was their refuge and a reminder of how Elspeth's death had changed their lives.

"I don't want to leave you." He warned. "If worse comes to worse, I'll let Geoffrey take the case alone. He as much as threatened to sever me if I didn't look to you first—and much I'd deserve it."

"Roger, I'd be certain to let you know if things couldn't continue without you for a bit." Hazel leaned up and kissed him through his beard, a gesture that always made him laugh. "Is there anything I can do?"

Roger bit his lip. "I don't know," he said slowly. "Would the family speak with you?"

"They've always been willing to speak with me," Hazel said with a coldness that was not directed at her husband at all. "I have simply chosen not to."

Roger took a deep breath. "I need something of Elspeth's. If you asked for it…do you think they would give it to you?"

"We can but try." She said simply. "And we will."

4: Take my Bones
"Heaven take my soul, and England take my bones!"
--William Shakespeare

Hazel heard someone rap at the door in the early hours of morning. Before she could even rise up, Elena was pattering down the hallway in her stocking feet. *Goodness.* Elena was normally a late sleeper. She wondered if the full moon was rising again; mad dogs, madmen, and Elena always reacted to the shift in the lunar cycle.

She re-settled back down under the warm quilts at the girl's low giggles. A familiar tenor answered back. *Geoffrey.* Hazel smiled to herself. A week couldn't pass without Roger and Geoffrey seeing each other. A shame they didn't often work together.

Elena skittered back and popped her head into the sitting room. "Mum," She beamed. "Uncle Geoffrey's here. Has Papa left?"

"He left at a quarter-past, dear." Hazel told her daughter—and to the entering Geoffrey Lestrade. "Elena, *what* are you doing up?"

"I'm trying another loaf of bread." Elena was put out. "It's not rising as well as yesterday."

"There's less warmth, sweetheart. The slower the rise the better the bread. Why don't you take the time and create a filling to roll inside the dough when it has set? You have nearly an hour before school."

Elena perked up and vanished as quickly as she had appeared.

Geoffrey traded a rueful adult look. "She never seems to operate under anything less than three horsepower." He noted. "Roger's at Bow again?"

"A late case. He didn't give me details, save that he had to go take a lesson on the language of Flowers, even if it cost him ten shillings or seven days." Hostess and guest shared mixed sighs. "And after that, a few telegrams, and then would see to some matters with the Bow Street Runners at the new station-house."[33]

"Tcha! He can't stay away! I'm lucky he spends three days at the Main Office as it is." Geoffrey set down a pasteboard box with an intriguing rattle and sank into his usual chair. "How have you been?" He asked.

"I shall be glad to get up." Hazel said fervently. "I am tired of being tired." She allowed her hands to twitch over the smoothly stitched fabric. "And I am close to nausea to think about sewing, or knitting, or tatting, or all of the other things."

"How about glue?"

"Glue?"

Geoffrey opened the lid of the box and held it out. Hazel took it; the weight was more than expected. Inside rested a box of assorted shells in a wide variety. "I'll have you know, your loving husband sent me halfway to Cheddar to pick this up."

"Oh, bless his big awkward heart." Hazel said with feeling. "And bless yours for being so easily swayed."

"Swayed, bosh. You're his sanity. That keeps *me* sane." Geoffrey grinned.

"I shall make something creative." Hazel decided. "Bring the lap-table over here."

---

[33] Language of Flowers: Listening to Magistrate Flowers at the Bow Street court. The man was known for his solution to offences: "Ten shillings or seven days!" Bow Street Runners were one of the earliest versions (1746) of the London police. They evolved from the "Thief-Takers" who tracked criminals for a fee, and took government wages. Their building (25 and 27 Bow Street), was completed in 1881 and unfortunately converted to a boutique in 2007

Geoffrey obliged; Hazel poured a handful of shells into the corner and began sorting "Geoffrey, what is this matter?" They both knew what she meant, and though she was a Northerner of the island and he from the Southern, they were both too old-fashioned and polite to mention the dead by name in a casual conversation.

Geoffrey never bothered prevaricating with Hazel. It did no good; it never did. He sighed and wished for a cigarette. "We were given some information from an unexpected source," he spoke delicately. "It will be long and complicated, I fear. And I also fear for Roger's well-being. But if I hadn't included him..."

"He would have ended your friendship." Hazel finished. "I know." Her sharp eyes sank into his flesh like daggers. "And you have the look of someone already troubled?"

He stared at her without speaking, unsure of what to do. Long experience with Hazel finally won out. "I just..." His hands moved over the hat in his lap. "I'm already disturbed and that's because of things that necessarily ought not to do with the case." His cheeks pinked under his normally sallow complexion, and he stared down to give the threadbare drugget a firm examination.

"Geoffrey, you are just going to have to explain yourself now." Hazel's bright mind flared in the hope of something to think about.

"I've been studying a bit on...people with more fingers and toes than..." He cleared his throat hastily. "Than most." That last was said out of consideration for the absent Bradstreet. "They're called polydactyls...I thought I might fathom the motive of someone who would want to kill a child because they were so...different." He looked further past her, from the floor to the opposing wall. "I don't like to talk about it."

"I shan't think anyone would be." Hazel answered him. "And forgive my saying so, but this already sounds dangerous. If a person would kill a child for scientific edification, they couldn't possibly hesitate at killing a grown man." Hazel Roane Bradstreet was a composite of all conceivable warm shades of golden browns. It made her eyes gleam like a fiercely intelligent cat's. "A policeman would be seen as the means for such a man's destruction. They will defend their sorry lives, Geoffrey."

"I'm not about to let Roger stick his neck out any further than he must." Geoffrey took a deep, deep breath as he spoke. "I am worried that he will journey into personal territory. I plan to be there at his side *the entire time.*"

Hazel chuckled. "Good for you, but you know as well as I do; when my Roger is in action, nothing less than a freight train can pause his motion." At her ersatz brother's grimace, Hazel laughed out loud. "He needs this, Geoffrey." She sobered softly. "If this can help heal the rift in the family, he won't hesitate. "

"The rift should have never happened." Geoffrey snapped. "I *am* sorry, Hazel, I know they're your cousins, but all of this was wrong."

"*Far* cousins, thank you. But, no…Grief can take on forms as hard as a rock," Hazel replied softly. "And one can dash themselves to death upon them. I would say the same about your own family, Geoffrey, but you seem to feel their censure is justified."

He set his lips tight. He was not about to argue with Hazel. Not here, and especially not now, but this was their oldest argument, during which Hazel truly *did* sound like one of his actual sisters. Jenny, mostly…he missed her sharpest.

"And with that said," Hazel said smoothly, "I know you will see to Roger. You're supposed to be a bit smarter than he is…but don't think you can persuade him of doing something if he doesn't want to do it."

"How well I know." Geoffrey sighed at the ceiling. "How well I know."

Lestrade hesitated between the hard concrete of Bow Street's corner to Hart Street[34] and the dry awning of a tiny honey-stall. The vendor was an old veteran of the slums, a dark-skinned East Indian with foreign vowels in his speech. The men traded nods over the table of small casks and the old gentleman went back to instructing his art to a young boy in training.

The wind picked up, weak against the heavier weight of the mixed snow turning to rain. Lestrade pulled out "his" cigarette case (a beaten tin box he used for himself; the fancier one for showing amongst the social public was larger, engraved silver, and flawless). Smokers were never discouraged in these small establishments; their habit discouraged the equally filthy presence of small flying pests. The old man smiled and waved a greeting to a passing hawker bawling the mid-morning news: The end of the season's apples and pears were nigh, but Samuel's was happily taking orders for March's cucumbers, spring greens and onions and Polish radishes (guaranteed sweet meat with no pith). And not to fret, dear housewives—rhubarb was on its way!

"How goes the business, Mr. Husher?"

The old gentleman beamed under his turban, his mouth a tessellation of alternate teeth. "Right enough, Mr. Lestrade. Right enough." He finished cleaning the bit of table, and showed the boy how to drizzle a continuous stream of golden liquor into a smaller cask for selling.

---

[34] Hart Street was renamed Floral Street in 1895

Lestrade hoped Mr. Husher kept his business. Hart Street was full of illegal brothels and very enthusiastic pubs and the markets were often of low value. The Bradstreets shopped here for the safety of the children and the quality of his honey, which was pure and single-cut.

"If you wish to buy some honey, Mr. Lestrade," Husher announced, "I have just lowered the price."

Lestrade turned his head to study the newly-chalked slate. "A tuppence pound?" He lifted his eyebrows. "Are you that worried about the Lyle's refinery?"[35]

Husher only smiled his crooked-path smile, his head moving from side to side (he never could quite get the British method of shaking his head). "It is a wet day, Mr. Lestrade. The honey likes the wet. I must respect my customers, for today they will buy more water than they will on a dry day."

"Is that so? Can't you just put it all into casks on a dry day?"

"We could, but who wants to buy honey sight-unseen?"

"Ah. True. "I'll take a pound-cask of your wildflower."

"Not your usual chestnut honey?"

"It isn't for me." His landlady would be plotting and scheming with her spring menus, and she had never quite forgiven him for 1) hating most forms of sweets and 2) liking sour treacle and bitter chestnut honey. A bribe was necessary once in a while.

---

[35] Right now, Lestrade and Husher only know a Scotsman by the name of Abram Lyle is settling down to the business of refining sugar, and that will put a pinch in the local markets that will not compete with their own sweet goods. Lyle's Golden Syrup, a viscous leftover of the refining, will arrive in 1883.

He'd sheltered just in time. Smeared-up yellow-grey clouds cleared their throats and began the evening's main performance with a sour rain that only emphasised the general dirtiness of the city. The little detective cupped his hands around his lucifer[36] and trained a wary eye on the atmospheric ceiling looming over the battered rooftops. His strong, hot breath mixed white vapour with the barely-thicker white of his tobacco. Soft lumps of rotting black snow fell from high rooftops and burst at his feet, dislodged by the rain.

The little detective felt about as dirty as the clouds above him. Only once in his life and once in Roger's life had they ever dealt with a *personal* case. Such things were not encouraged, and every sensible detective worked very hard to avoid that situation.

In his case, the end result was telling the truth and watching his own brother swing for murder as his last brother went to the madhouse. For that success, his family disowned him.

Between the two men there were some bedrock differences.

Lestrade did not question his father's judgement. It was as simple as that.

For Roger's case, the end result was admitting he couldn't find his sister's killer. For that failure, his surviving family had disowned him (The Northern pride was too stiff to take back words said in haste). Lestrade definitely, positively, and wholly questioned, criticised and disapproved that judgement. He would contemn[37] it for the rest of his life because the ostracism had been superfluous against the self-blame Bradstreet held for himself.

---

[36] match
[37] View with contempt

"Here you are, Mr. Lestrade." The old man passed over a tiny wooden cask, clean and dry and wrapped well in clean linen sacking. "Be sure to come again. I am selling as much of the cherry-blossom honey as quickly as I can pour it. The spring coughs are troublesome."

"I'll keep that in mind, Mr. Husher."

"You must be careful. Horseradish syrup and mallow-milk will keep you from getting the city in your lungs." Like many immigrants, Mr. Husher mentally lumped all of the ills of the city under the name of London.

Bradstreet's youngest had died coughing; pertussis passed on from someone in the outside world. Lestrade tried not to think about it…or say something sharp to the old man who meant well.

He waited a bit for the coming lull in the rain. He blew a smoke ring, mostly to see how it would behave in the heavy air. It floated awkwardly, like a bicycle tyre needing a patch, across the street until a passing cab splashed it back into vapours. A man lumbered by, either too drunk to walk right or crippled. In a veil of rising dank mist Lestrade noted and approved of a passing PC lifting his glove to the old derelict in salute. In the city of millions he was surprised to feel a stab of isolation.

Lestrade's isolation was permanent. Nothing would bring back his brothers. For Roger the conditions had been as neat as they were cruel: *Find her murderers.* Find her murderers and all would be forgiven. Lestrade bowed to the inevitability of Roger's desire to make peace with a family that didn't deserve him, but he did hope that they would be kind to the children.

Being exiled had freed Lestrade from the day-to-day worry about his work affecting his parents. In the self-doubting hours before dawn, he sometimes wondered if it also freed them from worrying about him. Lestrade knew anger. Much of his job was spent cleaning it up. Anger was fired in origins as murky and dirty as a London fog...but its flame was bright and clean.

He only hoped the flame would not consume Bradstreet.

The Elegant Barley:

Getting a certain Arthur Holyrood out of his beloved work for a simple meal--even on the excuse of a private talk--was never easy. Lestrade saved up the tiny bits and favours owed before he turned his in those slips; he also kept an eye out to the schedule. This close to wages, Holyrood might be up for a free supper plate in the interests of clearing his chips.

His offer was duly accepted. They met at in a discreet corner of *The Elegant Barley*.

Lestrade had known Holyrood for years; he'd been a casualty PC since a skirmish with the Hooligan Gang,[38] but luckily his injuries had not completely disabled him like so many others. A good memory, honest warmth and a love of work had created his post as a specially trained doorman[39] at the Yard's officially titled "Prisoners Property Room" better known as "back room", "Black Room", "Hall of Horrors", "Collections Room", or "Black Museum." It was not the post for the squeamish or the superstitious, for he was neither. He was simply a man missing the full use of his left foot and neck.

---

[38] The Hooligan Gang actually existed—a knot of young, tough and often motive-less malefactors who may have inspired the introduction of 'hooligan' into our dictionary. At this point in time they are not yet completely notorious; in 1904 Lestrade will read from his notes to Holmes and Watson: *'It seemed to be one of those senseless acts of Hooliganism which occur from time to time, and it was reported to the constable on the beat as such.'* (The Adventure of the Six Napoleons)

[39] Holyrood is a custodian or janitor.

Whilst appointed officers kept up the work and dealt with the public and the proper release of objects for court and investigation, Holyrood's humble task with humbler pay was to ensure the facility was kept neat and clean, the books in place and the files in alphabetical order and the objects of murder in proper order and respectfully shown. His reduced livelihood gave him enough to live in the old inglenook of a stone tenant building, and once a week he paid for the foodstuffs put into the community pot. At night he hired himself out to write letters for the illiterate. With tips and gratuities he had no reason to leave his posts.

Lestrade liked the man and admired his pluck, which was large enough to choke a peacock, but there was something about him the little professional found terrifying. He did not think his own will and faith was enough to keep going should his lots be cast so low. At times his enjoyment of Holyrood's company was spoiled by this remainder, but Lestrade's stubborn thinking caused him no end of grief when he didn't have a case to puzzle. Holyrood was a man who found satisfaction in his work, no matter the work.

This small, lean, quiet man with thoughtful gaze and shabby clothes tended the Museum's objects of murder intended or accidental: A horseshoe cast off by a nag had killed its owner and rested by a knife that had fatally stabbed a cook by a slip against the chopping-block. A stone a man had tripped upon to his death (the court couldn't decide if the stone had been deliberately placed by an angry heir) tucked in a box against a child-sized bludgeon crafted by an enterprising street harlot. There were *hundreds* such objects and they only represented a part of the real number—which Lestrade was certain was innumerable.

These silent things harkened back to days when all acts of death were punishable by death, but who could prosecute a dumb, inanimate object that had taken a life? It had no place amongst decent people, for a thing that had human blood might grow thirsty for more. It needed to be destroyed or put away— but it couldn't be left out or even re-used. Metal used for murder could be melted down and re-forged into a completely new implement, but the taint, the echo of death would still be there, waiting for the chance to make more crimes.

It was a sad fact for all policemen, collectors and museum curators that the mute, rusted, dust-collecting items fascinated the public. When any object had a story attached to it...someone was willing to own it. The darker the story the stronger the pull, and people stole what they wanted when they couldn't get it honestly.

It takes a mind that is half-catalogue to keep track of such things. Holyrood had thrown himself into the world of macabre acts with his usual enthusiasm and never looked back.

Lestrade lowered his newspaper (society; barely fit to wrap a fish) and waved as the stiff-jointed man in sombre slate blue stepped unevenly to the table. (He no longer 'belonged' to the Force, but dressed like a plainclothes out of camaraderie). Holyrood grinned around a neat hedge of square beard and equally boxy eyebrows, so light they were transparent in the lamps.

"Good to see you, Lestrade." Holyrood accepted the offer of smoked smelts. "I never get enough of those," he confided.

"I can't blame you. They're perfect." Lestrade neatly separated a small fish from its spine and anointed the tender meat with sauce. When he was alone he chewed bones and all, but that appeared to be a behavioural anomaly among Londoners. "I hope my note made sense to you."

Holyrood shrugged. "Your question ain't so odd. Seems as long as there are objects, someone'll want'em."

"And here I was worried you might think me fanciful."

"You? Fanciful? I daren't." Holyrood did not laugh at the notion, but Lestrade flushed anyway. "Ah, well, as t'your note, we have to keep a special eye out on any *human* relic," Holyrood made a face, clearly distasteful of the topic but not enough to stop his meal. "Standin' orders from the highest authorities. 'Twuz made clear that anyone who works in that portion o' the building has to be 'alert and forsworn to act if they see too much...interest,'" he coughed lightly behind his hand, "in sech."

"Always?"

"Permanent status."

"My word, I hadn't known."

The crippled man tipped forward, his forearms making a decent fulcrum for his spinal level. "We don't often talk about it," his voice dropped low. "Not that it bothers *us*, but it does bother the Them Upstairs a great deal! They're terrified England'll see a Lacenaire come upon us."

"Lacenaire..." Lestrade repeated without blinking. "That flash faker?" At Holyrood's warning glance he dropped his own voice. "I'm sorry," he apologised. "But you've shocked me, man! What does the worst criminal in France have to do with *England*?"

Holyrood made a low *heh-heh* of wry amusement. "I take it you're familiar with the facts of the case?"

"Who damned well *doesn't*?"

"Truthfully? Quite a lot! And the Home Office would like to keep it that way."

Lestrade studied his friend, but the man looked serious and it wouldn't be his idea of a joke... *He has a reason to say this*, the little professional reminded himself.

"Well." He tapped his fingertips upon the table-plank. "He was executed before I was born. But I remember the old fellows talking about it. He was well-educated, good family, more chances at success than any of *us* would ever imagine…but meant nothing to him, and he turned to petty crime and the petty crimes turned to a double murder. Honestly, when you look at the particulars, he *must* have been the least competent criminal on the Continent! It's clear he had no head at all for law-breaking." He made a 'bah!' gesture with his free hand, the other firmly attached to his drink.

"And yet for all his stupidity—which appears to be unmatched—he was a first-rate writer on his own behalf. He became a genuine celebrity; an artist."

"I remember his portrait was painted as he waited for the guillotine." Lestrade scowled in distaste. "Shocking, how people revered a killer."

"We can't pretend to know why or how the public became so smitten o'him, Lestrade. *But the fact is they did.* And under a normal case I'm sure the Home Office would just say, 'That's the French for you.'"

"That wasn't a normal case!" Lestrade had a bad feeling he knew where his friend was headed. "Englishmen were caught up in him as well. They wrote about him, made up poems and bits in the papers…made a bust of his likeness…"

"And when he was executed, they sold his blue coat to a grabby-handed collector. They cut off his killing hand, and preserved it like a piece of art, and they took his skull, defleshed it, made engravings of it, and made a phrenology map of his plaster head, trying to find the precise location where the evil slept in his brain." Holyrood had no explanation for what humans did. "The man is still a celebrity. The first and most eager voices on his behalf were those anxious to study him in death."

Lestrade shuddered.

"So there we are. A pretty problem."

"More like a horrid mess."

"That too."

"Still, human remains..." Lestrade scowled. "I'd say the closest we've gotten to sensationalising that sort of horror is...Carney Ambisinister. Which happens to be most of the reason why we're both here."

"Now, *that* was before my post," Holyrood confessed. "Just before, actually. I heard plenty about it."

"There was plenty to talk about!" This was not a compliment.

"And you knew him before he was caught."

"I hate to say it, but yes."

"Is it true how he got his name?"

"Very. No one knew what made his right hand twist around, but it did give him the impression of having two left hands instead of one." There had also been a livid white scar along the wrist, moon-shaped and full of its own legends.

"Did the carnivale really drive him mad?"

"Who knows? As a part of the show, the man was decent enough...at least until something happened into his mind and he took a knife to half his fellow workers one night as they slept." Lestrade shrugged helplessly. "No one ever learned the whys, and he went to the noose not telling." He looked down. "There really was no warning. He was a man who said hello at every chance. He was a good enough fellow...on the outside."

"And then his body was stolen right after he was hung." Holyrood mused.

"We found most of it a few hours later by the river. Bad day for Mr. Dolan! The twisted hand had been sliced off at the joint, along with a quantity of body fat from his thigh. The Office said it was clear that his twisted hand was going to be made into a Hand of Glory."

Holyrood tipped his head from left to right, like a metronome. His frozen neck allowed no other movement. "The one we have left is bad enough." He mused.

"Hold a—you've got *another* one in there?"

"Mmn…it ain't listed as such—someone rescued it before the cultists could finish making it into a Hand. You wouldn't know it from any other severed and smoke-dried human hand."

"Sev—sm—?" Lestrade cleared his throat.

"I don't let delicate clients view it—I don't care what they say or how much they offer me in the way of a bribe!"

"Should be buried; that's what would be decent." Lestrade lectured.

"No approval. Now, we *do* have approval t'bury Mr. Ambisinister's missing bits…but the approval came a little…late."

Lestrade winced. "Right. I'm going to ask you the big question, my friend."

"Have at me." Holyrood leaned further across the table, fingers withyed into a loose basket by the mustard-pot. Over his thin lenses, rheumy brown eyes twinkled.

"In dealing with a case…that has at its heart…" Lestrade spoke slowly because damned if he could risk being misunderstood, "body thieves… and…ghouls that are willing to pay for whatever strikes their unclean fancies…" (Holyrood couldn't help but notice that the un-Catholic Lestrade was letting his fingers scrape a bead-like abstract in the ring of moisture by his drink.) "What are the odds, d'you think, that this…*client*…might be able to send us on to more ghouls?"

"Depends." Holyrood said simply. "Your odds'd be good—that beast earns his bread and cheese on a diet half informer, half backstabber. The one with the most to lose is the most likely to inform on his peers, who might have *less* to lose! Horrid system of human-remains-black marketing, where the guiltiest have the merest slap o'the wrists, whilst the lightest of the offenders are the first to see the shadow of the gaol."

"How could there possibly be not-as-guilty people involved in a market that sells *people?*"

Holyrood harrumphed. "That'd be the criminally naïve, Lestrade. You know they're out there...Bless 'em." He tapped the emblem on his watch-chain for good measure. With a little jump, Lestrade realised it was of a tiny skull on a stack of books. BRUNO was the only lettering he could make out. *I'm starting to see bones everywhere*, the Inspector thought.

"Young, earnest students," Holyrood was going on, "believin' that a good specimen will be the skeleton key to break into their respected standing in—what?" He caught on to Lestrade's gape. "Oh." He grimaced. "Forgive the pun. I ain't really that clever on purpose. Where were we? Ah. Students. They'll want a specimen of their own, and they'll want it badly. A decent draughtsman can elevate his standing by some sharp sketches, or experimental photography...I'm told that in training, nothing substitutes for a real specimen save another real specimen. Sometimes the pressure to collect can be worse when they're from medical families—they'll be expected to stand apart...distinguish themselves. Dear old Dad isn't going to just hand over his own skull when the son graduates; he has to find his own." He made his imitation of a shrug. "And they feel that we owe em, in a way."

"*What?*"

"Y'heard me. Part o' the reason why criminals are sent to the medical tables after they die is their reparation to Society. Ever wonder why you see the same names and faces in a case that brings in dead orphans or the street-crawlers? A few pence or a tot of gin is enough to make payment for any corpse. And y'know how it is when a man thinks he's owed something."

"Bloody hell. Yes, I do. It means that when he doesn't get what he wants, when he wants it…he goes looking."

"Got it in one."

"It really means that much to 'em." Lestrade had never been able to wrap his head around things that didn't make sense. Thank God, the Law had never required his understanding—just his obedience.

"I have it on good authority." Holyrood's gift for mimic meant he could drop into another person's character from one breath to the next. "Though I'll admit, most purely medical men aren't interested in 'relics of superstition.' Science is their bloodless God. It would take another Dr. Roanoke to keep 'em all sorted."

Lestrade shivered. "Now, he was a lot of help! He told us human fat is worthless within a very short amount of time, and the thieves had to have been planning it ever since his execution was announced." Back then, Lestrade wouldn't have been able to eat and talk at the same time.

"There are markets, *and then there are markets*," Holyrood said slowly. "The problem is that you got the medical and scientific worlds pointing fingers at the side that holds to superstition and illiteracy…but in truth the poorer folk have just as much right to point fingers right back." His light eyes clouded. "The burden is on our betters but we needn't go there." He leaned back and took another fish. "I get plenty of inquiries, you know, from people who want a 'specimen' in collection. One knows what they're *really* asking for so discreetly. They want me to sell them something curious or fantastic."

Lestrade harrumphed disapproval. "As if we don't face the suspicion of corruption every day as it is." He muttered.

"Very. At any rate, as soon as I refuse a query, the next thing I do is put the object in higher safeguards. It could be a week from now, or even a year. But those people aren't going to forget they wanted something. They see it as an investment, you know. What's months of waiting if they get what they want? There's a horseshoe that killed two people; flew off the horse twice. I wound up nailing a fake horseshoe into the exhibit-box." He chuckled under his breath. "Stolen about four times last year."

Lestrade's chuckle faded too soon. Behind the brief smile rested his natural countenance.

Holyrood cleared his throat meaningfully.

"Ah." The little professional looked down at his hands. "What d'you think, then?" He asked. "From one man to another. What are my odds?"

"What will you get out of this, Lestrade?"

Lestrade thought of Elspeth Bradstreet first, and his closest friend second. He thought of how he couldn't express his truest wish without mentioning either. "I want a lead," he said instead, choosing the next on his list. "I want a lead that will give me the names and faces of men who rob the dead for a living, so that I can make a list of those names, and go down it, one by one and syllable by syllable…until I find someone who can tell me who would have paid to defile Carney Ambisinister's remains." Caught up in his confidence, he leaned over his side of the table until the two men were nose to nose.

"I've thought it through, Holyrood. Body-thieves *can't* just up and steal a body. They go through a lot of risk for what they do—they aren't going to add to that risk by keeping their swag hidden until they get an offer. Every day they've got it is dangerous—they've got to get rid of it fast. They need to have the market set up and waiting for them. S'like those high-mark jewellry thefts. The person who really wants the stone but not the gaol is going to pay someone good to do all of that for 'im.

"Someone wants Mr. Ambisinister's hand, he's going to tell his rotting contacts what he wants, and how much he's willing to pay. Whoever stole his hand knew what they'd get from the deal."

Holyrood tsk'd. "Now that's your turn for a nice turn of words."

"Eh?"

"Deal. That's an old northern name for the Devil, for he does know how to make a bad deal."

"Ah. Well...so if we go by this reasoning so far..." Lestrade energetically lifted his hands, caught up in the enthusiasm of his theory. "The buyer isn't going to just up and ask any Johnny Jump-Up in the market! He's going to go calling and use his contacts...make discreet inquiries...a friend of a friend. Someone who knows someone!"

"That's all very well and good, Lestrade, but a theft for a Hand of Glory...that's...filthy-dark. If someone's going to keep their mouth shut, it's a member of a cult."

"I don't think a cult stole his hand." Lestrade's excitement was bubbling like the springs at Bath. Now that he finally had an audience, he was beside himself.

"Well who *else* would steal a Hand of Glory? A rival museum?"

"*We have no proof that his hand was a Hand of Glory, Holyrood.* We have a missing hand, and a missing portion of fat off the thigh. You'd think that it was for a Hand of Glory, wouldn't you?" He shook his head, grinning like a Hallowe'en turnip. "*But a Hand of Glory is usually made from the left hand—the* sinister *hand—and the left hand was still on the body.*"

"A Hand of Glory *has* been known to be cut from the right hand." Holyrood demonstrated his own knowledge of infernal *obscura.* "Especially if the right hand was the hand used for murder. Like Lacenaire's."

"But it wasn't!" Lestrade very quietly hammered his fists on the table. "That hand was worthless—he couldn't even hold a pencil with those fingers! No, the Inspector on that case completely missed it! If they were going to steal anything, they would have stolen his *left* hand—because it was left and because it was the hand used for killing all those people."

Holyrood's gossamer eyebrows popped up into his wrinkled brow. "A theft of science masque as a theft for the Black Mass?" He rubbed his chin. "Lestrade, you got a head like a Swede's turnip, but this is the most stubborn I've ever seen you. But. Your notion fits..."

"It all hinges on cracking into this network of body-thieves." Lestrade's temper had cooled with his outing of thought. He ate a few more smelts, his jaw set. "We never found the thieves, because we were looking in the wrong direction. We should have been looking to the educated men who hire grave-robbers—not the cults."

"You're very certain of yourself."

Lestrade had reached a stopping point in his meal. He wiped his mouth with his napkin, which gave him a moment to collect his thoughts (good manners helped keep his head cool when his temper wanted to get the best of his tongue).

"I'm certain I owe Mr. Holmes an apology, *that's* what." He said at last. He signalled for another cider and waited for it before continuing. "I must have lost weeks out of my life trying to track down Ambisinister's ghouls outside of the Inspector's wishes. I went wading in the dregs of mankind, hoping they would give me a lead to the mess...All that time, Holmes—still a newcomer to London—had already known all there was to know about that side of the city. I can see him now, younger and skinner, smoking his pipe and telling me I am just wasting my time, and I didn't listen to him!"

"Not even as a consultant?"

"He wasn't a consultant. We...er...lucked into each other on different reasons." A collision might be a better word. Lestrade narrowed his eyes at Holyrood's skeptical face. "He's changed a bit since the man you know now, man. Back then he did most of his work out of his rooms. If he went out you hardly saw it. Just your basic armchair-consultant for hire. And for the record, I did ask him if he would be interested in the job."

"What did he say?"

"He said he didn't work for nuppence."[40]

"Holmes said *that*?" Holyrood hastily wiped up his drink-foam off his face.

"He was in disguise." Lestrade explained. "I didn't know at the time that he stays in character as long as he's in disguise. And as it turned out, we weren't allowed to bring in a consultant for the case."

"Oh." Holyrood relaxed and gave his cohort a reproachful snort. "Don't scare me like that, man!"

"I didn't think it would put a fright in you!"

"I've worked with the man too!" Holyrood riposted. "Didn't you know, Sherlock Holmes in nothing less than precise speech is one of the Six Warning Signs of the Oncoming Apocalypse?"

Lestrade laughed into his collar, and the thickened mood about their table was broken.

The little man's good humour was not lasting. He glared into his drink as if it would scry a proper future for his hopes. "I was so bloody sour at the end of it! I wanted to find the guilty, and I wanted to find the guilty amongst the carnivale. I had my reasons, mind! Who else would want to strike out at a dead

---

[40] No pennies: No pay.

man? The only people he killed were the people he worked with! He didn't kill any of the customers, or visitors, or idle passers-by. No, it had to be a crime of science, and the Chief knew it because he didn't let us bring in consultants. He was afraid there'd be a scandal out of it." Lestrade looked tired at the memory. "You wouldn't believe some of the people—and things—I encountered in that search."

"I'm certain I wouldn't want to." Holyrood told him. "Fortune-tellers, Gips, the people who dabble about in things outside of the Church?"

"They're not all bad," Lestrade was quick to correct. "You've got the ones like Old Three Eyes who keeps to her own kind and keeps us alerted to any troubles." He shrugged in that peculiar Lestradeish fashion that often perplexed his comrades. Holyrood always thought it looked like a cramped-up version of Gallic bafflement. "There you go, Holyrood! I was so caught up in that case I really was looking in the wrong direction. S'taken me what—years!—to get back on the right rail!"

"If you are right, and you do have your car on the right rail," Holyrood assured him. "You don't need to be told you'd best keep on your toes!" He waggled a finger. "Whoever they are, *these men are dangerous.* Make sure they don't lie just to tell you what you want to hear. They've gotten away with this for so long…don't think they'd hesitate to commit another one to keep it hidden.

"*And watch the Crows,*" the other man added in a sudden afterthought. "Most of'em are clannish—their first thoughts are for themselves and their kind!"

Lestrade agreed with his mouth, but he had already decided to trust Dr. Watson all the way in the case.

It wasn't as though he had a lot of choice; the man had come to him after all, and unlike some people who reported a crime and then had second thoughts…Watson looked as though he knew full well what he was getting into with tattling on another member of his profession.

And his being military...a Major...well. Policemen were usually seen as unthinking beasts of the Biblical field; the serving staff that kept the Home Office a well-oiled machine. Most of Watson's ilk wouldn't have given a copper so much as the proper time.

But Watson was giving the Yard respect.

The Yard owed him nothing less than the regard they gave the public...but they also owed the young man a good sight more because of the way he treated them in turn.

Lestrade respected the complications that rose in such a breast as Watson's. Doing the right thing wasn't easy when you were taught there were different kinds of right and wrong. In the bottom of the well rested the truth: This was wrong and needed to be corrected.

The detective turned to the rest of his fish and conversation as they moved on to more pleasant things—ending on a friendly note—as his mind was already in another direction, thinking hard: The miserable Ambisinister's case had closed as a failure. If he could only close it...find some answer to the missing limb.

It wouldn't hurt his reputation at all, but behind the shell of professional vanity lurked a more human selfishness: It stung his pride as a young and eager policeman that the killer's body had not gone to rest intact.

The Police force had many advantages to it, if a man was willing to make the sacrifice. It was a meritocracy, so if a man didn't advance he was swiftly dismissed. Lestrade did not see himself as growing old, but he had no family and he had precious few friends. If he was rendered helpless he didn't want to finish his life destitute in a gutter.

If this case could help him track down Carney Ambisinister's missing hand, it would help him close a chapter on his past...and put his own personal wolf at bay just a bit longer.

"...I said, are you finished for the day?"

Lestrade rescued his wits in the nick of time. "Near enough. I promised Brother Jerome I'd stop by tonight."

Holyrood made a face better suited on an ogre's. "Mind your step on *that* street." He muttered.

"It isn't that bad, man."

"It isn't so good either!"

Bow Street:

Mr. Bradstreet was so tired he hung up his coat and thought to himself, *Hazel's laughing. Oh, good.* A moment later his treacle-filled brain asserted, and he was hustling down the short hallway to the cramped sitting room.

His wife was sitting up, a small lap-desk of shining things before her, and swatting at the grasping hands of their daughters. "Get away, I told ye! My word, it's no wonder the sponge had t'be punched down again! You need to pay attention to what ye started!"

Another swat as a narrow hand inched to the tray. "Mr. Bradstreet! Tell your daughters to keep their grasping little hands to themselves or go hire out as pick-pockets!"

"What's all this then, ladies?" Roger growled deep in his beard. "Are you being plaguesome again?"

"Plaguesome, pestiferous, and penitent-less!" Hazel exclaimed. "Tell them to go see to that bread!"

Roger recoiled. "Me tell a woman what to do in the kitchen?"

"It *is* my kitchen."

"You heard the Queen, girls." He tagged them on their heads as they grumbled past; when he grinned back at Hazel, his eyes were shining. "I see Geoffrey got the box."

"Do I want to know how you came about this?" Hazel was a generous person, but giving her something in return was a problem; she was full of restrictions and brooked no tolerance for something that was too frivolous, too expensive, too troublesome, or too sentimental.

"It was simple. I had Geoffrey pick up a box of assorteds the last time he was sent to the coast. He didn't even have to pay anything; he says he traded a box of cigars for the lot."

"They're lovely." Hazel held up a stickpin. Tiny green pea-shells had been glued together to form a small stalk and three oval leaves. "This only wants a flower-head to go with it. What do you think?"

"Mmmn...How about something early? A snowdrop or a rosebud?"

"A rosebud it shall be." Hazel set to work. "This should answer all the worries you men have on spilling water inside your pockets when we go dancing!"

"Better make one for Geoffrey too." Roger advised.

"Hmph. He's a better dancer than you, Roger, *and* he's got a twisted foot!" Hazel scolded almost absently as she picked through the shells. "A small cowry," he heard her mutter. "That's what I need..."

Paddington Street:
Lestrade pulled out his case-notes as soon as he built up the fire. A contrary crack at his sill made his desk chilly; perfect for keeping a bottle of cider. He set his chair by the grate and was into another hour of study when the door rattled from the knock

of a large knuckle and Roger popped in head-first, snow and ice melting on his face.

"Thank you, old fellow."

"Not at all." Lestrade twisted around. "What are you doing on this end at this hour? It's a bit late for work. Come in by the grate; you're all nithered!"

"Ah, right." Bradstreet eyebrowed a droll look at what was on Lestrade's desk, and his friend half-scowled at him, half-daring him to produce a large, Gilbert and Sullivan-style musical on his own habit of bringing his desk home on his back. "I just came to give you the new news." He settled himself into the guest chair whilst Lestrade, without asking, rose to dig out the flask behind the book-end. "Got a telegram. The evidence that Dr. Watson asked for will be delivered to us by post by the end of the week." The information was met with a grunt and a nod. "Geoffrey, you have a distracted, dowie air about you." He noted the little book at the corner and picked it up, turning it over and over.

"I'm sorry, Roger. I just feel like this is going to be hell on ea—oh, put that down," Lestrade said hastily. "Horrid little thing." He muttered. "Where was I…Oh, I was feeling like this is going to be hell on earth."

"I don't feel, I *know*." Bradstreet tutted and frowned at the book. "What's the matter with a book of doctors?"

"They're *specialists*. Horrid stuff. Pictures of men of science posing with skulls…and…model heads and…and glass eyes…and…and things like that. And I do *not* like the fact that we not only have to work with a civilian in this, but we have to allow him to take some personal risk. The Chief will not approve when he reads this in the report."

"What are you reading all that slop *for*?" Bradstreet wanted to know.

"There's a picture of our suspect in there…"

"And you think I shouldn't take a look at him?"

Bradstreet's voice was patience itself. A bad sign.

Lestrade puffed out his breath, flushed at his friend's knowing look, and picked up the book again. "Here you are…" He grumbled, and opened it, but clearly forced himself to let Bradstreet hold it in his own two hands.

The big Runner stared deep into the glossy paper, trying to see God Knew What on the other side of the ink. It did not escape Lestrade's notice that his friend's pulse had quickened, nor that he was making the effort to breathe calmly.

"He looks…" Bradstreet hesitated, but there was no getting around the truth. "I don't think I've ever seen a more harmless-looking man in my life! He looks more harmless than the priest who baptised me!"

"If that's the same Pastor Jones on your wall, that's harmless indeed." Lestrade felt depressed. He leaned back in his chair and stared at the ceiling above his nose.

Bradstreet ground the image into his brain with about fifteen seconds of intense staring, his face without any expression, and handed back the book. Lestrade clapped it shut and stuffed it into a drawer.

"Problem?" Bradstreet queried coolly.

"It's got me edgy." Lestrade told him with a perfect lack of shame. "I'm not used to it. To them those are all just…tools. And like any man with a tool, they'll take it out and show it off like a workman would a new brass hammer, or…or a garden spade."

"Ay, but they were human once, and there is a part of them that is human still." Bradstreet said softly.

"Yes. I'm all sickish inside, Roger." He wanted to pace, but his tiny room wouldn't allow it. He clasped his fingers together instead, and ground his palms together.

Neither man spoke for a minute.

"Don't read that book, Roger." Lestrade said at last. "Please."

"I promise."

Lestrade lit a cigarette from his personal tin and (since they were friends) threw the tin at Bradstreet. "Back to our conversation...I honestly can't think of Watson as a civilian. If anything, he thinks *we're* the civilians." His mouth bent around his smoke at the purpled indignity of Bradstreet. "Once a Major, always a Major, and I'll bet you money, marbles, and chalk that if he didn't hold his medical profession to be higher, he'd be *still* using his military title."

Bradstreet grumbled as he leaned forward to light his smoke off Lestrade's. "Still..."

"Oh, I understand completely." Lestrade leaned back. "But he's no civilian. And as far as risks go, you've seen what Jezails can do to a human body." He put his hands in his pockets as Roger puffed, and stared out the window.

"Well, then, what's bothering you if it isn't the fact that we'll be employing the only human being that can make a human being out of Sherlock Holmes?"

Lestrade snorted softly. "Fancies." He said curtly.

"I'm glad I'd already swallowed." Bradstreet stared as his drink struck the little table. "Geoffrey, the word is exclusive of you. You have no imagination."

"For which I'm grateful. I don't need an imagination." Lestrade did not mention that his nightmares might possibly qualify as imagination, but he didn't like to think of them either. He pulled his hand out and stared at his nails. "I've been going over the old tales of the Selkies... Watson seems to think they're important."

"You're in a bad mood because you're reading fancies?"

"No...No, that has nothing to do with it. I don't see these things as anything more than...colourful, muddled, and side-tracked reports." Lestrade rubbed at his forehead slowly. "Have you ever looked at a fairy tale, Roger, really, *really* looked at it?"

"Every day. Especially when I'm interviewing a suspect for mental evaluations."

"Well...I'm starting to see some of these fairy tales as...a very muddled account of things that really happened. Oh, I don't believe for one moment that humans can turn into seals!" He lifted his hand. "But I've been pretending I was examining these accounts for Scotland Yard."

"Go on." Bradstreet urged. "You've gotten my curiosity."

"The old accounts call the Selkies, Finmen, from Finland, which even the old writings say is actually the Orkneys. The people from those islands were a mixture of Greenlanders, Nords, and sea-faring travelers that wandered by. The men and women were both capable of using those skin boats to travel on." "Lestrade picked up a page and read from it:

> "It may be thought wonderful that they live all that time and are able to keep to sea so long... His boat is made of seal-skins, or some kind of leather; he also has a coat of leather upon him, and he sitteth in the middle of his boat, with a little oar in his hand, fishing with his lines.
>
> "And when in a storm he seethe the high surge of a wave approaching, he hath a way of sinking his boat, till the wave passes over, lest thereby he should be overturned."

Bradstreet listened with both ears. He tugged on his left moustache. "It sounds like the way a seal swims...The kayaks of those Greenlanders would behave in that manner. I've seen them flip upside down just to make the visitors squeal. Those skin togs of theirs leave'em high and dry and grinning every time."

"That's what I thought. One thought led to another." Lestrade put the paper down. "The Finmen were blamed for bad seasons; I suppose that's strategic sense. If you've going to go out for fish, you've got to be in their own element, and someone in a skin boat can certainly go where a large craft can't." He was looking increasingly uncomfortable. "What do you recall of those old stories?"

Bradstreet shrugged awkwardly. "They aren't stories I'd tell the children...they'll hear them soon enough... Mostly the old tales everyone seems to know about: That if you take the skin of a Selkie woman, she'll have to stay with their land-man and be their wife. Most of them did stay, and bore children, but even years later, when the fisherman carelessly let her find out about the location of her skin, she'd steal it back and return to the waves."

"Mmn-hmn." Lestrade held his eyes. "What if that skin of the Selkies is actually the skin that's hung over the wooden frame of their single boats...and their waterproof clothing that lets them get out into that frozen waste?"

Bradstreet slowly turned the numbers over in his head. His eyes widened a little. "It would make sense." He blinked. "Perfect sense."

Lestrade poured himself another drink. "Well, there's no proof..."

"Huh. That circumstantial evidence is strong enough to hang the Brothers Grimm!" Bradstreet huffed. "The polydactyl trait must hail from a Greenlander with that trait; probably a poor woman who was kidnapped by someone who wanted a hard-working wife who didn't speak enough of his language to ask for help." Bradstreet snorted. "No fashing wonder the explanation is all about seals."

"I beg your pardon?"

"Geoffrey, have you ever had to deal with a missionary or three moving in? The first thing he does is pull out a pen and start "transcribing the quaint customs of the area." Bradstreet pulled a long face.

Lestrade copied him. "Yes. It seems like the Church recruits an awful lot of would-be scientists."

"And have you ever seen anyone play the game for their own amusement?"

"Many times. The old people would tell those priests all sorts of things--outrageous things you couldn't possibly believe, and they'd dutifully write them down as if it were Gospel--pardon the accidental pun."

"Not at all. It's a perfect pun. I'm just thinking that a fairy tale about a fairy wife can be overlooked. Kidnapping a bride can't be."

Lestrade flinched as if a bolt had hit him. "It happens." He snapped.

A moment later, Bradstreet remembered who he was talking to and could have kicked himself. *Damn.* It might be a blessing to have extensive family records...but bad stories were inevitably with the good ones.

The Runner fervently kept talking to move things along. "I'm thinking I need to start looking at Garrett's reading." He said aloud. "Lad's too caught into the fanciful stuff as is." He set his glass down with a sigh. "And speaking of reading...will your desk be clear in a few days?"

"Absolutely." Lestrade answered. A bit of tension bled out of him. He sighed. "When your correspondence comes in, we'll talk to Watson."

"Speaking of fanciful...how's he going to keep this particular little problem away from Mr. Sherlock Holmes?"

"Lord only knows; I don't." was Lestrade's fervent reply.

A pall settled over the room; some of it was the factual weariness that intruded upon the mind whenever the concept of persuading Sherlock Holmes of anything was offered. The men settled into individual brown studies, Lestrade playing with his little glass more than he sipped, and Bradstreet stretched toes-out to the small fire lapping at his wet soles.

Baker Street:

Watson woke up hours earlier than his usual habit in a mood as foul as the overcast sky. His body ached and throbbed from the remnants of the war; he more rolled out of bed than got out of it; one of the fouler phrases from his barracks-days came to his mind and he just as viciously stamped it down.

Why was it, he wondered darkly, *that the Army insists on sending home men who are still capable of pulling a trigger?* God knows, the urge to pull that said trigger was strong today. He could take his Adams and retire to the practice-range...

But not in this weather. He scowled as he clipped his moustache for the day. Even Mrs. Hudson's plane-tree looked abashed in the small courtyard. *And if it wasn't this weather, I wouldn't have the urge to go practice!*

Holmes' solution, which was a panoptic redecoration of the room in bullet-pocks, was no solution at all.

He yanked on his waistcoat and found a clean handkerchief for his sleeve. Away from the light chill of the window the warmth of the fire penetrated the floor-boards. Knowing Mrs. Hudson, there was hot coffee or tea on standby. He shot his cuffs and descended the stairs amid the warm smells of a busy kitchen, expecting Holmes to be smoking up the Drawing Room if he had not gone to bed.

But the Drawing-Room empty and the atmosphere free and clear.

Watson felt his brows float upward, buoyed by surprise as he stepped into the uninhabited room. The bedroom door was half-open; Holmes usual habit to let him know he was out.

This was a little out of what Watson had grown accustomed to for his friend's schedule. Under normal circumstances, Holmes would have been fixing his pre-breakfast pipe by now with his morbid collection of all the unsmoked tobacco fished out of the bottom of his bowl during the course of yesterday.

Watson looked about; Holmes was still not there. The drapes were pulled open presenting a wide view of the chilly wet street.

A folded paper torn out of one of Holmes' unlined notebooks rested on the breakfast-table like a dozing butterfly.[41]

Curiouser and curiouser… Watson flipped the card over.

Watson,
Will be gone until the following Tuesday.
H.[42]

"Huh!"

For someone who was capable of the most amazing verbal creations, when it came to writing Holmes could be as brusque as an unsanded plank.

---

[41] Holmes' copious notes and extensive collection of personally-collected information is legendary, but Watson records few instances where Holmes actually writes things down. Perhaps he fixes his data temporarily into his amazing memory?

[42] The details of Holmes' absence will be clear in future writings.

Holmes had left the early-morning paper by the note; thoughtful of him. Watson couldn't face the thought of going outside just yet. He poured water out of the pitcher and mixed himself a packet of acetylsalicylic powder. The cloudy drink was bitter and sour, but he drank it from long experience. It wasn't enough to take away the edge of the pain.

He was down to the worst of the gritty bottom-dregs when Mrs. Hudson emerged with the breakfast tray—set for one. He replied to her usual good-morning queries with his usual manners, knowing she deserved that much courtesy when Holmes could barely remember if he had eaten. He was glad of the coffee, and was pouring himself his second cup when his landlady arrived, too early to take the tray.

"Begging your pardon, doctor, but this just showed up at the door for you." She pulled a neat little envelope out of her apron-pocket. By now Watson had come to recognise various hands from the Yard; they were economical on paper. He thanked her and snipped the lip of the flap open with a snap of his fingernail.

> *Doctor,*
> *We have the materials you requested.*
> *You may see me at yr*
> *convenience.*
> *G. Lestrade*

Excellent use of discretion from Lestrade; and here Holmes wasn't even around to appreciate it! Life and its myriad ironies...the doctor caught himself smiling. Why was he smiling? His heart rate had increased; he was facing the prospect of something grim and dire, but he was looking forward to it at the same time.

His smile faded. Holmes was gone. He was guiltily relieved. *There is no need to feel this way. If I can solve this appropriately, he will never know the shame of my profession.*

Scotland Yard:

Bradstreet's smoking had increased after Hazel's illness. Lestrade mentally shot up a prayer of thanks that the man's intake had cut down markedly in the past 24 hours. Thinking of a problem often did that to him—that and knowing Hazel was beginning to pull through.

"I wouldn't trust those maps," Bradstreet was saying. "Sure they go back far enough, but the coordinates are nightmarish. How's one supposed to find a missing tombstone when the boundary between two graveyards was separated by a white cedar?"

"I'd look under the cedars myself," Lestrade noted. "You just think how big they can get. And the roots could be causing all the upheaval...could very easily crush the grave-markers to rubble in a short period of time. Well, I could be wrong. What're the stones made of?"

"Yellow soapstone. It was local over there. Almost slippery to the touch, soft as butter when it comes fresh out of the ground, which is why everyone wants all these elabourate decorations? But it isn't permanent."

"Goes against my grain, friend. But then again, so much of *my* family has themselves for a sexton.[43] I've not known many courteous enough as to die on the ship instead of off it..." Lestrade glanced up and belatedly noted Dr. Watson was standing in the doorway, hand lifted (and frozen) in the act of

---

[43] A reference to the unknown numbers of the drowned amongst the English Channel, 'the great churchyard, where every man is his own sexton,' meaning they have buried themselves in the sea.

knocking politely on the frame. His expression was a sight to behold.

"Oh." Lestrade cleared his throat. "We were, ah, discussing a missing graveyard, Dr. Watson."

"A missing *graveyard*." Watson looked like his ears had betrayed his mind.

"It's not what it sounds like. It appears to be a property issue, and it's come to the point where both sides of the border are about to go to war. Figuratively."

"In which case, at least we know where to put them." Bradstreet grumbled. "Mostly."

"Oh." Watson was still looking wary.

Lestrade thought back to what else he'd just said. "A lot of sea-farers in my family. Some of them were actually law-abiding." He had the air of a man who has told tales on himself too long to be affected by it now.

Watson relaxed. "I'm surprised you aren't in the Thames Division."

Bradstreet hooted. "That's what everyone says! Just because of that one ruddy inch."[44]

"I'm the black sheep." Lestrade explained. "I hate to get my feet wet."

"I've heard worse." Watson said wryly. He limped inside the office with his damp hat in his hands. Bradstreet rose and began pouring tea.

"Lestrade made this," he warned. "Since he came back from that undercover work with the Tinkers, he's been unable to make a decent cup."

Lestrade blew a smoke ring at his best friend. "If it doesn't kill you, it should do all right."

---

[44] There was a 1" difference in the minimum height requirement between the Thames Division and the other police.

"I've never had a Tinker-brewed cup before, I confess." Watson stared down at the cup, his natural eagerness for the spice of life warring with his natural desire to avoid a relapse in his health. Somehow, Lestrade had managed to make it strong enough to pull the theine[45] out of the leaves; the oils glistened on the surface, and the doctor knew without trying that half a cup of the stuff would send his heart to racing like a shot of cocaine; a break-out of sweat would surely follow. "I might need a bit of milk and sugar with this," he said faintly.

"There's no 'might' about it." Bradstreet commiserated. He dropped three lumps into the brew. If anything, it looked even darker. "Lestrade likes sweets as much as Christ likes Moneychangers. You're always on your own for that around him."

"It keeps me on my feet." Lestrade was obviously immune to his coworker's emotions. "Well, Roger, I think I owe you a Mag.[46] I really would have thought Mr. Holmes would be here with the doctor."

Watson swallowed his tea, thinking that the painkiller of this morning was nowhere near as effective. "He's off on a case. I'll hear all about it in terms that are hardly to be fathomed, and he'll probably be the thinner for forgetting to eat."

Lestrade frowned lightly. "His weight's better than it was when I met him."

"Surely you jest...no, surely not. You wouldn't make a joke out of that." Watson shuddered. Lestrade shrugged with his pencil. "At any rate, I'm off work today, so I thought I'd come over."

---

[45] Before caffeine was discovered to be in both tea and coffee, theine was named of the active stimulant in tea.

[46] Ha'penny

Bradstreet was nodding as he went to the back of the office and pulled down a tightly-built cardboard box. It was the sort for mailing packages, strong as thin wood and almost as heavy. "I remembered that our old village priest used to make hand-prints of the children when they were a few years old. The prints were sort of a...well; I suppose you would say a prayer record."

"Go on." Watson's brown eyes lit from within, like a flame behind a cognac bottle.

"Yes, we'd hardly any children, due to the parents moving off to work, so the elders celebrated all births." Bradstreet did not look into the box as he pressed it in the doctor's hands. "I thought he'd just made prints, but he did one better. A few years after he'd done my age, he moved to plaster."

Lestrade had been bracing himself for this, but Watson had the look of a man who already knew what he would see. He gently lifted the lid and poked aside the padding of soft papers. Lestrade, from his vantage point, saw the doctor's face spasm as if in pain.

That's it. Lestrade didn't know why, but something very important had just happened.

Watson pulled out the plaster-cast of a child's hand and held it as lightly as if it were his own. Bradstreet had clasped his hands behind his back and was turning to stare with great fascination out the window. Lestrade had been trying to ware himself for this since Bradstreet had intimated the contents of the box; it was still a shock. The thin sheets of plaster for the webbings between the fingers were delicate as sea-shells. The cast had every detail of fingernail and whorl.

It unsettled the little detective, most severely, and he didn't blame Bradstreet for not looking. Those hands were the only real physical trace he had left of his sister unless Watson was successful.

And they're real enough, he thought.

Under his moustache, Watson's mouth had set. He was pale underneath the browning of the desert sun, and scoops echoed under his eyes. Those eyes glistened as they lifted up to look at Lestrade.

"This is what I need." He said steadily enough, but he cleared his throat before he could continue. "If I may...Inspectors...this is a difficult question I must ask of you...if it makes it any more palatable, think of it as...a writer searching for research material."

Bradstreet and Lestrade looked each other, but they were both in the dark. "Go on, doctor." Lestrade prompted.

Watson thrust his jaw out, just a bit. "The case in question means going to Edinburgh. How should we do this?"

Lestrade felt the blood drip out of his face. In the corner of his eye, Bradstreet was turning on his heel, eyes wide and hands open.

"I...I *wouldn't*." Lestrade whispered. He looked at Bradstreet and found support there. "Scottish Laws aren't exactly the same as English Laws. You have to be very careful. All one needs is a single misstep of jurisdiction, and...and then you just see how many policemen find themselves ruined!"

"Lestrade and I know *English* law inside and out." Bradstreet rasped. "And we know some of the differences in Scottish law and English law, but it's enough to make us leery of stepping on anyone's toes, however accidentally."

Watson had paled too. "I...had hopes, gentlemen," he said stiffly, "That—"

Bradstreet's large hand shot up, halting all attempts at conversation.

"No, it isn't hopeless, just requires a bit of extra planning. We'd have to call up someone we knew from that end...someone who knows us enough to give us a little leeway, and they'd help us do the job. The only thing is we'd be sharing the responsibility of the case."

"MacDonald?" Lestrade suggested.

"Without a doubt." Bradstreet agreed.

"If this is a case of murder within the North," Lestrade hedged, "We'll be walking a tightrope." He studied their guest a breath longer before adding, "The more we find on this killer, the better."

"I can assure you, the odds of the man stopping at only one illegal collection are very small." Watson whispered. "It is much more likely that he has more crimes."

"The more that is found, the stronger our standing. But if there is a *chance* that an English citizen has met a foul end with someone on the other side of the wall…We do need to be there." Bradstreet clutched at his teacup.

Watson nodded. He set the plaster casts down inside the box as gently as a sleeping infant, and went to the wall where Lestrade had a large map of London. He stared at it in silence whilst the Inspectors watched him.

"I have to return to Edinburgh if I am to smoke out our murderer. I'm not certain where it happened…but I believe the proof will be at his residence." Watson's back was hard as a rock under his coat.

"Dr. Watson," Lestrade made his voice as careful as he could. Bradstreet was a powder-keg, primed to explode. "Perhaps it would be in everyone's interest if you explained a few things about Dr. Parker?"

Watson's face was still white, which made the ghastly set of his face all the worse. "A man," he murmured, "that I was once pleased to call my mentor."

Lestrade felt his jaw drop. At a loss, he stared at Bradstreet. Bradstreet's expression, he was sure, mirrored his own. Watson's reticent horror now made terrible, perfect sense.

5: Envy

"Envy Rots the Bones."
--Proverb

Bradstreet, surprisingly, spoke first. "Doctor, may I trouble you for a moment whilst I speak with my colleague?"

"Oh, of course." The ever polite Watson began to leave the office, but Bradstreet stopped him.

"No, not at all. We'll bring in some coffee whilst we riddle this out. I don't know about you, but this tea isn't doing it for me." (Lestrade's mouth fell open.) "Inspector?"

"Coffee, doctor?" Lestrade managed not to stammer.

"Actually...yes. That would be a good thing to have." Watson glanced down at his leg as if he suddenly hated it.

Lestrade waited till they were up against the wall where the small stove kept the pot percolating. *"What was that all about?"* He hissed.

Bradstreet wiped his face. *"Did you see the look on his face?"* He hissed back.

"I saw," Lestrade protested. "He's upset, man alive, but he looks to be in control."

"You think?" Bradstreet shot back. He still spoke very softly. "Geoffrey...can we trust Watson on this?"

The possibility had simply never occurred to Lestrade. It must have shown in his face, for the bigger man sighed.

"I *know*, he's living—and working with—Sherlock Holmes. Holmes usually gives us a fair deal, when he's not with-holding evidence, or making us feel as though we're back in school, or just insulting us to our faces...but what's Watson like in a Particular, Geoffrey? Have we seen his mettle?"

"What more can you test from an Afghan fighter?" Lestrade wanted to know. "Look, Roger, I know what it is you're asking, and you're right to do so." Bradstreet didn't react; he was standing with his arms folded across his chest, hiding behind his thick mustache. Lestrade kept on. "Roger, I don't think Watson's that kind of man who would let his personal feelings take priority over structure. He's military; just look at him. We must look like anarchists in comparison to the life he's used to living."

"That's just it. You've seen how personal some of these veterans can get when things go harsh. What if he's like that once he's the one under fire? Can you say for certainty he wouldn't react on impulse?"

Neither man ignored the fact that Bradstreet was worried about *Watson* being too-personally staked in this; policemen were often called to worse than a murdered sibling. Bradstreet simply didn't know if he should add Watson to his own burden.

Lestrade swallowed dryly. "You're right, of course...but, Roger...the same could be said about the two of *us*. There isn't a day when we're told not to let our feelings get in the way of a case, and then we run right into someone turning a blind eye to procedure and bashing a confession out of someone!"

Roger grimaced, for 'confession-bashers' were the rule, and not the exception. "At least we've got the two of each other to keep ourselves narrow, and we've got our oaths of service." he pointed out if in a garbled way. "And Watson? If anyone would keep him on the path, wouldn't it be Holmes, whom we are not bringing in to this case?"

Lestrade sighed and poured the last of the coffee. He didn't know who brewed it; hopefully Dagg or Mirren... "Watson doesn't want Holmes innit because he's trying to protect Holmes from a bad situation. I don't question Watson's loyalty to a mate. For that matter, I don't think the good doctor would do anything that would bring Holmes' to attention to this bloody mess."

"You think he'd behave to keep Holmes out of this?"

"You heard his reasoning. This is a matter for the medical community, and he needs it to be as discreet as possible. Now, I get the feeling that a part of him is just plain ashamed that his own mentor was proved rotten, and he doesn't want Mr. Holmes to know he once kept bad company…but…he'll keep his mouth shut and his hands to himself to keep this from getting out where it shouldn't."

Bradstreet's dark eyes were shrewd. "There's something else, though, isn't there?" He guessed. "You've got *that look* on your face again."

"Perhaps." He admitted slowly. "Mind you, I'm no expert on the way doctors and surgeons and physicians and whatnots operate, and I just don't have the urge to learn much more than I do know." He sipped the top off his cup gingerly, decided he could live with it.

"They remind me of the peerage, actually." Bradstreet said surprisingly. "You know how they can get; inclusive, shut-mouthed, and loyal to a fault."

"Yes, that *does* sound like our betters…" Lestrade said wryly.

"Pshaw, I've been introduced to some surgeons who may as well be a Peer of the Realm!" Bradstreet sniffed.

"And that may be part of the reason." Lestrade reluctantly held out the sugar bowl to Bradstreet and tried not to watch him pile it in. "I think…Watson may be wanting to protect the innocent." He met Bradstreet's look of astonishment in silence. "I've had a few examples of medical scandal explained to me, Roger. This is…this could be a powderkeg." He shook his head, not satisfied with what he was saying, but unable to make it any clearer. "If a doctor is placed into disrepute, it isn't just the doctor who will be tainted with the scandal. His family, his friends, his very school and the students who respect him will all be affected. His work cannot be cited without derision or scorn; any good he's done with his innocent students will be completely negated by the scandal; his students will share in that shame." Lestrade took another drink of coffee. "Call me wrong if it feels wrong, but I think Watson's craving for the proof to be set forward by another doctor. As a matter of honour…even if it could bring about his own destruction of reputation."

Bradstreet's shadowed face suddenly infused with the light of comprehension. "Well, I suppose I can see why he doesn't want Holmes to know about it."

"Beg your pardon..?" Lestrade paused, his bitter cup suspended before his lips.

"I've seen these scandals too." Bradstreet's fierce gaze was backlit from a taut satisfaction at un-riddling Watson, and his large fist gently ground into the pestle of his palm. "If word gets out Mr. Holmes knew about this mess, the public would avoid him like the plague. They'd lump him with Watson's crime of reporting his teacher in murder."

Lestrade closed his eyes and pressed his forehead. "You're right. Watson wouldn't want to put that at risk."

"He'd be down to the level of a shill, or…working for the Foreign Office and I can't say which would be worse." Bradstreet breathed his relief. A mystery was solved and he could rest. "A man like him needs to choose his clients."

"So we just remember…if it all explodes in our faces, we just make sure Holmes can truthfully say he didn't know what his fellow lodger was doing." Lestrade did not share his friend's satisfaction. The whole thing tasted sour as old mash. "All this…all of this…this coddling," he spat, "to protect the future sensibilities of a man who wouldn't return the courtesy."

Bradstreet's blocky face was so deep in thought even Lestrade couldn't read him. "He's a dangerous man, this

Parker. There are those who would say that the consequences should have kept him from his actions. And yet, you and I know humanity does not live up to its ideals."

"No...no it does not." Lestrade sighed. There was no reaching Bradstreet when he started waxing philosophy. "When a man thinks of what he intends to do instead of what he is doing...that is where the worst crimes take root." He came to himself and put sugar in Watson's coffee. "If he's behind the murder...would he stop when someone else caught his fancy? I suggest we see what sort of plan is formulating in Watson's mind."

"You think he has a plan?" Bradstreet asked doubtfully.

"Not sure he *needs* to plan," Lestrade said thoughtfully. "Throw him into a disaster, and I can imagine he'd rise up swinging. But telling him there's a disaster to come into...*that's* different.

"I know how procedure *should* be followed." Lestrade scowled. "And I'll keep to it. Watson is sure as sap and we can believe him—but unless the proof is hard and fast, he won't say it. He wants our assistance in getting this proof; very well, we ought to give it to him."

"Once the proof is there, it'll be our turn." Bradstreet stared at the wall behind Lestrade. "We've used assistance before, Geoffrey, and I can accept that. But if it looks like he's in trouble, we should be there."

"What we need is a hard excuse of our presence in Edinburgh. Start thinking, Roger. Can your intra-office ties explain it?"

Watson smiled slightly to see that when the Inspectors returned, their expressions firm in a new unity in the situation.

"We've glanced over a few codes." Bradstreet explained. "We don't know where Elspeth may or may not have died," he stopped to take a deep breath, "but she *was* a citizen of England. That and a few other fine details ought to give us the leeway we need. There's also the fact that your man Parker claims double residency in Scotland and England."

"He hasn't used his English address in five years, but he still keeps it up." Watson scowled thoughtfully. "I didn't think of it." His self-disgust at missing the small detail was actually rather gratifying to the policemen, who daily faced the accusation of laziness or stupidity for overlooking the smallest detail.

"We'll keep it in mind. His double-residency will go a long way to helping us carry the authority. What we can do is file the initial report based upon your statement—which can be kept in confidence for now—and get a warrant to search the English address. That will allow us to tie-on an additional search upon his Edinburgh address, but you seem worried?"

"Not for the English address, no." Watson said quickly. "He can't get to his possessions in time. No, I am concerned that if he is surprised by a search of his house, he can…damage our chances of finding the proofs of his crimes."

The Doctor squared his shoulders backwards, his still-brown hands lacing together at the front of his waist. "His father was suspected for years of collecting…but in the end it was only the proof of that one attempted murder, and a stolen skull that convicted his actions. If the whispers are to be half-believed, there was an entire room of such things, kept in secret."

"You mean sneaking in and finding the swag." Lestrade could not completely hide his admiration—or his disapproval. It made his voice do queer things.

"That," Bradstreet attempted diplomacy, "Sounds…a little…chancy."

Watson only looked at him.

Lestrade cleared his throat and coughed into his fist. "Well." He muttered. "We've done similar things in the name of the Badge, haven't we? Bradstreet, what's your recipe?"

Bradstreet grumbled a bit. "My responsibilities in Bow allow me some jurisdiction, but Lestrade will be the figurehead and the ultimate authority." Bradstreet nodded to the little man. "As long as it doesn't interfere with his professional duties, he's allowed to take on private cases."

"And my desk is clear." Lestrade told him. It was only a little white lie; it would be clear if he pulled the night in the office, but he'd done worse for far less reason.

"What is your fee?" Watson startled them by asking, rising to his feet with a hand to his waist.

"Already taken care of." Lestrade said quickly. "There's been a reward posted by the family and I can use that as an excuse." *But I wouldn't take that ill-offered money if it was dressed in a peerage.*

Watson nodded slowly. It was obvious his personal sense of honour was tainted at the notion of taking an advantage, however false, or a family's grief; but he was prepared to go along with a necessary ruse.

"So…what are your intentions and how can we help you?"

The doctor gave them his brief summary of intentions, and was grateful to see they had no objections to what he was planning. Bradstreet shook his hand in parting. His grip was dry and strong.

Outside, the London fog was building pressure; Watson felt the dull throb in his bones and wondered again if he had cast his lots to a foolish wind when he chose to come here. He still felt vulnerable and naïve in this city, a cesspool indeed. He liked people; it was a fundamental part of his being.

Yet, there were times when he wondered if he was completely out of his depth with the Study of Man.

Going to Dr. Parker's house again might be another such activity that would be listed as "out of his depth." He slowly limped his way to the attentions of the nearest cab-driver and listlessly gave his directions to the chemist, the Stationary's, and finally home. Trafalgar Square passed by his window, the endless throngs of homeless huddled against the cold.

Despite the winter air the reek of the unwashed wrinkled his nose. His face stared out of the glass, tired and stupid. The gaze of another veteran like himself looked up, his once-alive eyes flattened and dull.

That might have been his fate all too easily. At best, he might have been one of the recruiters...one of the men who had set his steps to the Army.

Culp had been the man's name. He paid out of pocket for things his wages didn't cover: the cleaning of his uniform for being all day in the soot of the cities, and even the Queen's Shilling that sealed the deal. He cut a fine figure in the corner and spoke with pride, but he was a Shabby-genteel underneath his brass buttons. When Watson had accepted his shilling it had been a measure of trust between them: too many young wags had taken the shilling and never returned, leaving Culp all the poorer.

Would he still be around? Would he still be on the recruiting corners?

Watson leaned his head backwards, staring with eyes that did not want to quite focus on the dirty scenery as it rattled past. He clenched his teeth as the cab turned to a rougher cobblestone; electric threads of pain charged his nervous system. Putting his injured leg straight out helped, but he hated how it bent the rest of his body like an old man's.

The cab ground to a slow halt inside a pillow of sloughed-off snow and sluggish pools of melt. Watson stepped out with his hands death-gripped upon every support he could find, but when he turned around to hand up the fare he was unprepared when the driver hopped down and helped him with his parcels. Flustered attempts to pay him extra were met with a firm no and a nod. "Not at all, sir. We remembers our soldiers."

Watson was left standing, staring after the vanishing man and his horse with his goods neatly set upon the door-step. He did not know the man...but somehow the man had known him. Was he on display? He shook himself and took the key to the lock.

Strange how his bachelor lodgings felt like they were home; and his moody, wonderfully brilliant, disputatious lodger with their already long-suffering landlady, family.

Perhaps I feel that way because my own family would have never understood. Not that what he was doing would be *illegal*; Watson could not imagine himself performing any such activity. It was hard enough to see himself defeating a lifetime of upbringing to enter a man's household--a man once respected--as a guest under subterfuge. He was very glad his parents hadn't lived to see this day. Their own personal sense of honesty would have never noticed the *purpose* of his actions; they would have only noticed that he was operating under false pretence. From such actions, they held, no good would come. Dishonesty begat dishonesty.

They had been blessed with the comfort of a narrow outlook. Small wonder they had not turned a hair when their second son, the son who must make his own way, went to medicine for his career, and from there the Army. A bullet in the desert, or a falling brick off a roof—one's destiny was all the same.

Perhaps it was the new awareness of Bradstreet's own estrangement, but the doctor was worried about the Runner. The man's bereavement was clear. As a doctor, Watson had granted his name to many a babe by grateful parents without knowing if the child would ever survive. He knew one of Bradstreet's twins had been named after Lestrade. What a loss for everyone.

The doctor wrenched his mind back to the business at hand as he took his packages one step at a time to his rooms. He had no sister himself, but if anything had ever happened...he was not certain he could be as contained and controlled as the big man.

You've plenty to do without taking on another's problems, he scolded himself; Bradstreet would not welcome that sort of kindly invasion. He tried to make himself as comfortable as possible in his usual corner and waited for the familiarity of Baker Street to settle into his bones. If Bradstreet—or Lestrade—had seen him at that moment, they would have been surprised at how silent and still he had suddenly grown.

For his part, Watson had learned the art of doing nothing the hard way; it is very difficult to come to a useful plane of mental power when one is near-mindless with pain and blood-loss and thirst in the heart of a desert war. Later on in the Army hospital he began to recollect some sense of himself, but all the hard efforts were laid waste with enteric fever (enteric fever— what an ironic term for a man who did nothing 'enteric', but laid insensible three out of every four days of his illness!).

The third blow had come when the Medical Board deemed him unfit for serving again; logically, Watson could not blame them. He would have rejected himself out of horror. But the Army had been his chosen world, and one he had thrived in with an unknown sense of self-worth. Losing that world had been painful in the extreme. At the same time, he was facing another form of rejection in terms of what family he had left.

After a certain amount of disaster, *one more* severance of the past becomes nothing more than flat and two-dimensional. Faced with his inability to prevent the dissolution of his relationship with his brother, Watson merely swallowed that along with all his other imagined failures. Whilst he would have never admitted to it, being the second son with low prospects had set him up to accept this sort of thing years ago. Hamish had been the bright star, promising and intelligent. Hamish had been the only sensible choice of heirs.

And now, Hamish was…what Hamish had chosen to be.

And he was…not what he would have chosen.

He could not help but feel that rising above his brother (however accidentally) was somehow a refutation of their parents' hopes.

It was the lot of his life.

Back at the Yard, the two policemen were still a little shaky at the magnitude of their looming project.

"He had it all figured out!"

"Roger…how many times have you said that?" Lestrade asked in his exasperation.

"I'm still not completely believing it. After all of that…that…" His large hands winged through the air like so many baffled birds. "That…plotting and scheming we did…he'd already figured out what to do!"

"Man thinks quick; perhaps because he cuts to the quick." Lestrade stared into his empty cup. "Nice trick. I wonder if he's always like that."

"God Alone Knows." Bradstreet was slightly horrified at the notion. Such thinking was for paranoid malcontents, criminals, and strategists—not decent law-abiding folk.

"So we get his statement filed—you'd be the best man to let the Chief know about it. He's less likely to fuss at *you*." Lestrade gnawed on what little was left of his thumbnail as he thought aloud. "And I'll pick up the rest of the papers...we can meet up with our fellows in Edinburgh...and stand back and let Watson go into the lion's den."

"That's no ordinary lion." Bradstreet pointed out.

"Quite all right. I'm sure that's no ordinary Watson."

Edinburgh.

Watson had once thought (not so long ago) that he would never return to the Athens of the North. The bad memories remained bad, and the good memories were painful as his now-constantly throbbing leg and the duller weakness of his shoulder.

His last visit had been largely under the hours of night; "Auld Reekie" (Old Smokey) was its most well-deserved name then, for the stench and infernal glow of the coal fires created huge glowering bellies in the sky above the city.

But, in the light of day he surprised himself. He'd forgotten the impression of the city's vast collection of medieval structures. *Auld Greekie* was another name, a pun on its intellectual capacity and thriving subculture.

Robert Burns called it *Edina* for its Latin name; Ben Johnson called it "*Britain's Other Eye*" (tho' he was less poetic in his treatment of the oats eaten there), and Sir Walter Scott, descendant of the Wizard Scott, won all the prizes for linguistic tomfoolery when he called it *Yon Empress of the North*.

He could not have lost himself in these streets. He was too well known by his face, his actions and his surname. Even the subterranean catacombs of Old Town wouldn't have let him lie quietly buried from prying eyes. He'd no choice but to choose another large cesspool, and only London fit that description.

And it was working; he thought bitterly. *It had been working.* But yet...here he was back in this, with a trained accent that fooled no one. A Northerner knew another Northerner by his face and his name and his mother. How he spoke as judgement was a queerly English conceit.

John Watson lifted his head to the murky sky above, feeling the weather on the skin of his face. Since the 1500's they'd been building multi-storied structures, *lands*, as tall as fourteen stories in the days before the refinement of iron. He could not lose himself in aerial worlds either.

He crossed the broad street cautiously, his step uneven and awkward on the cobbles; a paper-hawker was chaunting his public to buy and thus support the Scotland National Rugby Team. Watson hesitated, but found himself unable to resist. The game was his only honest addiction, and it had been part of the city since '71. He passed on a coin without checking its value and took the newspaper that warmed his palm.

There had been a time when he'd counted every tiny coin that came his way. The war had taken that from him too. He knew of course that his depleting funds were due to his inability to hold on to money...but Maiwand had taught him the worthlessness of cash. Cash meant nothing when the throat clenched up for water. The month's pay in his pocket couldn't purchase a lost limb, or ease the pain of the man screaming next to him for morphine (God, the screams were with him yet). Money, then, was only the means to the end--one should criticize those ends, but not the means.

It gave him a new perspective to the definition of money being the root of all evil. Money was the coin of need and desperation. Even when his spendthrift ways curbed his livelihood, he couldn't justify himself to think much of the losses. As long as he could work, he could bring enough in to live on.

Although he was relying more on his pen than he'd ever imagined...

The paper was advertising the next-season's ice hockey recruitment. Watson scanned the slightly-bizarre language of the article and decided '*haranguing*' was not too strong of a description, but hockey-players were like that. He snorted at a critical assessment of the last bout of cricket. Yes, of course; *everyone* knew it took Scotland 80-some years to even join the tournaments, but when they did...every schoolboy knew Scotland trounced Surrey by 172 runs! Watson bitterly regretted the end of the Scottish Cricket Union's clear demise; by next year it would be gone. He didn't know what would happen after that...

He stuffed the folded paper under his arm and this time, crossed the street without reversal or interruption. His satchel swung awkwardly from his good hand. A wind from the dry, cool east was coming up. He welcomed. His appetite stirred, ready to replenish after an entire day of switch-overs and delays on the rail--The Flying Scotsman had been unusually inefficient.

Watson picked a promising Old-City tavern that advertised "clean rooms and water" as well as its ability to treat the illustrious clientele of the Royal Observatory. A solid table was chosen against the battle-scored oak wall that let him face the world. He set the paper aside and dickered for a plate of savoury oatmeal sausage and a tankard of roasted barley beer (ignoring the vile Shandy-gaff[47] being swilled not far away). The innkeeper set both down with considerable pride, stared Watson's too-thin body up and down with a scathing look, and sniffed, offended that his guest had let himself go. "S mairg a ni tarcuis air biadh," He leveled the challenge. *He who has contempt for food is a fool."*

Watson dipped his head. "I agree," he held up his fork with a genuine smile, mouth already watering from the rich odours of lovage, sage, coins of leek and razor-thin slivers of carrot and parsnip into the ground meat and a goose egg to hold it all together. Peppery winter savoury coated the top of the dish with dried thyme and the barest dash of lemon zest. The mound of buttermilk and mashed potatoes was only a gild upon the lily after that masterpiece.

The innkeeper nursed his scowl, turning skeptical and solicitous under this thick beard. "Cockaleekie tomorrow," he answered. "T'won't last long. Barley bread too."

Watson enjoyed having control over his eating. Back at Baker Street, meals were often taken hastily and in the process of running, engineered by a man who felt his pipe-tobacco a more necessary source of sustenance.

Not that Watson would ever call Holmes a fool. Not in anything. But Watson had never seen him approach a meal with anything less than a perfunctory obligation. He took his pleasures in other areas…all of them were either cerebral or a manifestation of the cerebral…such as his running down clews in a mud-drenched field…

His strength aggravated by the trains, full of a good meal with dark ale, Watson took to his room. It was a simple, basic fifteen-square foot affair with the luxury in the small things: the quality of the bed, and the silence of the thick walls. The window was small and solid, masking a good-natured polemic

---

[47] Mix of ale and gin

on the street between elderly draughts-players. Candle-sticks provided illumination (it was clear more modern illumination would enter this establishment in full protest). The maid brought warm water and supplied the location of the nearest Turkish bath. Watson thanked her, and passed on a tip for her troubles.

Alone, he satisfied himself that the satchel was safely underneath the bed...his face dulled with dread for the future, but the true agony did not know what would actually happen tomorrow when he paid his calls.

He missed Holmes, but he was also glad he was not here. This was like standing in a battlefield all over again; invisible cannons yawed before the doctor, full of terrible promise and he didn't know which would fire first.

He did miss Holmes, but they were alike in the oddest of ways.

Neither liked to ask for help; it was better to offer it before putting the other in the quandary.

And in this...

Just as Holmes did not include his friend on cases for his own good...so Watson ought to return that courtesy.

Watson slid the satchel deep under his bed with his foot, and was asleep almost as soon as the clean sheets were drawn over his chest.

Sleep he needed. The hard work was about to come...

Bradstreet and Lestrade had taken a later train. It gave them time to arrange the possible hasty search of Dr. Jonas Q. Parker's English residence at a moment's notice. This of course meant Bradstreet had to wax his most persuasive and invoke a large amount of trust with the superiors—Lestrade knew better than to try such tricks. The Chief was a fine man and a hard worker, but his loathing for Lestrade was rooted deep in a quarrel going back at least three generations and six wars. If he approved anything, it would be in the hopes that his hated little officer would be on his way to disgrace and dismissal.

(Gregson was always happy to remind his rival that this guaranteed him the 'honour and satisfaction' of being the first on the Chief's Special List—a blessedly short and depressing tally of cases no one was expected to solve in a thousand years).

Thus, despite Bradstreet's success in getting the pre-arranged warrant and the approved search, they were crippled at the restricted time. It was hoped in the strongest possible language that they would find their answers at Dr. Parker's northern residence within 48 hours of arrival in Edinburgh.

They'd sent their pre-planned ciphered wire to MacDonald and took up the lodgings he'd arranged for them. It was a quietly reserved inn directly across the street from Parker's address ('pure coincidence, but handy,' he'd said). At the moment, they were more grateful that it gave them the time to wash off the layers of English soot that had collected on their persons during the trip.

Inspector Alec Macdonald was that most unusual creature: a completely fair-haired, fair-skinned child of the Hebrides. His mind for detail was enviable, as well as his ability to draw those details together to come up with a scenario. Everyone knew he was doing the work of two men on a regular basis but he never once lost his good-hearted cheer and willingness to help.

Which was just as well, Gregson had remarked once with great jealousy, for the man had the ability (either from sheer physical presence or from personality), to siphon all but the most minimal amounts of oxygen out of a room once he entered it. Combine that with an enviable Aberdonian education, and you had a fearsome package inside a frame that was more bone than flesh, and more brain than muscle.

Edinburgh was one of his many hats; he had family in the city and that gave him an easy excuse for being here in the off-hours, sipping tea on the bench and chatting away the idleness. He was planning a transfer to London in a few months or by the end of next year, depending on the health of his father; Scotland wanted him to go as a good example they could be proud of, not to mention a reminder that Scotland was an asset to British justice.

MacDonald listened intelligently around the obstacles of scrubbing and quick bites of food and asked pointed questions about policy and research; he was fascinated at the intricate details of the case and confessed he was curious to see if the rumours about Parker were true.

"Seems like you'd have a better chance spying at the back." The tall man offered at last. "Especially if there's dark doings. Should I try to see if there's a better address?"

"We're already *here*." Bradstreet didn't have to remind the others that extra expenditure meant extra censure from the Office. Nothing stifled initiative as quickly as the ice-cold prospect of having a case thrown completely out the window by someone sniffing 'abuse of privilege.'

"Watson's signalling us by cigarette. He can't really signal us as a gentleman from the Back Door." Lestrade grabbed up the last bit of toast from his tray, checked to make sure it wasn't contaminated by Bradstreet's sprinkle of sugar, and chewed away.

"Huh, you're right. This is going to be a snorter, isn't it?"

"One of these days, you're going to wear out that word." Bradstreet grumbled.

"I'll just have to buy another 'un." MacDonald didn't turn a hair.

"Or find cases that don't apply." Lestrade couldn't resist.

"Now that's daft talk." MacDonald told him. It was exactly what Bradstreet had been thinking. "Where would that be? The Lost Umbrella Department?"

"Now, that *can* be interesting." Lestrade said sadistically. Talking whilst chewing helped him concentrate on a perfectly straight face. "Wasn't it last year Bellows reported an old brolly on 'Fourth that was being used to hide State Papers?"

"Hidden up in the handle, wasn't it?" Bradstreet proved his knowledge of small, deathless details as well as a willingness to add to MacDonald's torture. "Then again, where else are you going to hide things? The stalks aren't very big."

"Makes one wonder how many other brollies are being used for ulterior means."

"And there's what—4,000 unclaimed brollies in the department at any given time?"

"Well, would you claim a lost'un if you were using it to pass on swag?"

"We'll never know...until someone subjects all 4,000-plus to a thorough search."

The Londoners turned and looked expectantly at their ersatz host.

MacDonald scowled at them.

"I'll be outside," he announced grandly. "Doing eemportant things. I'll see you tomorrow." He rose and with long-legged dignity, made his way to the door. "And speakin' o' umbrellas," was his Parthian shot, "mebbe want to take your own. The weather does what she wants up here in the North."

BANG went the door.

6: Bones Dried Up:

"Our bones are dried up,
our hope is lost,
and we are cut off."
--EZEKIEL 37:11

Watson awoke that morning to the tune of the little street-urchins calling for work or alms. *Today* he would begin.

The morning news was not very interesting—that in itself was interesting, as it was Watson's experience that Edinburgh could make a *duck* a newsworthy event.

The memory could make him smile now, but at the time it had only caused gastric upset; a flying eiderdown mallard (and from only the Gods knew from where or to where), had aspired too high of a height whilst passing over the city. Unlike the Icarus of mythology, his wings had not melted but iced over, sending him plummeting to what would have been a death by normal standards if its loss of control hadn't coincided with a passing waggon of construction-sand for the local ironmongery.

Having been inordinately proud of his introduction to Blackheath, Watson had been more than a little nauseated to find his brief moment in the sun eclipsed by an unlucky sea-fowl who later wound up as a pampered pet at the waggon-driver's cotter.[48] *His* story had received exactly one paragraph of text. The mallard (replete with evilly beady eyes and a serrated beak which gave it a most unscrupulous leer in the illustrations) received three square inches of paper.

I really was arrogant, wasn't I? Watson asked himself with a wry shake of his head, smiling at the newsprint just as

---

[48] Lowland word for crofter

the tavern-keeper slipped a platter of black pudding to his elbow, side-dressed with a steaming mound of eggs. *Expecting them to write up my achievements! A duck plummeting hundreds of feet and surviving really is a more newsworthy event; rugby players emerge on a daily basis!*

Still smiling at himself, he put a fork into his breakfast whilst a clustre of idlers mused aloud on the tribulations on a weather front that couldn't be predicted by time or tide. The more things changed…

"Do I know you, young sir?"

Watson looked up into the face of a younger, much hairier version of last night's tavern-keeper. "I don't know," he answered honestly. "Perhaps, though I haven't lived here for a time."

"I mean no offence," The man assured him. Watson lifted his left hand from the table at the wrist, conveying he understood. Family was not just a way of life and a reason for a blood-feud; family connexions were constantly lost and re-forged. "You simply remind me of a man I once knew…a teacher…he would tutor some of the boys with promise, even tho' they never had much money." A wistful note threaded through that smoke-roughened voice. "I was one of 'em." He said. A hammerhand thumb lifted up, touched his forehead. Watson noticed this aberration in fascination. "But I cannae remember ught I should…was hurt in the wreck o'the *Yarrow*. I don't know his name, but…well you remind me of him somehow."

Watson swallowed hard. "There was a teacher, his name was Watson." He cleared his throat. "I fear he's gone now."

"Ah." Old sadness crossed the face. What Watson had taken for age was in fact, a very hard life and the weathering parchment of burn scars that a salve of goose grease and knitbone[49] had not been able to cure. "I allus wished I could thank him for his kindness to me. But I was ashamed for him to see his lessons had been wasted with the fall of a mast."

"Did you enjoy his lessons?" Watson made a stab in the dark.

His applicant was startled. "*Of course I did.* I still remember the wee gemstones of his teaching. His numbers…Oh, yes, my life was the richer for it."

"You could have given him no higher compliment, sir." Watson said softly. "I should know."

The doctor watched the man walk away, his step more confident whilst he himself was shaken. He had dreaded such a confrontation. It was a consequence of living in Edinburgh. And, of course, being so thoroughly a *Watson*.

The weight of the satchel rested at his feet; he would go nowhere without it. The *problem* was the next step in all of this. The doctor frowned as he thought. Even though he knew he was doing it, he couldn't seem to stop. The basic sense of unease was still there, but fainter for having a decent meal and a good night's rest.

Deceit was not Watson's nature, though he *was* clever. Somewhere in his life he'd gotten the impression that the quality required a high craftiness he did not possess. Most people who met him had him pegged for *intelligent* at first line-up. But the sort of cleverness that could combust the air with lies…well, *that* was a different story.

Why *couldn't* life be more like the lessons of open warfare? There was a reason why Holmes called him a romantic. Watson responded to the intricate rules of behaviour fronted with forthright conduct on an emotional level. *They made sense.* He disliked the feudal method, but his personal

---

[49] comfrey

beliefs in a meritocracy were part of his attraction for the Army.

No matter how much he tried to puzzle out the problem, the solution never came. Shaking his head, he rose to his feet, placing his weight upon his walking-stick. His leg suddenly throbbed, like a dead thing forced to move reluctantly against his will and the young man set his teeth. The hard-won optimism was melting in the face of the old pain.

He would have cursed…if only there was any good in it. Sadly, cursing did no more good than it did begging for water in the desert, or wishing for morphine as one woke up from the surgery-table.

John Watson stood outside the raised porch-step of the small tavern, breathing quietly in the cool of the morning air. About him a soft grey fog swirled an undulating twist before his eyes, each dirty water-droplet heavy and pale.

On the other side of the street, a mere yard to the left, he could see a beggar perched on another such step as the one he was using. The man was missing his left leg, and he was the colour of the fog. Watson could see the shine of war medals above the bowl he kept for begging. His clothing was falling apart to rags, and yet he was polishing his medals to a shine.

God in his wisdom, have mercy on us…

He was beginning to see how much he missed his life in sooty London, cesspool though it was…and…his life with his new friend. *London is more home to me now than this place. In a way it feels strange. In another…* In another way he could not quite define…London felt like the place he had been meant to live in all along.

The newspaper-sellers were cantillating about a new art-show featuring the works of Britain's favoured and controversial artists. Watson had no taste for such fare; the very thought made his insides lock up under his ribs and sting the water to his eyes.

I will not stay here. He knew this to be true. *I no longer belong here. Mourn me, but let me pass,* he paraphrased the snatch of prayer from his childhood. The heavy satchel pulled his wrist all the way to his shoulder and neck. It added to the ache in his leg, made his step one-sided and awkward. Humiliation made him even more awkward: he stepped off the kerb and all but fell onto the street. His cane saved him.

Embarrassed, Watson lifted his eyes by accident to the silent veteran begging on the other side. The old man's pale brown eyes were calm and quiet...and knowing. In one moment, both men understood each other.

Watson lowered his gaze, knowing the beggar would never accept money from the likes of him. He too, had served and given enough.

Once on the street, Bradstreet horrified his best friend with the purchase of a hand-held pie stuffed with a ground meat that was no more identifiable than the accompanying vegetable. Lestrade devoutly hoped it wasn't turnip, but the odds were...

"Just because they make you ill doesn't mean the rest of the world has to do without, Lestrade." Bradstreet had enough attention to give him a halfhearted scowl.

"It doesn't exactly make me *ill*, Bradstreet. It just...I used to eat a great many turnips when I was younger."

"Crop-failure of the '70's?" Bradstreet guessed. "Yes, as I recall, kitchens were a bit limited that season." He chewed and swallowed peacefully. "At least we had a choice of turnips, turnip greens, mustard, cabbage-turnips,[50] Swede-turnips and parsnips."

---

[50] kohlrabi

Lestrade made a sound that managed to combine agreement with digestive opinion. "Yes, Bradstreet...I vividly remember."

"At least there *were* a few beetroots. I rather liked the yellow ones...and the mangel-wurzel..." Bradstreet propped his feet up against a chunk of broken street-rubble that the road-workers had not yet noticed. In the tiny slip of park it was possible for two men in clean but battered clothing to enjoy an early cup of tea as a clustre of children attempted a complicated-looking game that appeared to be a combination of road bowling, palle-malle, hurley, and 'dodge-the-traffic'. Lestrade, who had no children of his own (much less the intention to marry), was flinching at every third or fourth movement. Bradstreet, well accustomed to such things, only paused from his eating long enough to bellow well-meaning advice to the poorer players. Lestrade thought by turns that his best friend was making it worse.

"Are you trying for manslaughter?" Lestrade finally asked.

"Scotland doesn't have manslaughter." Bradstreet said with infuriating calm. He took another bite of awful pie.

Anyone who didn't know Bradstreet would be worrying about his mental state; he appeared too calm and casual for the subject at hand. Lestrade knew better. The man simply reined in his emotions until the conclusion of a case. No matter how exhaustive or horrible, he remained coolly remote and professional. It wasn't until after the last report was written, stamped, and approved that he would blare up like a foghorn.

Lestrade had been around his friend before and after these events...and he honestly dreaded the conclusion of this one. For now he was relishing the quiet before the storm.

And he was studying the house in question.

Parker's address was…impressive; a three storey example of foggy stone and taut architecture with a ropework of vines climbing up the facing. Lestrade supposed it was a change from the usual ivy carpets...

Despite the clear age of the old relic it was well tended and money—lots of it—had been spent to keep it with the quality of its neighbors. MacDonald had given them a battered old booklet of Edinburgh's distinguished houses, and they knew it had served its time as a school twice, a hospital once, a mortuary, and, until Parker the Elder had gotten it as part of his wedding dowry, a place for the rebellious elites to mingle so they could discuss politics and art at the same time with the same officious tones.

That bit about serving as a mortuary, even briefly to meet the noble needs of the city during a Regency cholera epidemic, had Lestrade particularly interested.

"Mphm." Lestrade tapped him on the arm. Both men studied the world from the top of suddenly-elevated newspapers. "Here he comes." The little man whispered.

"He doesn't look like he's even looking for us." Bradstreet muttered under his breath.

"Look at the way he's walking, Roger. This weather does nothing for those wounds."

"I would say not. It's hard enough on my joints."

The Yarders waited quietly. The doctor was dressed with a mind to the ways of Edinburgh, and they had never seen him look so anonymous in the crowd. His head hung down and his eyes barely looked up from the placing of his heavy feet on the sidewalk. Even from down the street, it was easy to see his tight, painful set of the jawline.

"Man's going to age before his time if he keeps that up," Bradstreet murmured, almost too softly to be heard.

"Least he doesn't have far to walk," Lestrade answered in the same voice. A moment later Watson was nearly abreast of their bench, separated by a sudden knot of cab-drivers who objected strongly to the rough game. The doctor stopped; his eyes barely flickered, and the Yarders knew he had seen them.

They saw him tighten as his wounds reasserted in his nerves, and he braced himself yet again, turned his back to his audience, and painfully plodded his way up the freshly-washed concrete steps to the carved door on the top.

Bradstreet hadn't realised he was holding his breath until Watson's patient knock was answered; the door parted to show a black gloom and a pale butler. The two consulted with each other a moment, and then Watson was stepping inside the large door. It shut with a mahogany tone.

Lestrade hissed next to him. "All right, he's gotten this far. Now we have the difficult part. Staying here and waiting for the signal." 'Staying put' meant 'torture' for Lestrade.

"Or," Bradstreet reminded him, "waiting until he's failed to come back out."

"Let's just hope that doesn't happen."

"Someone will notice if we don't. Surely?"

"This isn't like London, gentlemen. Anything going on in Edinburgh may be noticed…or it may not."

The bearer of this cool advice from behind, Inspector Alec Macdonald had made his morning appointment.

Lestrade pretended to read a garrulous newspaper whilst eyeing the innocent-looking Brownstone that had swallowed up Dr. Watson. Bradstreet had all but abducted a tea-cart and enforced a promise of frequent returns for cups of the strongest brew the little detective had drunk outside a Gipsy caravan.

The tea-vendor had the look of one of those mixed-blooded Tinkers. Lestrade was tempted to patter at him just to see if there would be a reaction, but he wasn't certain of MacDonald's possible reaction. Local police *didn't* like it when outsiders talked with 'their' people so much…it was like poaching. Or bigamy.

"Don't try what they're selling as coffee." MacDonald warned softly.

"Why? What is it really?"

"There might be a few spoonfuls of the real stuff in it…but the rest is roasted dandelion and chicory." MacDonald sipped blissfully. "A great favourite of our oldsters, who canna' have the stimulant. Not sayin' it's not good, but it doesn't wake a man up in the morn."

"*Anything* on this bird at all?" Bradstreet wanted to know past the pleasantries. He didn't want to sound desperate, but last night was a courtesy for MacDonald; it was now their turn to get data, and he didn't like not having it.

Macdonald pursed his lips and shook his head from side to side. "Not *officially*." He said quite carefully.

Bradstreet's eyes sharpened. "*Unofficially?*"

Macdonald shrugged. "That's the snorter," he explained. "His father was suspected for extensive body-thieving. And he was friends what was some gentlemen caught up in the case over in Forest Hill—some snatchers wanted some money in a hurry, so they started turning fresh corpses over to sell to some of the doctors."

That *was* a snorter. Lestrade shivered. Next to him, Bradstreet had stopped breathing. "Just how fresh were the corpses?"

"Let's just say one of the specimens was insufficiently dead when they got him. That was one of the reasons why the laws overturned the mandates against supplying schools with bodies."

Bradstreet rubbed at his forehead. He was holding himself in as tightly as a piano-string. "But there's nothing on the son."

"No. He pays his taxes, he goes to chapel, lives alone, lives simply in that dusty old house of antiques and everything his father handed down to him. Family investments keep him cozy—he doesn't have to do anything he doesn't want to. Mostly retired from teaching, but he does a two-day lecture once a term for the students on pathology. It's a lively topic, for all that his slides are a bit on the disturbing slant." MacDonald sighed. "I take tutorin' when I can gentlemen, but one o' that man's seminars was all I could take."

Lestrade took another drink of brew. He was going to keep his mouth shut on *that* as much as possible. "What's your reading of these particular tea-leaves, Mac?"

Macdonald scratched his new winter whiskers. "On or off the record?"

"Yes." Lestrade speared him with an eyebrow.

MacDonald grinned, but quickly sobered. "There's something wrong with a man who is so...so *sterile*, gents. Nothing we've noticed outright. But I'll warn you now, that's how his father was. It was just luck and a tip and a policeman who wasn't too footsore and cold to answer up on that tip one night at the graveyard." He rubbed at his new beard again. "You think of growing up in that house. He'd be seein' his father break the law to suit his own ends...would he think anything less of it?"

Anyone else would be asking why the police weren't keeping a tighter eye on the man. The Yarders knew better. Overworked and understaffed, a lowly constable was responsible for hundreds of citizens, or sometimes the entire population of a small town. The Inspectors had it no better, being responsible for the Constables and working liaison for victim, victim's family, criminal and criminal's family.

"Dr. Watson is dead certain this skeleton is an illegal possession." Lestrade said carefully. "I haven't known the man long, but he doesn't make things up. He's as painfully honest as a tooth-ache.

"How queer," he added in afterthought, "that this Dr. Parker would be so reluctant to talk about something he's so proud of."

"There were accusations at Dr. Parker's father," MacDonald cleared his throat, "I'm not trying tae taint the evidence in the case, mind you, but nothing was ever found."

"His family seems awfully clean, doesn't it?" Bradstreet shook his head. "Wouldn't we all like to believe that families like that really exist."

"We're in the wrong profession to say that." Lestrade grouched. "Keep going, Mac. He was clean, but not so clean to the eye of the public, was he?"

"Several families were convinced he was behind the opened graves of their loved ones…but…no proof." He sighed and pulled out a thin, sealed filing envelope from inside his coat. "This might help add to some illumination." A blunt finger tapped the paper meaningfully. "The men will be patrolling about same as usual, but as soon as Auld Reekie goes dark, we'll have a few more on post in the shadows. When do you get your signal?"

"Tonight at dark." Bradstreet answered.

MacDonald leaned forward on his knees. "This case you're on, you shouldn't have trouble getting your bird back to London. Dr. Parker claims English citizenry, especially when s'more convenient fra him to be English than Scottish--so that's a bit more in your favour. Also: Least little bit of a breath of a scandal and the school will *beg* you to pack up the cause of the trouble and trot him out of the city, *fast*. They don't want to be the site of an outraged scandal." He cleared his throat. "And the fastest you do it, the better."

That was an unexpected spot of luck. The two Londoners traded looks with each other. "We rather didn't expect that," Lestrade confessed. "What about extradition?"

"Man, you're a Runner aren't you?" Macdonald grinned at Bradstreet. "Bow Street's still the only office in charge of extradition. And believe me, when it comes to avoiding the kind of screaming Edinburgh can raise, we *will* overlook procedure. Just this once. Until, that is, the next time Edinburgh threatens to scream."

"That's odd." Lestrade scowled. "I never heard so much as a dust-up over the way Edinburgh handles things."

"Oh, you never were on the other side before." MacDonald spoke so seriously they knew this was no light matter. "This is one of the largest cities on the island; it's the most eemportant city in Scotland. *The* most, gentlemen. One of the Seven Cities of Enlightenment; one of best places to live and all that…People come from all over the world to live here or visit here because they want the advantages of London without the disadvantages. It's not as crowded as London because there simply aren't enough chances to work up here.

"And you know, the University rather *likes* it all that way. It likes the reputation for learning and science and architecture; the literature and fine arts—and they operate under the very strong fear that if something makes the city look bad enough at the wrong moment, the Home Secretary might renege on his intention to work into the Scottish office; they say it might even be enacted as soon as '85.

"Anyway, if we lose status as the Jewel of Scotland, then Parliament, should-it-ever-be-restored-God-Willing, could go to *Dunfermline!*"

Lestrade exploded with laughter and just as quickly clapped his hand over his mouth at the glares from his companions. "I *don't* think that's all *that* likely," he strangled. Tears were forming in his eyes. "*Really.*"

"Some people believe it, though." Bradstreet pointed out.

"Some people also believe that England and the United States will reunite someday!" Lestrade pointed out. "It's *still* rubbish. It doesn't matter if you've got a person as smart as Mr. Holmes believing in it; that doesn't mean it's *going* to happen. Canada is as far as we're going to get, except for possibly that land Senator Webster gave back on the New England border in a drunken stupor. Why can't we have politicians like *that* anymore?"

"Oh, that is an extreme example." Bradstreet admitted. "Besides, Canada's been prepared for another war with the States since 1812."

"Good for them." Lestrade snorted. "I'd be too. I'll bet the Red Indians will volunteer. Very well. So we can do some sneaking around and get this fellow over to London. *If* we can prove there's something on him. That's lovely. But in the meantime, we have a man in there who is *not* a policeman, whom we can only trust will confirm the proof is inside. Hopefully he won't be hurt in this."

"He is from Baker Street." Bradstreet grunted.

"And he's a Watson, eh?" Macdonald murmured. His eyes caught a faraway look; a memory perhaps, and his fingers tapped against his thigh in thought.

"You've met him, haven't you? At the Regatta Parade last year." Bradstreet commented.

"He's a different one." MacDonald said obscurely. "Not as different as the man he shares the rent with, but *still*. Different."

Lestrade risked pulling his glance away from the front door. "In what way?"

"Man's a Scot. But have you eever noticed, he uses the word "Scotchman" and not "Scotsman?""

Bradstreet frowned, then his eyebrows slipped straight up as he realised what Macdonald was saying. "You're right. That is different."

Lestrade needed a moment to catch up with them, but he soon enough grasped it: The word *Scotchman* was correct English in all ways, but it was almost exclusively used by people who were outside the race. Scots hardly ever used that word…save as a wry joke or a disparaging motion.

"Why would he use an outsider's word?"

"Oh, there are a few reasons." Bradstreet admitted. "Scots aren't like the English, Lestrade. There's much less importance placed on dialect. But for you to use an outsider's name for yourself, well that usually means one was taught to be ashamed of themselves in some way."

7: *Bone-grubber*

> (*A*). A person who grubs about dust-bins, gutters, etc., for refuse bones, which he sells to bone-grinders, and other dealers in such stores.
>
> Socially as low as the people who collect dog-dung for the tanneries.

You can do this. John Watson felt his heart cease to beat as someone fumbled at the other side of the door; a light scratching of metal, before the door opened. The dried-apple face of the old butler blinked up at him, unused to the daylight of Edinburgh.

"May I help you, sir?"

"Hello," Watson was lifting his hat as he spoke, fingers gripped around the handle of the satchel in a death-lock. "I apologize for my abrupt arrival, but I was wondering if Dr. Parker was available for a social call."

The butler's eyes—dried-up looking too, like black haws or sloeberries left to desiccate on the branch, peered into his face.

"Lieutenant-Colonel Watson?"

"I'm afraid it's only the Major," Watson was patient—he had given this speech at the last visit. "My apologies for not minding my manners."

For just a moment, the brittle exterior thawed on the old face, and Watson knew he had struck home, as it were, on his entrance.

"I have my card," Watson lifted the rectangle of paper as he spoke.

"Not at all, *Major*." The butler spoke so smoothly it could not be seen as an interruption. "The Watsons have standing welcome in this house. Please do come in side. Dr. Parker will be made aware of your arrival. If you recall the solarium?"

Now that he was alone in same said solarium, Watson took a deep breath. He took another. No doubt the many green potted tea-plants in the warm, sunny room appreciated his contribution.

He'd stopped thinking when the old man let him in. For a moment the identity of John H. Watson had vanished and a blank slate had appeared. He was not an actor. But he could, at least for a brief time, submerge himself into another's personality. Most people had that ability on some level; he'd had reason to practice it more than most.

Now what? Alone with his thoughts, the familiar cauldron was bubbling to the surface.

From somewhere distant and above, a door shut behind two foot-falls. Watson shifted his weight to his stronger leg and lowered his bag.

"John Watson!" Dr. Parker shuffled forward with his own version of war in his body; an uneven spinal column underneath his sober black suit and a large portion missing from his hip-bone. The visitor had often felt the man had never really resembled anyone's ideal of manhood with his long, cobweb-like whiskers curling in silver bows off his narrow nose, and large red ears like the ears off some book-illustrator's fanciful concept of a gnome or household-brownie. His body was designed for scuttling, and before his wounds (it was rumoured) he carried the erratic, lopsided patterns to movement. Even as he entered the room his hand was extended for a shake. Watson took it with an inward swallow. The hand was dry as a stove-top and bulky with three different rings.

Watson knew it was common for a man to move his wedding ring to the opposing hand once he became a widower...but displaying the fact he was widowed thrice over...*that* was something one didn't see every day.

The old man's eyes gleamed, bright blue-green and energetic. "So good to see you again—and so soon! What brings you back to us, Major? Surely not my scintillating conversations about dry old dusty bones!"

Watson smiled with more confidence. "I've always enjoyed your conversations, sir."

"Pshah...I have no real cleverness. I merely stockpile ten to twenty variable topics, and I go down the list." Parker waved his grasshopper hand to the low benches resting in the solarium; they were wood and carved to mimic bamboo canes. "Have a seat. What have you been doing with yourself? How is the Lieutenant-Colonel?" The title was given lovingly over the tongue, and Watson had been expecting this, but it still scraped against his nerves.

"I've been up to no more than last time; training and working on my career—."

"Are you going to set up your own practice?" Parker broke in rudely.

"—er, soon enough, I hope. I've been using my wound pension for more than the horses."

Parker laughed. "I know the truth of that! You *should* have stayed with the Fighting Fifth," he waggled a finger at Watson. "I know the Berkshires are a good lot, but nothing like a Fusilier in a tight spot!" He dropped his hand into his lap, sudden as a meteor. "But you've heard that enough, certainly. What is your brother up to now?"

John was now better prepared. "He is still caught up in his own affairs," he assured his host wryly, and it would take someone as sharp as Sherlock Holmes to notice there was little in the way of warmth behind the eyes. "You know how he is."

"Too true, too true. There's a genius in every family!" Parker laughed again. "But don't tell me it was business that brought you back. Not this time of year when so much of the roads are swamp."

"Well, no, not precisely." Watson permitted himself to lean back a bit, and took the offered cigar. "Most kind. Thank you…"

"Not at all. It's good for the plants, you know. In the good months I just open the windows and let them purify a bit of the Auld Reekie, but when things are like this—, " Parker shrugged. "I make my own reekie fog."

Watson laughed shortly. "I confess it was a puzzle that brought me back, Dr. Parker."

"A puzzle?" Parker's quick eyes popped alert (everything about that man was quick; it was like talking to a grasshopper that would far rather stretch its legs). "Not from anything I said, I hope."

"No…no, not at all." Watson found a tray for his cigar resting underneath a large fibre-banana tree and pulled his satchel to his feet. Parker leaned forward; arms perched on his knees as Watson pulled a small key from a chain around his wrist and delicately prised the mechanism open.

The satchel opened with a stiff creak of leather, not unlike that of a large frog. Inside rested a thick padding of crumpled soft rice-paper. Watson fished around carefully for a moment, and then slowly drew out a plaster-cast object.

Dr. Parker's quick little eyes expanded as his mouth formed a serious little O underneath his wispy whiskers. His large ears flushed red, catching the sunlight in the little room and as Watson watched, the red spread like a flowing stain across his papery cheeks to settle to the high points just below the outer corners of his eyes.

"Why, good heavens, John. Wherever did you find this?" Awe mingled with several other emotions in the man's scratchy voice. John was fairly certain he sensed a thread of worry.

"A surprising gift," John admitted. "What do you think of it?" He did not wait for an answer. "I was told the owner was a child of about five or six years of age when it was cast."

"Five or...*six*...?" Parker repeated gently. His own surprise tingled his voice. He looked at the imprint of the small, webbed hand more carefully. "It is very small," he admitted. "I don't suppose you have the other hand cast?"

"As a matter of fact, I do." Watson agreeably obliged; Parker's own hands trembled as he rested each imprint upon his knees. He looked like a child facing a treat. The fact that it was the marks of a child's hands that he faced so eagerly made things all the more disturbing.

"This is...clearly a Selkie," the old man said carefully. "But I must say, it is most pronounced. And an extra finger! I really thought my specimen was the only one."

"Well, you only have a skeletal specimen," Watson said slowly.

"*Wherever* did you find this, John?"

John pinked up. "I'm afraid it's a bit of an unlikely story." He started carefully.

Parker laughed. "Of course, if you're the one telling it!"

Watson felt scarlet crawl up his neck at long-endured japes at his love of writing.

"But do go on!" Parker pressed.

"It is not a very absorbing tale, I fear. I was merely performing some services for an old man who was once vicar for a little church somewhere north of London. Rheumatoid arthritis." Parker nodded to show he'd understood. "He lacked the funds to pay me, and I wasn't really paying attention; I told him we could always barter, so I didn't think anything of it." John shrugged. "He returned a few days after his visit, raving about how the treatments had helped his joints, and asking if I would take payment in some plaster casts of pathology. Once I saw what he had, I thought how marvellous it would be to begin a small collection along the lines of your study."

Parker picked up the child's hand-cast, his eyes shining as he stared about him. Watson was convinced he did not imagine the spark of sudden malevolence in the once-kindly face at the thought of a rival collector. "John, John. This is marvellous. You have no idea how amazing this is."

"He said he had another set of casts made of the child a few years later," John said almost absently. He kept his eyes on the small white objects as he spoke; it helped hide the need for his feelings to come out.

"How remarkable! Did you tell him you were interested?"

"Of course. He was an intriguing fellow." Watson pulled out his little notebook and frowned at the small pages. "Name of George F. Carmichael, vicar of Lerwick's Church of the Cove."

"John, this is amazing." Parker was back to peering at the small white things in his hands. He looked rather too eager about his work. "Would I be too forward in purchasing them from you?"

John let the silence drag out to awkward proportions. "I was rather hoping to keep them for myself...eventually donating them to the Museum when I have finished my studies." He smiled charmingly. "So few students have the advantage of a decent collection, you know."

"Oh. Of course. That would be quite good of you, John. Quite good." Parker hurriedly lowered the little casts. "May I have a little time with them to take some measurements?"

"Of course, Dr. Parker." John had found his cigar cold and was busying himself with re-trimming the end and lighting it. "I thought it important enough to take them straight to you for perusal. No one else even knows about them."

"Really." Parker's eyes gleamed. "John, I must say that is passing kind of you."

"Not at all. I recalled your fascinating monographs—not to mention your lectures—of the past." He puffed quickly, grateful for the thick smoke-screen that had suddenly risen between them.

Parker shook his head in admiration before lifting his water-clear gaze to the younger man. "I shan't need more than a night with them." He said quietly. "Please do stay with me for supper and the night. Unless...you have other obligations?"

John sensed the other man had sniffed the bait. *Now to let him run.* He shook his head. "I'm afraid no one else even knows I'm still in the city," he confessed. "I did all my familial duties the other day. I would have been on the *Flying Scotsman*, but the weather..." he grimaced and reached for his throbbing shoulder. "Well, it has been rather discomfiting. I was forced to change my plans at the last minute."

"Of course it has. You should make yourself comfortable." Parker rose, but not without tightening his grip on the tiny plaster hands. "I needn't more than a few hours to make written notes of these...please do stay the night, my dear young fellow. I'd be most pleased to put you up."

Bait drawn. John rose slowly, exaggerating the stiffness of his leg. "That is most kind of you, Dr. Parker," he said with a smile. "Most kind."

Bradstreet had drawn the short straw. He wrapped tight inside his heavy wool coat and dropped to sleep by degrees whilst he trusted Lestrade to stay awake.

Little worry about that; Lestrade had something broken or deaf in the part of his brain that controlled sleep schedules; that was rather obvious to the Yarders who had to operate with him. Lestrade functioned without sleep and even less kindness.

Whilst Bradstreet slept, sharing the warmth underneath the shelter of the boxwoods, Lestrade smoked from an unfamiliar packet purchased on the street-corner and wished he'd selected a less-pungent brand (he daren't risk smoking something that smelled 'outsiderish' and had bought from the first tobbaconist by the inn). The casual eye would pass them by as two nondescript men, wrapped in dark clothing and sheltering from the night, but being polite enough to stay off the street so as not to offend the eye of respectable people.

Over their heads loomed Dr. Parker's address. On occasion the clatter of the staff shuffled back and forth; windows opened for inspection and shut again with distant clangs of wood upon wood. A military man, Parker was the type to batten down the hatches at every chance.

Lestrade normally hated the stone silence of a skulking patrol, but his head was unusually crammed with the disturbing contents of MacDonald's file. Instead of fidgeting restlessly and percolating like a factory brewery, he was hammering point after point home in his skull and smoking to keep from compulsively checking upon his watch at every count of 120.

Condensed to the most basic of portions, the case of Dr. Parker, Senior, had been left on a puzzle.

Families were *insistent* that Dr. Parker had been the force behind the looting of their loved ones' graves. This was back-benched by the statement of one of the grave-robbers who wanted a lighter sentence bestowed on his sons. If there had nearly been a riot before, there had been a narrow miss with three as the approval to dig up the graves in question had been given. Three graves were empty.

But other than the man who had been "insufficiently dead" and a few relics in his study, *nothing had been found*. The case had been hushed up. Quiet voices and probably quieter papers had turned a mountain into a mole-hill. Lestrade didn't like that. The courts hadn't liked it much either, and the families hated that there were no actual proofs of their beloved dead in his possession…but luckily there had been enough with the one cime to put the man behind bars for the rest of his natural life. The son had neatly escaped all threat of scandal as he had been finishing up his schooling in (of all places) Switzerland. The little detective had no understanding of going through the bother of travelling so far just for an extra letter or three to attach behind one's name, but he was quite used to not understanding that isolated breed called the academic.

Watson might have been more suspicious of Jonas Parker if he'd known anything useful about the father. It was a clear case of silence in the Hallowed Halls. In burying the past the entire medical community had put the future at risk.

Proving again that God *did* pay attention to the lives of mortal men (if only to leave a *Punch*-like comment), Parker Senior's natural life ended sooner than anyone's expectations. Intolerance with his own boredom had led the man to an unhealthy habit of window-gazing in the dead of winter, and his natural arrogance had refused the (base-born) prison doctor's treatment when the cough moved downward. He died under the same frozen conditions that had ironically prolonged the life of his last victim, for the extreme cold of the night had left the body-thieves thinking there was no warmth of life within. In a last note so fitting it needed no words, Parker's body had gone to the very science that had served him in life.

But to be extra-sensitive to the issue, Scotland had hastily donated the corpse to the English physicians, claiming the neat excuse that the Parkers were English citizens (MacDonald had penciled in the margins of the paper that the skull remained under lock and key as a study for the dangerously insane, but the body had been lost).

Whole or intact, Parker Senior's soul was long gone by the time the son had returned from a life abroad and set up his practice whilst making horrified reparations to society. Society had been all too eager to help him bury the business in good deeds and generosity. This lasted barely a year before he shipped out as a surgeon for the Crimean War and returned another year later, permanently crippled from a potent admixture of enemy viciousness and savvy Russian snipers during the Battle of Sebastopol. In the fervor of the Light Brigade (which had mercifully for him been at Balaclava), Dr. Parker had gained popularity, respect, and admiration. From there his career had risen quietly and without any real murk, until finishing into dusty old and sleepy retirement.

These facts and many more slipped through Lestrade's head as he rested under the boxwoods.

"Roger!"

His best friend's tenor hissed into his ear over the sound of a clot of ersatz street-performers.

"Roger Thomas Bradstreet!"

Breath reeking of peppermint floated down his neck and the big man struggled to sit upright, looking for the entire world like a man who had fallen asleep in quite another era.

"We've got to head for shelter," Lestrade was saying just as a low, underbelly growl of thunder thrummed across the city's cloud-cover.

"Oh, my...G—" Bradstreet scrubbed his face awake with both hands, his dark eyes thoughtful and worried. Over their heads a very un-seasonal blanket of fog was rolling off the coast. *"How long has this been happening?"* He demanded.

"It hasn't!" Lestrade snapped, angry that it might be implied he was remiss in his duties. *"It just started boiling up, like soup from the bottom of a cook-pot, lessen five minutes ago!"*

Bradstreet rose up quickly, licked his finger and held it up. The result was less than encouraging. *"This wasn't in the weather report."* Even as he said it, he blushed to think of the sheer inanity of his observation.

Lestrade only stitched his mouth shut and glared about the swiftly deserting city as if some intelligent deity had conspired against them, just to see what they would do. *"Where do you think we should go? I smell rain."*

"Cut across the greensward back to our tavern--It won't be the best place to look out, but it's mostly a straight-view and it is better than nothing." Bradstreet nodded, lowering his head into his bowler and began walking.

Lestrade followed behind, out of respect for his clearer wisdom on the layout. They did not quite make it before the rains.

"I do miss your dear brother's company. Is he adjusting to his new condition?"

The question, to all appearances innocent and courteous—froze John Watson to the bone.

Rain hammered against the window...or was it the blood in his ears? The doctor forced himself to swallow down the potatoes in parsley. "He was always a bit pragmatic," he said at last. "I would daresay that is his aid in his trial."

Dr. Parker made a sound of agreement. His fork rested unemployed in his fingers. It was only the two of them in the small dining-room, but Watson had never before felt the presence of too many people. His brother hung between them, the ghost at the feast with his silent accusation.

"He used to come up at times, you know. Adored those conversations of geology and geography. The science of soil was ever fascinating to him, which is all to his credit. There wasn't so much soil at the Watson *villa* as there was rock, was there?"

"What little soil we had, I guarantee you he had it all mapped and analyzed!" John laughed to himself at half the memories in his mind. Good memories. "He had so many different hobbies....that he could keep track of them all was a marvel."

"But you were the one who could always keep up with him."

"Well, if I couldn't I assure you it was not for lack of trying." He tried to make light of it.

"You were always a good deal more intelligent than you let on, John." The professor's light eyes twinkled over the table. "Everyone took your brother for the genius, but I would say, 'don't forget John, he has depths.'" He poured a clear yellow wine out of a narrow carafe with a contented sound.

Three drinks from that carafe had entered Parker before supper was even served, and that had been just as lush: smoked turkey, cloche salads and potatoes with parsley had led to a meal such as he had not had in a very long time. Watson wasn't completely certain he could have eaten at this table a month ago; Mrs. Hudson's cuisine had balanced out anything overly fatty in concession to her invalided lodger, and he owed her from moving past the thin soups and strengthening broths that were only a step above hospital fare.

Watson hated being the topic of conversation, especially when the converser was imbibing. It made him uneasy, and that in turn made him a little prickly. "I can't say I ever gave it much thought, Doctor." he said gently, hoping this would be the end of it.

"Oh, John, you do yourself a discredit." Parker waved his hand. "You're *quite* a person. Unique." The blue-green eyes were just beginning to swim in the shine of alcohol. Watson thought of little buoys bobbing in the ocean. "Something anyone would be proud of—I mean someone." He tittered. "Excuse me, I said you were something. That was a bit off, wasn't it?"

Watson's skin prickled. The table between them had become a black chasm; its space loomed menacing and chill around Parker's little bonfire of willpower and charm.

Once, Watson had to pretend to the Afghani he did not know their language. They had been planning to kill him as he headed home from their village in retribution for a man his own army had shot. He was convinced it was their own inability to read the mannerisms of infidels that saved his life.

"But, come. I'm keeping you from supper." Parker waved. "When we're both finished I should like to show you my *Kunstkabinett*[51] again.

"After all," he added. "With the weather being what it is, we shall have to make our own amusements."

---

[51] *Cabinet of Curiosities*: A traditional name for a collection of items that had not yet been properly quantified in their status within the scientific world. This centuries-old practice is the earliest forerunner of modern museums.

"That would be most kind of you, Dr. Parker." Watson lifted his water-glass in a softly-smiling toast.

"Blast it all…"

Lestrade emerged from his turn in the hasty bath to find Bradstreet all but sitting in the narrow window, peering sideways down the street. He had nicked Lestrade's tiny field-glass and was trying hard to see anything with it in the glowering atmosphere.

Bradstreet's scowl reflected badly in the murky glass as the rain commenced.

"Nothing?" He guessed.

"Nothing I can pick out, but then, this is not the best view." Bradstreet hammered his fingers against his thigh as he brooded. "I'm going back out," he announced—not to Lestrade's surprise, but Bradstreet looked astonished at himself for the loss of control. "I'm not about to let anything slip through us tonight."

"We'll both go." Lestrade said patiently. He'd rather be going back out in the thick of things, weather and all.

"You just got clean."

"It's not London, Roger. I might be able to stay clean *more* than an hour for once."

Bradstreet sniffed to cover his nerves. "Never saw your like, you know." He complained as they made their way back down the stairs. "As fastidious as you are, you work in the filthiest city in all of Britain."

"Part of my charm, old fellow." Lestrade sneered using his best imitation of Gregson's arrogance. It was worth acting the fool for the result: Bradstreet snorted like a draft-horse and clapped him on the back. But Lestrade could tell through the brief contact that his old friend was trembling.

Don't do anything foolish, he thought hard to the other man. *Don't. Let me do it. Not you.*

"Incredible."

Watson was unable to keep the astonishment out of his voice. Beside him Dr. Parker beamed proudly with his back to the endless rows of books and papers in his library. He appeared almost avuncular to his former student.

Watson finally turned the object in his hands back upright. "I've never seen a skull-drum in person before."

"They aren't commonly found on this side of the globe, I assure you. But I was more interested in the cranium than its musical ability. Its owner was allegedly a monk of the Himalayas."

Watson nodded once, his fingers tingling at the contact of something that looked like ordinary bone...but felt like ivory. "I've never seen such an eburneous example of human bone."

"They're quite rare," Parker admitted. "Partly because we know so little about the disease itself. This was even more unique; I'm told none of the tendons hardened, it was all in the bone. Hence, the person never really noticed anything happening."

"It's just like ivory—it is ivory!" Watson admitted. It was no simple thing to be absorbed in the thing in his hands, with unusual glass specimens and bones surrounded them on mounts and hooks...but it really was unusual.

"Chemically, it is probably closer to ivory than it is ordinary cranium calcium." Dr. Parker took the skullcap into his own hands. A thin membrane of goat-skin created the drum itself. "As I understand, this was a monk who was renowned for his poetic morning prayers."

Not seeing the face of the skull itself, Watson did not have a mental image of the man. He was glad. "I'd heard that they made drums out of their dead," he admitted, uneasy and unashamed of it.

"Part of their ability to remain unattached to the material world," Parker stroked the shining substance fondly. "They measure their worth in the un-measurable; the ephemeral and intangible. Our logic is quite backwards to their thinking."

"I would imagine." Watson could still recall the texture of the drum in his finger-whorls. It had felt just like elephant ivory, hard and dense and full of flint.

"Here's something." Parker suddenly gave the drum back. "Tap it and listen."

Watson was confused, but did as he was told. The soft echo was akin to an instrument stretched over an ebony shell: a softly alto D4 sang against his teeth, slow to dissipate into the air.

His unease growing, Watson suddenly could not return the drum to Parker quickly enough. The old man tilted his head to one side, blue eyes glittering with amusement and Watson flushed in sudden shame.

"They can adjust their drums to a perfect pitch," Parker chuckled as the drum went back to its shelf. "But they aren't without their superstitions...the monks claim to have the only ability to play these drums; all others must do so at their own risk."

"R-risk?" Watson wiped his hands on his trousers whilst Parker busied himself with placing the artifact back on the shelf just so. "What risk would that be?" He felt as though the vibration of that single tap was settling within his vertebrae.

"Oh, just one of their old-wives' tales that a drum made of man can wake the dead when sounded." Parker spoke casually, but it sent ice water across every inch of his guest's skin.

And he said only the monks could play this sort of drum...
How then did he acquire it?

"Oh, he heard himself saying. "That is an excellent specimen."

"Isn't it?" Dr. Parker beamed fondly. He forgot his precious drum in favour of a new marvel: the jaw of a child resting on a carved base. The child had been in the process of forming adult teeth, and the bone had been carefully shaved back to show the teeth in various stages of development along the jaw-bone. "Sheer luck for this little beauty," he said with evident pride. His fingers slid over the carefully-cleaned item with love.

Watson was glad there was no more of the child than what he could see. "Those are difficult to find," he observed, which was a polite way of noting it was a matter of expense as much as availability.

"Ah, again it was pure luck. An unfortunate casualty of the streets. The parents hadn't the money for a proper burial so I offered to do the honours." With a casual sniff Parker proclaimed his benevolence and his dismissal of the poor, who never did enough for the Society that tolerated them.

It was nothing Watson hadn't heard before, but it was the first time he'd heard this so blatantly from his old teacher.

But he hadn't seen him in his cups before either...

You just confessed to a theft of human remains, Watson thought in a slow-dawning creep of horror. *You just confessed to me, to me as a witness...*

...Because you think I am like you. Because you think I share your thoughts.

Watson buried a moment's more of nerve by dropping to his at-rest pose and looking around. The cozy library-study had once been a thing of awe for fellow students such as himself. A young man proved himself in his studies by an invitation to this room. Were it a matter of art alone, it would be a worthwhile goal for academic achievement: Parker possessed some of the rare anatomical folios of England and they were all wrapped in the luxury of fine paper or vellum with crisp ink and soft leather covers latched in brass. The mahogany walls hung bejeweled with fine oils and silver engravings; a skeleton each of the three major species depended from their wooden boxes propped upright, each with some unusual pathology. Against the main wall in rows of specially-purchased glass jars rested soft-tissue specimens, such as the usual unfinished infants or war-amputee's limb. But there were things set above the pale: the most famous was the femur of a man swallowed by a shark; digestive properties within the beast had made the bone so small and flexible it could be bent like an India-rubber tube and twisted to a knot.

As one of the eager young men, Watson had looked forward to the Sunday teas…but the memory was colourless and flat to him now. When he scrolled backwards in his mind the images were abnormally sunlit, like a child's innocence. All was pure and clear learning amid the wonders of the human body, unvarnished with age and corruption and cynicism.

Dr. Parker was prattling about his collection of eyes now. Watson let him. His own two eyes rested upon a fine Mexican bas-relief of a skeleton with a broad sombrero and serape and playing a guitar. The little skeleton grinned at him without guile or mischief or cynicism.

The tiny *Muerto* was frozen in the moment of innocence and the celebration of life with death; it was a carving. It was a remembrance of the semi-permanence beneath the flesh and a reminder of the future.

Watson was not a carving; he was a man, a representation of the clothing around the skeleton. He by nature had to change. And he had. With the war and the blood-sickness that followed, Watson had wanted nothing more than to return to some of his old joy in medicine, so a return to his roots had been logical. But the hope was ruined when Parker had pulled out his skeleton, and Watson had known it for murder by the score across the throat.

And as for Dr. Parker...

Watson braved another look at his genial host. The old man was showing him a string of curiously twisted vertebrae. Instead of cozy, the room's walls were narrow and tight. The gaslights cast dull shadows and wraiths into the corners. The wisps of lace curtain caught inside the lights, throwing sullen grey threads across the wall.

Holmes would call him fanciful. Watson would call himself a fly inside a web.

"Not so bad." Bradstreet decided.

Lestrade didn't dignify that with a response. They were huddled back into the scanty shelter of boxwood. It took the worst of the wind and rain off their shoulders but collected into their hatbrims like gutters and ran in thin streams down their fronts and backs in universally awkward times.

"I'm just glad we can see the doors," Lestrade admitted at last. "But I don't know how Watson is going to signal us in this weather."

In the beginning, it had been simple enough: Watson would plead a moment to step to the porch with one last smoke of the evening. A pipe if all was well, his thin cigar if not. And if he needed more time...

This sort of clime was against anyone stepping out. A host would insist on his remaining inside.

"We can hope he'll think of something." Bradstreet grunted. "Perhaps the rain won't last much longer."

"Just treat yourself to whatever you need, Major. I'm no further than the pull of the bell-cord."

"Mayn't I step outside for a final smoke tonight?"

"Certainly, sir. I shall leave the key in the door for your convenience; simply leave it as you found it, and I shall collect it the moment I have finished my rounds."

Watson nodded. "Thank you." He watched as the old butler quietly made his exit; he wondered if the man had once served.

Alone for the first time in hours, relief crashed down. He sank to the edge of the bed, hands in his lap as he studied the face off the little eight-day clock on the dresser. The rain was slacking but the hour was late. For himself, his throbbing leg and shoulder made everything an…experience.

Watson knew he was close to his personal tolerance for pain, but an anodyne was not permissible now. It was the main thing keeping him awake and alert.

The minutes dragged, long and sharp as his aching limbs grew heavier. About him the sounds of the old house creaked and settled and muttered as slips of wind pressed against the boards one way, then another. It might well have been the aerial complaints of disturbed spirits. After such an experience Watson was willing to dwell on that possibility…guilt could take many forms, and he might have well held an object of murder with the skull-drum. If not murder, thievery. Even now the high, stretching vibration of the note seemed to rest in the bones of his memories.

At last, he rose to his feet with a sigh of his decision. Bradstreet and Lestrade needed a signal.

He donned his coat against the night air, and walked quietly down the carpeted hallway to the front door. About him the house was dead and still of human life. The only animation rested within the sounds of the house itself. He re-opened the door and very carefully shut it behind him with a soft snick of iron. His back leaned against the damp brick and he reached deep into his pockets, pulling out his tin of Bradley's. The match scored light into his hand and he cupped it quickly, hoping the wind would not frustrate him. He needed the smoking to signal a detective he could not see. His nerves were over-ready for some sort of action to take place.

He could not see the policemen, but he trusted they could see him, and that they could see his signal for what it was: there was enough reason to come in and search. Watson would pretend to be as innocent and outraged as Parker at the rude intrusion, and there was more than a good chance he would ask Watson to vouch for him in incriminating language.

But that little jaw-bone…that is enough cause to bring in the Law. Watson was still sickened at the thought, and hoped his reaction had never shown. *Even if that is all we find tonight, I am glad.* He gulped hard, swallowing a harsh mouthful of smoke, and his eyes burned in as much anger as tobacco. He was not complicated enough of a man to justify the confessed trickery over a child's bones. Let him be seen as simple and short-sighted for science. He did not care.

Is it so easy to pretend? Is it so simple to lower someone's standards? It would seem so.

It went against Watson's every nerve to smoke at night when he did not want to be overtly observed; one might as well have a glowing target for their head. He'd declared enough sentries dead of their indulgence despite the orders of all the officers. A glowing coal was a perfect orientation for a rifleman. He shifted his weight from good leg to bad leg several times, pondering Dr. Parker. In the beginning, the man had paid no more attention to him than he had any of his other students.

Parker had met Hamish first; most people did. Hamish was as bright and obtrusive as the ideal British man. Whilst medicine had not been his forte'--indeed it was one of the few things in which he hadn't taken an interest--he had shared his curiosity with geology and geography with the interdepartmentally minded Parker. From there Parker had noticed Hamish' brother, and perhaps he had wanted to see for himself what operated under John's mind.

And John had not disappointed his teachers. Medicine was instinct as much as information; and he excelled in both. In a way, medicine was as thrilling as any sport or battle--well, it was a battle; a battle against the many forms of Death. To successfully conclude a case with a patient was a feeling he never tired of duplicating.

He would have stayed in the Army forever had his fate not rested in other areas. Rather than subside into a broken heart like his brother...he had become another sort of a soldier; one that saw disease and debility as his opponents.

Through it all, from triumph to tragedy and abject failure...Parker had made John uncomfortable with the vague and unspoken feeling that the man wanted to find something remarkable in him...which was one thing, but there were men who wanted to discover great things...simply to say they had been the discoverers. And with Parker...all the better to be able to say that he had discovered something remarkable within John Watson.

All his life, he had watched as people flocked to his brother, wanting his friendship and his approval... ...wanting to take him home for the same reasons why they wanted to collect something exotic. John had loathed it too deeply for envy, and now he realised he had made a serious mistake in not ciphering this behaviour out. Now that it was being focused upon him, he didn't know what to do about it.

He wondered if this might be the root of Holmes' erratic impatience with praise. He liked it well enough...if he had similar regard for the person doing the praising! If not...the phrase, 'damn with faint praise' could not begin to describe how his friend would react. Watson always dreaded the denouement of his cases when it had difficult clients. Holmes' temper was quick to break free when someone he despised insulted him with congratulations and admiration.

I should pay more attention, Watson promised himself. *Starting when we are both back at Baker Street.*

He drew the smoke inside his lungs and held it for a moment, needing the calming influence of the plant. His thoughts were still in turmoil; it was not unlike knowing the enemy would attack at dawn, but being forced to wait for that intermittent hour. He blew out the tobacco in a thin cloud, watching it catch the dying raindrops from outside the tiny porch eves. The storm was fading in uneven rhythm; it made a clumsy counterpoint to the singing.

Singing.

Singing? The doctor felt his face deepen into a frown of concentration. His heart pounded as he moved slightly against the edge of the porch-rail, listening for the source of that sound.

It was an old mode. Aeolian, rising and falling in the cadence of the minors' scales. Something about it was familiar...familiar and dark.

"As I was walking all alane,
I heard twa corbies making a mane;
The tane unto the t'other say,
'Where sall we gang and dine to-day?'"

Parker.

Watson felt his unease swell to exponential mountains. Where was the man? The sound was coming from somewhere below his own feet! He looked about him quickly, saw nothing--no sign of Bradstreet or Lestrade--but nor did he see the source of the singing.

> *" 'In behint yon auld fail dyke,*
> *I wot there lies a new slain knight;*
> *And naebody kens that he lies there,*
> *But his hawk, his hound, and lady fair... '"*

It was the oldest song in the English language; so old no one could even begin to guess. And it just *happened* to be a murder ballad.

> *" 'His hound is to the hunting gane,*
> *His hawk to fetch the wild-fowl hame,*
> *His lady's ta'en another mate,*
> *So we may mak our dinner sweet... '"*

Bradstreet stiffened as, through the curtain of box, Watson had suddenly grown as taut as Flag Manoeuvres on the green. The man's head whipped from side to side.

"He hears something?" The big man whispered.

"Look!" Lestrade's whisper was even softer, but it managed to cut through his friend like a knife. Watson was no longer looking about; he was looking down, but then with a swift jerk, was lowering himself off the porch, exquisitely careful to not click his soles against the stonework. As they watched in growing puzzlement, the doctor dropped into a crouch, heedless of anyone seeing him off the empty street.

For long moments they watched, baffled but knowing to be wary, then Watson very carefully rose to his feet again. It was difficult; his war injuries corresponded with each other, shoulder-wound opposing his leg.

His face was a papery mask as he glanced up at the street-lamp, and he carefully pulled out another cigarette, making a point of smoking it halfway down before he tossed it into the stonework ringing the porch.

"Hold it!" Lestrade hissed but Bradstreet was out of the boxwoods as soon as the door shut after Watson. The smaller man gritted his teeth, in for a penny/in for a pound, and followed him out.

Bradstreet had stopped at the spot the doctor had just vacated. He turned to look as Lestrade came up, and his face was milky under the dark of his moustaches. "Listen," he whispered harshly.

And Lestrade caught his breath.

> *"'Mony a one for him makes mane,*
> *But nane sall ken where he is gane;*
> *Oer his white banes, when they are bare,*
> *The wind sall blaw for evermair...'"*

"Where is it coming from?" He whispered. "Is it the sewers?"

"This is Edinburgh, man." Bradstreet's face twisted with an appalling knowledge. "There're more than sewers below the surface of the world."

8: O'er His White Banes

John closed the door behind him and froze, collecting information with his ears and eyes. Every nerve tingled; he was saturated with the song. It floated upward through the hallway, barely audible once he'd left the street.

Parker was in the Vaults of Edinburgh, and Watson was not happy about it but his Adams was in his pocket, and for all his growing proof of demonism, Parker eschewed the sort of violence brought about by any sort of ballistics. His war-wounds had been collected hauling the wounded to safety.

If he is in the Vaults, then his library would be unguarded...

The doctor slipped up the stairs, the pain in his leg momentarily gone in the flush of the hunt. Foolish of him not to think of the possibility, but he'd thought this section of the street was outside the limits of the old subterranean city. The street was outside the borders of Old Town, after all...

Absence of proof is not proof of absence. Watson scolded himself; another old teacher's words coming back to haunt him at the worst possible moment. It was a moment's work to detour back to his bedroom and build up an outline on the bed with pillows and his wadded-up coat. He lit the bedside-candle quickly and thrust the glass chimney around the wax in relief; the flame thrust his shadows across the walls. Closing his bedroom door after him he made his way to the library.

"Bradstreet, pretend I know nothing about Edinburgh. What are you talking about?"

"Niddrey Street," Bradstreet muttered, and appeared to sight something far away, as if drawing pictures inside his mind. "Edinburgh's got an underground city below the Old Town area...we're not far from it; perhaps the borders went further than most of us know. Maybe this is part of the original street..."

Lestrade was waiting with badly concealed impatience, rising up and down on his toe-tips, hands wrenched into his pockets.

"Build over a hundred years ago, Geoff. I'm sure I don't know why, but for years upon years, you had poor souls, mostly Irish, living underneath the city. Ten to a room no biggern' your little office-room, plus a stove to cook on. The garbage was awful even for *that* time, and disease wiped out whole families at once. The Vaults are supposed to be closed, but you hear thrill-seekers wanting to visit, and they'll pay for the trip down by a guide."

"Sounds like a sewer," Lestrade decided.

"It wasn't built to be a sewer, but you may as well call it such." Bradstreet smacked his gloved fist into his open palm. "That doctor fellow, he's down there. Watson caught on, and I'm afraid he's about to get himself into trouble."

Lestrade wasn't stupid; he was methodical. "The library." He breathed. "He said Parker would be likely to have his proofs in his library, and if he's singing underneath the city, he can't very well be in his house guarding it."

"That's what I was thinking." Bradstreet admitted, but the men traded uneasy looks.

Watson puffed his breath out in thought, hands on hips as he contemplated the library/study. Glass eyes gleamed back at him from behind glass displays; the real eyes floated listlessly in alcohol under jars, the colours of the iris fading gently over time. Ghostly eyes. He shuddered.

There should be something here. Elspeth Bradstreet's skeleton *had* to be hidden here. And if he could find that...he could find the proof of her murder...

...And there was a door in the wall where there had not been one before.

Watson swallowed hard. He held his candle close and limped to the wall, where the heavy oak panels doubled as fashionable cabinet-drawers. The gap was large enough for a man; a small one. He reached out, touched the edges of the wood. The intricate mouldings were also the handles and hinges; he tugged gently, and the panels opened further without a squeak.

It appeared to be a small dark-room or a re-constructed closet. More jars of preserved items met his eye, organic in nature mostly; but there were rice-parchment paintings of human pathology, hanging in bamboo frames and marked in red ink. Watson wondered where these were collected from; they appeared to be devoted to unique deformities.

He frowned at an image of a man with a flipper for a foot. In another cabinet rested the account of an African king struck by polio; he explained his warped lower limbs as proof of his ancestry as a merman.

He was scowling at a painting of a man with two pupils in each eyeball, wondering if the poor man's claim to pathology was floating in one of these jars, when a draft of air brushed against the hairs on the back of his hand. It smelt not of Edinburgh, but of a forgotten stockyard. The pit of his stomach churned.

Watson's head turned. A panel that he had overlooked as part of Parker's cabinetry for years because of its large size had been left ajar. Not much, but enough that the draught whispered over his skin cold and dank.

A secret passage inside a secret room?

Nothing for it.

He pulled his clasp-knife out of his pocket and in a sudden move, chipped the edge of the door with the blade, marking where he was about to go. A close inspection of the darkness behind the panel-door showed nothing but a void. That could mean his bringing a light inside would be an alert. Still…

Parker had been singing. He must be extremely confident…and he was without a doubt, drunk. That drunkenness might give him the edge he needed.

Watson slipped behind the panel and lifted the candle high, thinning the spill of light at his feet. Just barely, a winding set of stairs spiraled downward. The smell was stronger. Much stronger. Mould mixed in it. Old animal wastes. Lye and ammonia.

Grave-earth smells.

The young man swallowed hard as the ghastly vapours conjured old memories of the dead and dying. Everyone thought Maiwand had been a hot place, but no. He had never been colder than when he had lain in the earth, waiting for help or death.

Watson carefully closed the door in precisely the way he'd found it, but he was forced to step downward with his good leg, just strong enough to brace his weight whilst he moved. It was slow going; it was painstaking. It was maddening. But he kept the candle high with his good arm and stuck out his patience. The mildew became a stench. It burned his nostrils and he breathed out his mouth to lower the risk of sneezing.

The steps ended. The candle gasped against the volume of the darkness. Watson waited, thinking. That cool draft was going to his left; he took a cautious step across the black floor—packed earth, pressed into concrete density from the years—and felt the coolness penetrate his shoes. Faint as foxfire, the stone outlines of doorways caught on the threads of candlelight.

It was as silent as a tomb should be. He heard nothing but his own breath over the pounding of blood in his heart and ears.

Something pale tipped in the candlelight; a scrap of paper on the packed floor. Watson caught a stronger wave of ammonia, knowing it was not natural for this sepulchral limbo. He quickened his step to see a door, leaning open into the black hallway. Glass--*clean* glass—reflected back at him.

The footfalls spidered eagerly up behind him, but his wounds were too fresh and his balance, too fragile. Parker had enjoyed decades of practice after his crippling to learn compensation. Watson heard his own breath leave his lungs as the hands slammed into his chest, knocking him backwards and deeper into the room. His back struck the floor with a grunt of dizzying pain. The candle-chimney burst into fragments in the darkness; he blinked against the sting of shards and the door slammed shut; a final sounding click of a bolt-lock rang in the doctor's ears and with it, his heart forgot how to beat.

"I'm going to go in," Bradstreet announced. "You back me up."

"No, *I* am." Lestrade retorted. He met Bradstreet's glare coldly. "Don't give *me* that look, Inspector. I'm the one with the iron and you'd best think of what would happen if Dr. Parker claimed in court you'd thrashed him? I'm much more his size."

Bradstreet sniffed his anger down. "You're smaller than he is in both directions," A grudging admission. "I would adore the chance to see him accuse you of police brutality." The clever comment did not disguise Bradstreet's worry. "Be careful, Lestrade."

"Redundant grammar, Bradstreet." Lestrade turned and as one they grimly met Inspector MacDonald trotting up with a small army of silent policemen.

"He's signalled." Lestrade told the Scots. "And he feels there's cause to bring us in."

"God help us." Was all MacDonald thought of it.

The floor was stinking sawdust and flecks burned his eyes and nose but Watson was grateful. Its softness had saved him the injury of a heavy fall. He spat wood-shavings out of his mouth and fumbled in his pockets with trembling hands. He found his match-box inside a front pocket. He held on to the temptation to move before he could see anything and managed to strike a light after a few tries; his hands were still trembling, but it might have been from the cold and shock more than actual fear. The doctor's brain was coldly, mercilessly analysing his person and what it found was anger warring with humiliation, and a growing horror. The smell that had soaked into the soft sawdust was prevalent now; as a medical man, he knew the reasons for such a stench.

The match caught; he peered about the floor, found the candle and re-lit it with a gasp. The light was blessed. He felt himself relax, just a bit, now that he could see and he clambered to his feet by degrees, dripping sawdust grime and wincing at the pull of his wounds. *My God, will Maiwand never leave?*

He was in a collection-room…A very different room from the rooms resting upstairs.

Watson stared, his heart in his throat as he took in the fact he was sealed in a tomb with skeletons hanging inside glass cases.

Parker must have spent years building it up. *Years.* And his father had been in trouble for such murky dealings with human remains...how much had he *inherited*? What had he been exposed to as a child, to defray his sense of the sacred and create this sense of arrogant entitlement?

Elspeth Bradstreet's bones hung suspended in its box. She was a pretty child, with Bradstreet's apple-shaped face and firm nose and large, widely spaced eyes. Next to her floated the hunched-over skeleton of a very old man with an extra vertebra in his back. In life he had been withered; his bones were porous with osteoporosis. Most of his teeth were gone. He would have had pronounced cheekbones under his wrinkles, and a constant grimace of pain from the *otitis media* infection at his left ear that slowly killed him. The bones had been partially devoured by the disease; the candlelight caught the lacy filigree of the remaining bone. In his youth he had been handsome and evenly-shaped with a proud browline and strong chin.

Conjoined twins were mounted in a double box. He recognised Asia in their skulls.

A woman's skeleton hung, toes pointing downward. In life she had been young and beautiful with smooth, even features marred only by double canines in her jaws.

He could see all of their skulls. He could see all of their faces.

Watson forced himself to swallow. His hands shook from the weight of the candle and he got to the nearest table before dropping it. Cold sweat spackled the table-top from his brow. *Breathe*, he reminded himself. *You must breathe.* Even as Parker's devilish singing haunted his memory:

Mony a one for him makes mane...but none sall ken where he is gane...

O'er his white banes, when they lie bare / the winds sall blaw forevermair...

Stop, he reminded himself. *You are the Queen's Major. There is no wind here to blow, there is no wind at all. And until the door is opened again, there will be nothing in the way of air.*

He swallowed again, and made certain the candle was settled. He had to find something that would prize the door. Otherwise, Parker would win with a new murder under his belt, and gain a new specimen for his collection.

I thought him corrupted; I never thought he was mad.

"Careful."

Bradstreet nodded once, just to show he'd heard his friend's warning, and stepped without a sound into the room after Lestrade. In the hallway the two felt exposed and neglected at the same time. Behind them Bobbies rustled and jangled over the front steps, listening to MacDonald mutter his orders to spread out again, search again lads, look about, keep the truncheons out, and one hand ready for the alarm. Outside and off to the corner of the scrap of green clover a knot of servants huddled with each other and demanded what was happening. It had grimly amused Lestrade to note that there was a fundamental difference between rounding up servants in London: Here the little old ladies had no fear and were happy to treat the abashed Constables like overgrown children in need of a good dose of chapel.

"They're not in here." Bradstreet's face set tight. "I looked all over this side. The house is empty except for the staff."

"Watson left a form under his bed. He knew something was up and he couldn't risk telling us. I don't like this." Lestrade gritted his teeth. "Blast." He ran his thumb under his chin. "We *do* have Watson's permission to go in after him. That would keep it from being a closed case."

Bradstreet did not rail at Lestrade's study of procedure at a critical moment. The smallest incident could throw this entire case out of court, never to be tried again. They had to be careful. Everything was at stake.

"However many people are gone," he warned, "Eventually some of them are going to return. We keep this as quiet as possi--"

There was a scraping sound and Bradstreet was yanking Lestrade down hard enough to pull his arm out of the socket. A bullet burst wood splinters into the smaller man's neck; he yelped out of reflex more than actual pain.

Bradstreet swore and pulled Lestrade deeper into the darkness.

Alcohol.

A close inspection of the door was not encouraging. The door was thick and incredibly sturdy; the hinges were on the other side safe from tampering. But the sawdust floor...

Sawdust that was clean and new, fresh and dry. Going by its stench, it was made of pine and oak and maple—all woods quick to burn.

Watson set his lips. Parker's refusal to shoot him and give him a clean death would be his regret.

Alcohol in the bottles. Used to preserve the soft-tissue specimens, but alcohol was alcohol.

The problem was the oxygen. If he couldn't burn the organic matter in the earthen floor out within a very short amount of time, he'd suffocate all the quicker.

It was a terrible risk, but Watson was going to take it. A large bottle held a floating fetus with a badly misshapen skull. Watson paused only to shake his head at the ghoul his teacher had been, and as gently as possible in respect to the remains, poured the liquid as slowly to rest on the earth. The fumes were beyond belief. But...

But few people rarely step onto the actual line beneath a doorway. They are in the process of stepping *over* that invisible line. Hence the sawdust floor there was much softer and porous.

Watson's crippling had made him very, very contemplative about how people walked.

He watched as the alcohol soaked into the earth and cautiously set the jar back. Another match; he lit it cautiously and stretched his arm out as far as it could go before dropping the tiny flame into the dark wet stripe by the door.

And the floor began to burn. Sawdust. Charcoal scattered to eliminate odours. All flammable. The smell went from beyond belief to beyond description. He gagged; only blood made that tang. Only blood created that eerie wraithlike plume of smoke. How much of it rested over that new layer? How much had entered the floor over how many years? It had become part of the earth; bonded into the floor itself. And now...

He backed away as the alcohol burnt itself out. The air was hazed and thick; like a fireworks-factory inside a slaughterhouse. And a good three inches had softened up.

Eyes burning, Watson kicked off a leg from the table, gripped it in his fingers, and began digging.

"Halt in the name of Scotland Yard!"

Lestrade nearly felt his heart freeze in his chest at Bradstreet's roar. The Runner sounded in control...but only just.

The little Yarder mentally prayed that Bradstreet was not hoping to provoke Parker into doing something desperate. In this charged air, it would be too easy to make mistakes. Parker was a military man; he might have more than the one weapon. He might try to shoot at them or shoot himself to avoid arrest and disgrace.

Either way would spare the Crown the cost of a trial...

Silence. Bobbies sensibly kept back, out of sight and out of range, and a few were shielding Mac from closer approach. Smoke hung in the air, sharp and metallic. Someone was panting in another room.

"You heard me!" Bradstreet roared. "We know you're there, and we'd far prefer not to kill you in the line of duty! Now throw down your weapon and give yourself up!"

Something heavy and blocky clicked on the floor. "Very well, sir." The voice was high and thin and quavering. "I have lowered my weapon...I am coming out now."

"Keep your hands in the air, sir." Bradstreet was calming now; he sensed he had the upper hand when Lestrade did not. Lestrade threw his concentration all about them as the clouds parted outside the windows; in the soupy light of the city a lean man, elderly with wispy white hair was stepping forward, his bony fingers splayed out from his palms like sticks.

"Who are *you*, then?" Bradstreet growled.

"The butler." Lestrade guessed.

"How do *you* know?" Bradstreet saw the shock on the old man's face.

"If he was the owner he would have thrown his gun down to surrender. A butler is more worried about scarring his master's floor." Lestrade smiled terribly at the man's continued worry. "I suggest you be truthful," he suggested quietly. "I know everything you might possibly imagine about service. Where are Drs. Parker and Watson?"

"Dr. Parker went downstairs to the Vaults." The butler spoke firmly, but he still quaked inside his clothing. "I believe the Major went after him."

"Do you know what Parker was doing in the Vaults?" Bradstreet had picked up the gun and was holding it rather too tightly for Lestrade's liking.

The butler shook his head. "I am not allowed, sir."

"How does one get to these Vaults?"

"Through the Curiosity Room, sir. There is a door." A trembling finger pointed up the stairs to a blackened doorway.

"Moss, you keep your eye on the man, get his statement, rally Mac and the Constables, whatever. Tell Sidthorp to give me fifteen minutes and go after me as a back-up. I'm going down these Vaults, and I'll let you know if I need any help. Too many at once could make it all go Guy Fawkes." Lestrade had pulled his iron out and was checking it. It was a mean sort of satisfaction to see the butler's little eyes grow wide as he realised that *this* policeman were armed. The look was just as quickly replaced by a vague sort of betrayal that Lestrade was well used to seeing. The public wasn't used to the idea of policemen carrying weapons around.

He did not quite smirk at the man. "Tell me best how to get to the Vaults," he advised. "This has the look of an ugly trial, and you may wish to cooperate with us as much as possible."

9: Cover Our Bones

"And nothing can we call our own but death
And that small model of the barren earth
Which serves as paste and cover to our bones.
For God's sake, let us sit upon the ground
And tell sad stories of the death of kings."
--William Shakespeare

A few moments in the 'Curiosity Room' and Lestrade was satisfied neither doctor was present.

He waited a moment, listening. The hapless butler had been good enough to loan a bulls-eye lantern (it looked like something out of the Yard's Evidence Room, *circa* grand opening), and the wrinkled glass of the ancient globe cast watery reflections off the polished walls.

One wall was nothing but framed diplomas, certificates, and awards. Just the display was faintly sickening to the pragmatic little detective; it made him think of some sort of academic crowing; then again, he was a product of the Ragged Schools, and his fine diction owed to listening to the Master (also the sexton) talk more than what he was trained for (not that he'd be stupid enough to talk like the Master in his hearing).

The lantern passed over a grape clustre of eyes suspended in a brandy-coloured liquid; he nearly dropped the lantern as several floated to his direction, as if facing him. It gave him a very bad start and his fear for Watson trebled. Padriag Dooley, his Gipsy contact, said the eye held the last image it recorded in life. Better that than having to spend eternity in a jug, staring at a wall of paper bragging credentials.

He took a step deeper into the strange room--library, or museum, or medical laboratory? It appeared to be an uneven mix of all three. His foot sank down; something shifted without a sound, and the eyeballs wobbled again, mercifully floating away from his gaze. Ugh!

Wait a moment...

Lestrade's brows knit up over the bridge of his nose. He stared at the eyeballs even though he *really* didn't want to do such a thing...and stepped back.

He counted his heart-beat in the silence.

After the eighth beat the eyeballs moved.

Holding his breath, the little man took a slow step forward, repeating his earlier manoeuvre.

Ten beats this time. The eyeballs jiggled like raw yolk in the eggshell.

Ice crystals crept over Lestrade's hands, up his arms and across the nape of his neck into the base of his skull. A whisper across time pressed needles into his brain.

Davids, his old mentor, and his supervisory officer's bitterest foe. Davids' murmur of recollection breathed over the years past to present.

"We never would have found the swag, but the man had been to Japan and he learned how to trip the floor-boards so's he'd know if someone had been in his rooms!

"It was the weather-glass, y'see. He kept it mounted on the opposing wall from the door-way. If you didn't know better, you'd take a step forward into the room, and flat on the middle plank. And that would make the crystals in the weather-glass shift. Oh, it was bloody ingenious! We didn't catch on to the trick for nineteen years, can you believe it!"

Someone had been here, and recently. They had stepped on that plank, and they made the eyes move the first time... Lestrade gulped hard, not liking what he was seeing so far. Tall panel, left side…Lestrade mentally counted the butler's instructions and ran his free hand over the smooth wood, going against the grain for any tell-tale lines. A part of him was growing ever-more worried that this room seemed to have swallowed up two whole men. Thoughts of pit-falls and wired traps in the slums filled his mind, conjuring up old images of bloodied bodies and injured policemen. The criminal element, he'd long learned, could be clever in ways of causing harm.

Cool air brushed his fingertips and he caught on a flaw; he lowered the lamp to a neat little chip of wood gouged out of the edge-piece.

Watson.

Lestrade was impressed. The doctor was a man of surprises. He would never have guessed the man knew that little trick of the CID. It would seem he did his share of reading as well as writing. *He would be good at the Yard. I wonder if he would take us up on that offer someday.* It was such a tantalizing thought.

Lestrade dug in and the panel slipped outward without a noise. There was fresh oil on the hinges. Cool, dank air blew up in his face, strongly enough to move the hairs on his head, and with it, a warm reek of charnel. Lestrade's neck-flesh stiffened. It was wrong, that stench, like blood and mushrooms growing in a basement and...

His leather soles clicked softly against the fitted slate steps. They spiraled down like a castle's…not good. He did not trust ponderous architecture such as this. He held the bull's-eye high as he stepped down, bit by bit, and his nose stung from a queer scorching sensation. A burning abattoir mixed with the worst parts of a hospital, or…

Lestrade paused a moment, thinking. The odour had washed him back into a memory that was too close to his mind. Four years ago the *Princess Alice* had taken on water from a blow by the collier *Bywell Castle*, and over 640 men, women and children had drowned in the Thames eleven miles below London Bridge. It had taken days for the Water-Police, dredgers, and any able policemen to find the bodies. The processing-camp to identify the dead had smelt too like this: metallic smoke, mould, mildew, sewage, oil, high-fumes, blood, bile, and water...

It had been his first serious encounter with Sherlock Holmes as a private Detective, not a private Consultant (the first one delivering a message to the man for P.S. Roanoke, and the young man had struck him as mad even then). Holmes had stood apart so easily, for his idiotic nerve in moving among the corpses as well as his idiotic cleverness. He wondered if Watson had ever been told the details of that particular story.

Probably not...

Lestrade re-checked for his gun on instinct, slowly pulling it into his left hand. He didn't bother with pulling the hammer back; he was fast enough to pull it and the trigger within seconds of each other. A primed weapon was more dangerous—he'd far rather his blood be on someone's conscience than theirs on his.[52]

Death sounded in the history of his mind and faced him forward. Something was standing on his instincts with little knives, warning him of a very tangible danger.

Flesh of Christian, mends itself, he recalled his mother's proverb too easily. If Watson was in this, he was not well.

The small man stopped. His dark plainclothes suit blended his body in with his surroundings. There were whispery sounds, faint, but louder than his heartbeat. They were soft,

---

[52] Lestrade's attitude to guns was typical of his time even though a high number of policemen had served in the armed forces before joining the police.

delicate traceries against the ear, like the anxious breath of a dog wanting to slip its leash.

Liquid gurgling.

Panting of a large animal.

And now…scuffling, the heel against hard earth.

The sound of the mews; he was a horse-master's son. He knew that sound in his sleep. Lestrade came to a decision quickly; he'd had more practice than he liked with this sort of poor-light manoeuvre. He set the bull's-eye down and to the side and stepped out of its dull ring into the murky void. Its black depth seemed endless; mould glimmered on forgotten doorways and a second lantern, brighter than his own, threw shadows into the hanging cobwebs.

A huddled-up man in brown was hunched over a door. He was pouring the contents of a metal ewer into the floor, panting loudly from his effort. Smoke still curled up the bottom, rank and foul.

Lestrade watched, realising the other did not see him; his expensive lamp had blinded him to the old bull's-eye's weaker flame. The man straightened, and he clutched at the door to scuff with his heel. Contrary earth scraped up under his efforts, trying to seal the smoke shut.

"Stop this, Parker." Watson's calm, firm voice from the other side of that door—Lestrade had heard that tone of voice once—in the *Malmsey Keg*, when Watson demanded his own form of retribution to Elspeth's murderer. *"They know I'm here."*

"That they do."

Lestrade had crossed the floor in long strides, the earth carpeting his sound, and merely pressed the tip of his pistol into the man's neck above the collarbone. "Dr. Parker, you are now under arrest in the name of the Queen, and it is my duty to inform you that anything you say can be used against you—,"

His other hand yanked the bigger man up with grit-toothed strength as he rattled off the man's rights, and pushed him back against the filthy wall; Lestrade was used to dealing with the unsavoury lots twice his size, and before the doctor could finish his whimper his wrists were snagged. "Dr. Watson, is that you there?"

"I should hope so." Watson's voice sounded clearer; Lestrade saw a hole in the floor. Parker had been trying to fill it in. *"But I'd appreciate an open door, Inspector."*

"All right, then, easy enough. Might want to step away." Lestrade looked down at his captive, thinking to get a key, but one look at the shivered wreck of a man sobbing against the wall changed his mind. He sighed, dismissed him as worthless, lined up the hinges, and braced his weight to one side. At close range, the heel-kick sent the wood popping free from the metal housing.

The door wobbled open; Watson was on his knees, breathing deeply as a wave of smoke curled about him and limped out the door into the hallway, clutching at a grubby handkerchief. Lestrade pulled his hand up with a grimace. The young man's face was flushed but defiant and triumphant.

"Good to see you," he said through his teeth. And coughed.

"Bradstreet's upstairs with the butler," Lestrade informed him. "How are you?"

"I shall be fine enough when this is settled…" Watson was leaning on his good leg, and he shuddered once all over. "We have the proof we need, Lestrade. *More* than what we need." His voice was hollow and heavy with no joy to it whatsoever.

It was those words that did something to Parker's obviously frail state of mind. Despite the handcuffs, the man staggered to his feet, and with a single impressive kick, aimed for the back of Lestrade's legs. Before Watson could even finish opening his mouth in a shout the little detective turned to the side, and his own foot snapped out in a French-style kick. His toe caught Parker in the bottom of his chin as he flopped down to the floor on his own lopsided momentum; the man collapsed like a bag of sand.

"He can't hurt himself or others if he's out." Lestrade said grimly. He turned back to the reluctantly impressed Watson. "And I *don't* want him to be conscious. Bradstreet will be better that way."

"I see." Watson suddenly coughed. Black stuff came out in his handkerchief. "Perhaps you ought to see this...and not Mr. Bradstreet."

"Go easy on him," Bradstreet pitched his voice very low, so only MacDonald could hear. In the wet streets, the old butler was being settled up to ride to the station. "I rather get the impression he was serving because he didn't have much of a choice."

MacDonald set his lips tightly, his eyes bright with disapproval. "I should have thought of that," he said obscurely.

"Beg your pardon?" Bradstreet was startled.

"It's..." MacDonald sighed. "Well. It was a rumour. You hear so many that you just sort of decide which ones you want to believe in."

Bradstreet nodded.

"And this rumour had it, all the people working for Dr. Parker was working off their debts to him. Surgeries. Heavy debts, you know. He'd give 'em just enough pin money to live a bit, but the rest was their working off what they owed." The blond man looked very awkward for a moment. "Spent some time bragging about the man, you know. Used to work for the old palace in his heyday, very respectable."

"A personal debtor's prison?" Bradstreet stared as the other man nodded glumly. "Truly?"

"If no one complains..." MacDonald shrugged helplessly. The men looked at each other wearily, both of a height. "I'd say he doesn't have to worry about his debt to the man *now*."

"Small favours."

"Lestrade's still inside, as is Watson. I'm taking my lads in."

"I'll come with you."

"No; you take that poor old wreck in. He looks like he could use a good cup of tea and something to eat—and he can keep the rest of the household staff calm. They'll look up to him and do as he says..."

Bradstreet made a crisp motion as MacDonald turned and barked a quick order to a slight man, about Lestrade's size who was writing notes. The man stuffed his book in his pocket and trotted over.

"Sir?"

"McAlpin, whilst the PCs mind the ins and outs of the house, you go with Bradstreet."

"Sir." The man touched his helmet-brim.

"Are you sure you're all right?" Lestrade asked again. Watson was at least fully back on his feet, but his face was chalky under the smudges.

"I'll be fine," the bigger man repeated. He took a deep breath. "We have the proof." He yanked a fresh cloth from inside his sleeve--military style--and pushed it over his face.

"You had a close call," Lestrade said in his sternest voice. "The Yard is grateful, doctor, but we don't wish you to continue to risk yourself."

Anger flashed in those brown eyes, but Lestrade was well used to that, too. For a moment the two locked eyes and horns--literally--in the thick atmosphere.

Lestrade is not military, Watson reminded himself. *He follows his rules, as I must follow mine. His speech is no different than what I would have given to a civilian who wanted to help with an affair.*

But his pride hurt; to know that he was now a civilian only because of a Jezail and his choice of action.

If I was not half a man, I would still be a Major...perhaps higher. Watson whirled away, his teeth clenched against the truth he had no choice but to recognise.

"The proof is here," he said tightly. "I discovered it just before Dr. Parker tried to entomb me alive."

Lestrade spared a look of cold contempt to the limp form against the wall. "He's mild enough now," he said with a false sweetness. In perfect timing PC Sibthorp rattled up; the Inspector waved him over to stand guard over the prisoner.

"You don't know him." The younger doctor said heavily. "He can't endure direct death. I believe it was his plan to come back several days later, when I no longer lived."

Lestrade's look upon Parker was terrible. "Passive murder is still willful murder." He said coldly. "It is up to the jury to decide, but I doubt they'll see differently." He cocked his head, listening. "Ah, that would be Bradstreet," he added in satisfaction.

Watson was about to ask him how in the world he knew that, but the big man appeared in the smoky doorway, a PC just behind.

"Gentlemen," Bradstreet rumbled deep in his chest. His dark eyes flashed over his companions, and then settled, slow as leaf-litter, onto the senseless Parker against the wall. "I take it this is the man in question."

"Yes." Watson breathed in. "Inspector, might I trouble you to take him to the station?"

"Did you find the proof then?" Bradstreet asked, so softly they only saw his lips move.

Watson nodded. "We've found her." He spoke as a soldier, calm and direct and respectful.

Bradstreet nodded his permission.

Watson turned and stepped back inside the slowly-thinning room.

Bradstreet stepped after him, his stride long and determined. The doctor was stepping to the small skeleton hanging in the case.

Bradstreet stopped.

The big man took the sight of his baby sister's remains better than one might think.

Lestrade moved to his side without a word and made his face still against the pain as that big hand wrenched into his shoulder for support.

Bradstreet swayed slightly. His eyes glassed over for a moment and Watson studied the pattern of stone upon the wall.

"Proof of murder," Watson said as if under his breath. He held up his finger to the neck vertebrae. "Scarring upon the bone."

Throat-cutting. A doctor would know how to murder clean; this would have been a contract. Parker's inability to deal death personally was as obvious as the spectacle he made, an empty shell inside himself, all life burned out of him. The bonfire Watson had seen at dinner was gone and it was unlikely to return.

Bradstreet paused, and slowly turned his head from side to side looking about the tiny room. There were, Lestrade thought, far too many bottles and glass cases and cabinets.

"What's wrong here?" The Runner asked suddenly.

Lestrade followed his gaze to a headless skeleton hanging inside a highly polished chamber of thick glass framed with ebony. It was an appallingly outrageous display of money and death.

"What do you mean?" He wondered.

"All of these are...different." Bradstreet vaguely waved his hand around the room. "But that looks like a...well...I don't see anything different about that skeleton...and why have a skeleton without a head?"

"Damn, you're right." Lestrade flushed bright red to have missed something Bradstreet had not. He was too distracted— not a good showing as a policeman or a friend!

"You are right." Watson sighed. "And I confess I don't know about it just yet."

"No...because Watson needed a skull to see the face before it.

"Oh, dear."

Had he said that out loud? They were looking at him oddly.

Sweat broke out of the little professional's face as for one of the few times in his life, his brain leapt from thought to thought and finally a cringe-worthy conclusion.

"Bradstreet..." Lestrade cleared his throat. "MacDonald's report." He swallowed. "He said...when the senior Parker died...his body was sent to science...and that all but the skull was lost."

Bradstreet and Watson went as pale as Lestrade felt.

"You are certain?" Watson asked, quietly formal.

"It would seem," Watson voiced what they could not, "That he found his father in England and...brought him back."

"What he could find of him." Lestrade made himself breathe deep.

"What hath Thy death for sinners gain'd?" Bradstreet murmured in that sing-song way he did when he was quoting Wesley. "What hath Thy life to sinners given?"[53]

"If I may, Mr. Bradstreet," Watson cleared his throat. "I could use Lestrade's assistance in cataloguing this room. There may yet be something else in here."

Bradstreet nodded his agreement. He stared back at the unconscious Parker beneath the Constable's eyes one last time, not quite seeing him. His brown eyes kept sliding over that little mound and elsewhere. "Constable," He cleared his throat as the young man stepped forward. "If you would be so kind as to place him in your custody. I will speak to Macdonald."

Lestrade and Watson waited until they were alone. Quite alone. Lestrade blew out his breath, trembling inside his oversized coat. He reached up and rubbed at the bruise Bradstreet had left on his shoulder. "There's something else in here, isn't there." He said flatly. "Something you didn't want him to see."

"Not now." Watson agreed. His eyes were shining; small wonder. Lestrade's eyes were watering too. It wasn't from the smoke. "One moment, please." Watson slumped slightly inward, and stepped deeper into the room where a long waterproofed cabinet rested against a padded board on the wall. Lestrade hesitated to join him. Whatever Watson would have to show him, would have to be worse than the skeleton.

But the doctor stopped, his back to the Inspector, and his rested his hands on the table for a moment, head hanging down. "He wouldn't have kept just the skeleton," he said in a muffled voice. "A skeleton only tells part of the story."

Lestrade felt his heart freeze.

---

[53] Hymnal. "The Redemption of Man" by John and Charles Wesley. Bradstreet is a Methodist.

"Most bones are anonymous. There were enough questions about Elspeth Bradstreet's disappearance that he couldn't have the bones on permanent exhibit. It was a prized specimen; he only took it out once a year, like many researchers do." Watson snorted to himself in a display of self-directed contempt that Lestrade didn't recognise. "But at least he could show it. Show it off. That was important. A researcher is worthless unless he has some proof of his work." His throat moved over his collar in a swallow. "A Selkie has webbed fingers and toes." He said slowly, as if each word hurt him as it came out.

Horror climbed up Lestrade's chest and he gulped; the air left the room. The detective had walked among the dead by the hundreds and never so much as faltered; he'd seen his own brother swing for murder; he'd pulled bodies by the score out of frozen gutters in his Constable beats, and he'd had to tell the wife of his best friend that her husband would never come home.

But he'd never before seen an act of murder lovingly preserved in a jar of alcohol for eternity.

Watson set the two jars down carefully, one after the other.

Lestrade swallowed again. And again. "How..." He managed faintly. "How did..."

"He took the flesh from the bone, in a horizontal cut," Watson said in a dead voice. "And he stitched them back up together. I suspect he inserted pins inside to keep the shape of the extremities...the toes were particularly delicate...and then he preserved them in alcohol."

Now the pieces fit. "That's why you asked Bradstreet for the use of her hand-casts!" He breathed. "The casts were made before she disappeared; Parker would be able to show them off if he had those in his collection!"

Watson almost smiled; he was pleased the little man had figured it out. "I wasn't about to give him the originals," he admitted. "I gave him these instead." He picked up two small white objects from behind the jars and gently cradled them. Lestrade tilted his head to one side, puzzled. They looked exactly like the plaster casts the priest had made of Elspeth in life...but much, much smaller. "What did you do?"

"I made a cast of a cast," Watson nodded. "I had the cast of fine ceramic, and when it fired it shrank. Then I re-plastered the cast. The result was a smaller copy of the original. Parker thought the hands were of a five or six year old child, and he recognised the hands. It was...a bit of a long gamble, but...I had a suspicion."

Lestrade was a moment collecting his voice. "You were right not to show him." He said at last. "Bradstreet is a professional, Doctor. But no one should ever see such a thing."

"No." Watson agreed.

The smaller man ran his hand through his hair; a particular mannerism that fascinated Watson, for it went against the other's cat-like sense of neatness. "Is there some way we can put the rest of her up in a casket? Something that can be buried with the rest of her?"

"There is." Watson nodded. "Bradstreet needn't look."

"Good."

They set to work. The Murder Room--Lestrade couldn't think of it any other way--was not very large, but it had many objects. Watson's concentration was jolted when he heard Lestrade pull in his breath.

By this point, Watson would have to wonder what would startle the little man. He looked up from the act of opening a thin cabinet. Lestrade was yanking thin gloves out of his coat-pocket in a fever and pulling them over his fingers. That done, he reached into a black-lacquered box and gently pulled out a withered-up hand. The skin was black from preservatives and moved like dry leather. Inside its gnarled, grotesquely swollen fingers, a fat candle of an unwholesome sallow tinge collected dust.

"Lestrade?" Watson hesitated.

Lestrade did not speak or look at him at first. "Carney Ambisinister's missing hand," he said in a thin voice.

"Ambisinister the murderer?" Watson stepped over to take a look. "Are you certain?"

"I was on the case." Lestrade was still staring at the thing, what had once been a living hand, between his own two. "I'd know that moon-scar on the wrist anywhere." He was silent from the weight of his thoughts for a long moment. "I remember when they hung him, and I thought, 'now it's over,' for it's really quite a simple thing to take a life. It only takes a moment." The detective was pale as candle-wax. "But it never is over, not really. All you do is just take a life that's taken a life." He swallowed hard. "All the people he'd killed had been the work of a moment. No more. But the next day, when they called to tell me the body had been desecrated, all I could think was, 'it was supposed to be over.'"

Lestrade couldn't speak further than that. He was not as imaginative as Dr. Watson or Mr. Holmes; imagination was a pitfall in his career. But he could still see the facts in his mind. Rumours had circulated almost instantly despite the efforts of the Yard; that the hand had been turned into a Hand of Glory, a mark of witchcraft for who knew what sort of purpose?

"We need to bury him with his hand." He said at last. "So long as we keep mum. If one ghoulish collector knows, another will know..." Bitterness was thick as sea-salt in his voice. "We found it the first time...it was being sold on the market with sorts of things you'd never want to look at, doctor...and we put it in the Archives thinking it would be safe, whilst we pondered what to do. And there it was stolen again. The reporters had their fun with us." Something made him look down past the withered palm and his face changed, hot and swift as summer lightning. *"He left the ticket on!"* Lestrade hissed. *"I don't believe it! He left the crime ticket, still tied on to the arm-bone!"*

Watson shook his head. "This will take years." He said dully. "Only discreet inquiries will do, and they aren't as swift as the other methods."

Lestrade swallowed. He drew filthy air into his lungs until he calmed. "I'll be taking this back with me." He said softly. "Return it...under better guard."

"If Holmes were here," Watson murmured, "he would suggest a discreet burial posthaste with no one the wiser." A mixture of understanding and disappointment rested inside his normally pleasant voice.

Lestrade was too exhausted to fumble with words. "Mr. Holmes is not the law, Doctor Watson. I am as long as I wear the Guelphic Badge. And I must make my decisions within the law." He would ensure Holyrood was correct about the permission to bury this sad relic, but until then would keep quiet.

Watson's lips tightened fractionally under his trimmed military mustache. "And I am a soldier, Mr. Lestrade. I understand duties. We each have our own."

Yes. But Watson, though a soldier, was turning into something else.

He would have been a perfect addition to the Yard...if his life hadn't turned to Baker Street first. He wasn't aware of it, but his character was already more than what it had been when Lestrade first met him. Holmes' influence was all well and good, but the two waters didn't mix. Holmes had never struck him as someone who would obey the law if it didn't suit him. No. He would go to his own higher power every time. And from such mistakes, anarchy and corruption began in the Yard. It was inevitable.

The two men sensed the crucial hour in the room. They were united in their desires, but chasms existed between them in their methods. Complete trust would never be possible...not if both men hoped to keep to their own moral codes.

Lestrade lowered the relic back into its case. Watson turned again to his project. They went back to work.

It was morning when Lestrade stumbled into the small room he shared with Bradstreet. He wanted to sleep, and any wayward dreams had best go elsewhere for their business: he wasn't buying any of it.

After a few minutes of lying face-down on the scratchy blanket with his entire body buzzing like a beehive from nerves, the little detective rolled over and tugged his hanging coat closer, fished in the pocket, finally pulling out a familiar little book.

Parker's collection of specialists.

He leafed to a particular page in the back. Parker had *liked* the quote of the man on the other side: a spinal-injury specialist in the Western side, who had dallied in France long enough to make an in-depth study of the unfortunate Lacenaire.[54]

Or, rather, a particular part of Lacenaire.

The quote had been marked in pencil. Over and over.

And over and over.

---

[54] The Yarders would have known about the case for its unpalatable elements of cultish horror, class animosity, and manipulation of public sentiment.

Lestrade read the quote again. He couldn't help himself.

A study of Hands
--Theophile Gautier

Lacenaire

Strange contrast was the severed hand
Of Lacenaire, the murder dead,
Soaked in a powerful essence, and
Near by upon a cushion spread.

Letting a morbid fancy win,
I touched, despite my loathing sane,
The cold, hair-covered, slimy skin,
Not yet washed clean of deathly stain.

Yellow, uncanny, mummified,
Like to a Pharaoh's hand it lay,
And stretched its faun-shaped fingers wide,
Crisp with temptation's awful play;

As though an itch for flesh and gold
Lured them to horrors yet to be,
Twisting them roughly as of old,
Teasing their immobility.

A man who was truly mad might be stuck on a Hand of
Glory...but would they be honest enough to admit it made
them uneasy? Lestrade's guts told him Parker was useless and
cruel, but...not ...*irrational*.

Gregson, of all people, had a special turn of phrase for people like Dr. Parker. He called them "Incurably and cold-bloodedly sane." Lestrade had passed the days and inexperience when he would have scoffed at Gregson's wit. Like everything else, the man's wording was a fatal blow for its effectiveness.

The courts of law could put a man to trial or bedlam for his sanity...but they couldn't do a thing about a sane man who was missing a heart and soul. Hang him, yes, but could one prove a deviant of this...extreme degree...was actually sane?

If he was a less stubborn man, Lestrade would have turned the little book to the courts. But...Watson had told him he never wanted to see the book ever again.

And really, there was no proof that the penciling was Parker's, was it?

The detective finally put the book back. He needed to talk to someone when this was over—Brother Jerome, perhaps. This was a dirty, filthy, horrible, terrible case and he could trust the little friar to help him understand it.

Watson had been called as principal witness on grounds that his name would be kept out of the papers. Lestrade and Bradstreet hadn't expected the speed of the acquiescence of the authorities, but Watson had his wish.

"Either his name or his family name means something to someone," Lestrade muttered at the tiny book he'd been reading over and over since they'd allowed Watson the courtesy of a private moment. Through the single glass pane of the office they watched, blear-eyed, as the doctor signed his final statement with a crisp snap of the pen and passed it across the desk to the waiting official—some Gaelic title Lestrade didn't recognise.

"You knew anyone who'd share rooms with Sherlock Holmes'd be a stripe apart." Bradstreet muttered. "But could be they just want the case kept mum." He was living on cups of black tea and cigarillos the way his friend was living attached to his book. In the privacy of MacDonald's freezing office, they would watch everything through the open office-door. MacDonald had even pulled the rest of the specimens from Parker's little private Black Museum, so the two men were a little crowded. Still, it was a small price to pay to keep prying eyes from the pitiful remains until they were shuffled back into the morgue-storage where everything was guaranteed to be safe as houses.

"How are you feeling, Roger?" Lestrade asked bluntly.

Bradstreet grunted. He looked like he had a case of pink-eye, and shrunken hollows gave an appearance of lost weight and mass. "I don't look it," he muttered, "but I feel...I feel weightless." He flicked dark ash into the tray as he spoke. "It's like...well, I don't know. Like I can breathe again. And I didn't know I was missing that breath in the first place."

Lestrade nodded his understanding. At his elbow perched a battered box for blasting-caps, with hand-painted MONOTYPE SAMPLES over the lid in bright blue. No one would guess the last remnants of Carney Ambisinister rested inside it, wrapped in more cloths than would shame a mummy. The little detective was taking no chances.

Bradstreet couldn't stand the silence. "Why *monotype?*"

"Who'd steal monotype?"

More silence. Bradstreet tried to take the question literally. It was usually the safest thing with all things Lestrade. He was still composing a response when his friend stiffened up, his dark eyes upon the door.

The doctor's limp was less pronounced; perhaps his statement about having to "move it out" was true. Relief had lifted his spine and clarity was back in his thin face that had not been there since before their collabouration.

"I'll be attending the trial," he stopped as he came to the Inspectors, and waved them to keep their seats as he leaned forward on his walking-stick. "I also contacted some gentlemen of my acquaintance. After the full examination and recording, you will have your sister's remains. In view of the delicate circumstances, that should be within the next 60 hours. They promised to keep her name out of the papers, as well as yours..." He paused to cough into his hand. "Excuse me." He apologised faintly. "I believe there are still particles of sawdust in my lungs."

"Can you do anything for that?" Lestrade asked quietly.

"Oh, indubitably...just not in polite company."

"I'll contact my family." Bradstreet nodded, his face perfectly composed again. He had been preparing for this day for a very long time. "But, doctor, if I may..?"

"...yes?" Watson wondered as he tucked a fresh handkerchief into his sleeve.

"Dr. Watson," Bradstreet spoke one inch at a time, and his dark eyes were fastened deeply upon the tall, tan-skinned man. "Dr. Parker...was he...intending to collect you?"

Lestrade jumped slightly. He hadn't expected Bradstreet to pay attention to anything outside his own sphere...

Watson licked his lips and chose not to answer directly. Lestrade was staring from one man to another with an uneasy expression.

"He is not...sane, I think." He said carefully.

"No, of course he isn't. *Why* would he collect you?" Bradstreet persisted. His dark eyes were bright, almost feverish with the need to know. "All those...poor people down there,

there was something significant about them. You said in your report he accidentally called you 'something,' now that means something to *me*."

Watson did not want to answer. He would have rather not answered for the rest of his life. He closed his eyes and took a shuddering breath. "I was his student," he said heavily. "He was...fascinated by the wounds of war. Perhaps...because of his own." He looked down. "So few of us came back from the desert. Jezail bullets caused amputations as much as death...he wouldn't have had much to study..."

"Ghoul." Lestrade said under his breath. He was fixed upon the arm-bones of the tursh-toothed woman before him.

"You set yourself up as the trap. Perfectly done." Bradstreet said softly. His eyes shone with tears.

"I let Parker believe a few falsehoods," Watson closed his eyes, he was so tired. "I let him think those hand-casts were part of a set, and that the older casts were in the possession of your family's priest. I also intimated that the hand-casts were going to wind up in a museum someday."

"Well he wouldn't have liked that!" Lestrade stared. "You just as well invited him to kill you to cover up his murder!"

Watson nodded and turned again to the table, his fingers resting on the green blotting-paper. The foetus that had saved his life floated before him. Fresh alcohol had been added. It would take time to see how this child had been collected. By default of its location, it was doubtful it had been taken by the permission of the parents. Another stolen grave. "A treasure he could gloat over in private is not such a great treasure. The casts...they would have been a proud trophy. Forgive me, Bradstreet."

"Nothing to forgive." Bradstreet grunted. "If Parker is not insane, he is at least imbalanced. And," he lumbered to his feet to face Watson square in the eye. "You needn't be ashamed of your profession. Because as long as you're in it, the Yard will rest all the easier."

Watson stared as Bradstreet went back to the main office, his eyes suspiciously wet.

And...Lestrade was saddened to realise, the man was also astonished.

Someone taught him this. He wasn't born invisible, but he was taught to be. The little detective was too familiar with being the neglected son not to see the signs in another.

Beware of the invisibles. They have hidden depths.

They would never be full partners...but they could be allies. In a city like London where crime was as varied as the methods used to combat the same...it would be enough.

"A remarkable man." Watson murmured. "He has a charitable heart."

"Well, yes, but why do you say so?"

"I was thinking of how many other people in this world would bay for Parker's blood."

"If he did, he would be going against his faith." Lestrade said simply. "Also, it would throw off the courts if there was a breath of favourtism on his part."

"Still, it cannot be easy." Watson's speech was low, softly deliberate and very precise. Not unlike Mr. Holmes in one of his rare moments of reflection.[55]

Lestrade thought of his own experience. He told the truth and forced himself to watch his brother hang. "I dare say it wasn't, Dr. Watson." Watson shook his head, still marvelling. "I think it is easier for him that Dr. Parker seems out of his senses." Lestrade stuffed his little book deep in a pocket as he spoke. "I'm no man of great learning," he added with a wry

---

[55] Lestrade of course does not see this side of him as much as Watson.

twist to his lean face, "But if one thing operates without rhyme or reason…it is a madman."

"Perhaps the courts *will* declare him mad." Watson sounded tentatively hopeful, and as the idea took root, his shoulders squared back. A fresh gleam came into his dark eyes. The little detective wondered if he imagined the wisps of shadows clearing from his worn-out face. "It can be a difficult thing, to prove madness. There is too much we do not know about the brain and how it affects our motives."

Lestrade did not tell the young man it was at times like these the courts were *more* likely to decree madness just to quickly stuff a crime under a rug—not the nicest way to dispense justice, but a justice of sorts would be met. "It isn't for you or I to decide, but it does seem likely, doesn't it?" He rubbed at his jaw in sudden thought. "Perhaps he was already on his way to madness when he returned to Britain…"

"I can't imagine what must have happened to his mind when he decided to find his father's remains." Watson clasped his hands behind his back in a sudden military-like movement. His fingers clenched deep inside his palms. "It would have been a simple task…as a man of medicine he would not have been blocked from the usual venues."

"No." Lestrade had been trying not to think about this. "He found as much as the skeleton, but not the skull."

"It is most likely in the collection of some other scientist. Another man of medicine." Watson mused as he walked out of the room. "Or a specialist."

Or another bone-grubber, Lestrade thought. He believed that was more likely—a skull of a murderer would be worth much more in the market than that of a simple beggar's. *I doubt it really matters…looking for his father's head would be enough to put most people around the twist. What I wonder is when did he decide to start collecting people the same as his father?*

"That will be *that*," Bradstreet intruded into his thoughts as he returned. "And thank all mercies large and small." The big Runner had found his hat and was eagerly brushing the smells of Edinburgh Below off the felt. "What d'you think, Lestrade?"

"I think he'll be sent straight on to Broadmoor."

"I hope so. We aren't a hanging country, Lestrade, but I worry when there's a mess like this." He shuddered.

"And you? I expect you'll be talking to your family before the end of the day?"

"I did send a wire." The big man confessed. "I told them what they may expect…" He sigh-shuddered inside his heavy coat. "I'll be off to speak with them at the Church."

"Truce under holy ground?"

"Truce under holy ground."

"Need you a friend?"

"Not this time." Bradstreet spoke with regret. "Perhaps later. On the train back."

Lestrade patted his pocket where his own ticket rested. "I'll meet you at the station." He promised.

"See that you do." The corners of Bradstreet's mouth moved up without any heart as he left the room, leaving Lestrade alone at MacDonald's desk with the human remnants.

The little professional picked up the box holding Ambisinister's hand (he would not, could not give in and call it a Hand of Glory). With its recovery the burning need to find the thieves for the crime had dulled down. Or perhaps it was the memory of Parker in his mind.

He wasn't certain what he should think. Parker was in every respect all that his family had hoped to be...and all for what?

To be well educated, own his own house, answer to himself and be his own man, to run a household and be respected and admired...the man had even contributed to the charities about London and Edinburgh. Wouldn't that be enough? Couldn't that be enough?

It would seem not.

Within this insight, the Inspector could admit he had been on the brink of making the same mistake with one John H. Watson, Army Surgeon.

Watson would have made a fine policeman...if being a policeman was enough for him.

It wasn't. He could see that now.

Ah, well. The Yard's loss was clearly the gain of Mr. Holmes.

The small man smiled wryly as he tucked the box inside a heavy leather gripsack. He was professional enough to want to head back to London and the comforts of his office now that the case was mostly concluded...but he had a full day to spend before the train left, and he may as well do it proper.

"Excuse me, lad." He waved down a promising-looking young man. "I'm looking for the Episcopal Church?

The stripling nodded. "That'll be St. Mary's, Mr. Lestrade. If you stand on the front steps, the cabs can take you straight over."

"Straight over?" Lestrade repeated suspiciously.

A grin was his answer. "Especially if you tell 'em you wish to hear the Grimthorpe Bells."

Lestrade grinned as well. The name of the designer of Big Ben was allowed enough. "Thank you for that." He pressed a random coin from his pocket into the young palm, and strolled out into the cloudy air of Scotland. With luck he could get a minister or clergyman to make a prayer over his cargo before nightfall.

And from there…a little talk with Brother Jerome. The old fellow had been a policeman before donning the habit. He'd listen to the entire sordid tale without judgement…and he'd keep Ambisinister's hand secure as Lestrade filed the proper procedures to bury it.

Weary and craving the comfort of any bed, even if it was the back of a cab, Lestrade straightened his back and shoulders. Dr. Watson was just buttoning his heavy coat for the outdoors. The two men saw each other at the same time and nodded a final greeting…or a parting of ways.

Lestrade offered his free hand to shake and grinned when Watson took it with something like his usual firm grip.

"Do you have a place to stay tonight, Doctor? We'd be honoured."

Watson shook his head with a chuckle. "I'm well set up! I…ran into the friend of a friend at my tavern. We promised to talk of mathematics."

"Sounds…delightful." Lestrade felt his first laugh in days bubble up. "Now how are you going to keep this case from Mr. Holmes? He proclaims to read one's entire history on the trousers, cuffs, and shoelaces."

"And the boot-tips." Watson filled in. "He's still out on his own case. I don't think he's even in England."

"How disappointing," Lestrade mused. "I was looking forward to having one over him, just this once."

Watson's smile only grew. "I fear, Inspector, you and I will have to work a great deal harder and longer to claim such a victory."

Also from MX Publishing

MX Publishing is the world's largest specialist Sherlock Holmes publisher, with over a hundred titles and fifty authors creating the latest in Sherlock Holmes fiction and non-fiction.

From traditional short stories and novels to travel guides and quiz books, MX Publishing cater for all Holmes fans.

The collection includes leading titles such as *Benedict Cumberbatch In Transition* and *The Norwood Author* which won the 2011 Howlett Award (Sherlock Holmes Book of the Year).

MX Publishing also has one of the largest communities of Holmes fans on Facebook with regular contributions from dozens of authors.

www.mxpublishing.com

Also from MX Publishing

After Mina Murray asks Sherlock Holmes to locate her fiancee, Holmes and Watson travel to a land far eerier than the moors they had known when pursuing the Hound of the Baskervilles. The confrontation with Count Dracula threatens Holmes' health, his sanity, and his life. Will Holmes survive his battle with Count Dracula?

Also from MX Publishing

Internationally bestselling traditional short story collections from Luke Kuhns

The Untold Adventures of Sherlock Holmes

Sherlock Holmes Studies In Legacy

www.mxpublishing.com

Also from MX Publishing

"Phil Growick's, 'The Secret Journal of Dr Watson', is an adventure which takes place in the latter part of Holmes and Watson's lives. They are entrusted by HM Government (although not officially) and the King no less to undertake a rescue mission to save the Romanovs, Russia's Royal family from a grisly end at the hand of the Bolsheviks. There is a wealth of detail in the story but not so much as would detract us from the enjoyment of the story. Espionage, counter-espionage, the ace of spies himself, double-agents, double-crossers...all these flit across the pages in a realistic and exciting way. All the characters are extremely well-drawn and Mr Growick, most importantly, does not falter with a very good ear for Holmesian dialogue indeed. Highly recommended. A five-star effort." **The Baker Street Society**

www.mxpublishing.com

Also from MX Publishing

Dozens of short story ebooks

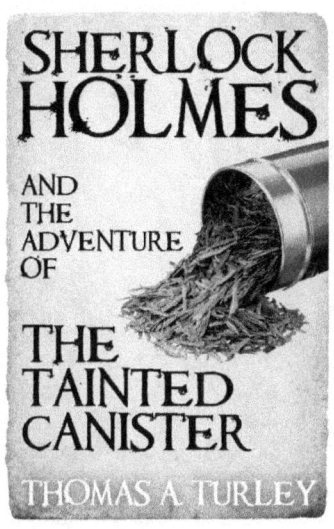

A lost chapter in the Holmes canon finally appears, as Dr. Watson recounts the mystery behind the tragic death of his beloved Mary Morstan. Join him as he attempts to bring a murderer to justice. Along the way, readers will encounter old friends and enemies from several of the other stories, leading to a startling conclusion that may baffle even Sherlock Holmes.

Available via Amazon Kindle, Kobo, Nook and iTunes.